The Filing Cabinet of Doom

MADELEINE SWANN

Burning Bulb
PUBLISHING

The Filing Cabinet of Doom
By **Madeleine Swann**

Burning Bulb Publishing
P.O. Box 4721
Bridgeport, WV 26330-4721
United States of America
www.BurningBulbPublishing.com

Cover illustration by Gwendy Gayle H. Delos Santos.

First Edition.

Paperback Edition ISBN: 978-0692245200

Printed in the United States of America.

CONTENTS

AMONGST THE DUST
AND THE MICE

I'd been at the London squat for two weeks when I realised I was disappearing. I first arrived in a van driven by a dreadlocked man I vaguely knew. I'd sat in the back on an old mattress while he chatted to a pierced girl beside him, and I was just starting to worry about my bladder when the phone rang. "Hello, is this Elizabeth Moreton?" The line was crackly but I recognised the director's voice.

"Yes, hello?"

"We'd like you to come in for an audition in Bournemouth tomorrow – it'll be at 12 instead of 3 I hope that's OK."

"Yep, that's fine," I squeaked, doing mental calculations of when I'd need to be up.

"Fantastic, and it's for local actors only, London is just too far."

I swallowed. "Oh, I don't live in London."

"Just gone through the Dartford Tunnel!" called the dreadlocked driver.

There was a pause on the other end. "Right, well, we'll see you tomorrow at 12." It was typical that this would happen after my decision to move to the capital, but I was certain it could be worked out. It took two hours to get to London from Brighton. I stepped through piles of tires and logs in the concrete courtyard and let myself in through the graffiti-sprayed front door. I climbed three flights of paint-cracked steps to the rooms at the top, passing the kitchen. "Don't be a numpty," exclaimed one cupboard door in black felt pen, "buy your own food and leave mine alone." A trio of stick seagulls flew around the text, adding a touch of joviality.

Wandering the dusty floorboards of the abandoned pub was like stumbling through a funfair crooked house; something was always off, something odd. The empty barroom was an intact but dusty relic haunted by illegal residents and mice, their little hands scratching and scrabbling in the walls.

After the following day's audition in Bournemouth I returned to my new room. It had no curtains or furnishings so I lay my mattress on the wooden floor and hammered a sarong over the weak winter sun. With the TV in place it looked almost like a student's room, were it not for the lack of heating. I kept warm by making a log fire in the grate, sitting hunched like a chimp looking for ants. It was then that I first noticed the chipped gold of the poker through my hand. I dropped it and stared at my almost missing digits but they didn't reappear. I shook my head and grabbed my mobile phone from my coat pocket with my good hand. My thumb hovered over my friend's number but something stopped me. My friends and I had become an old money family, each has a grievance with another but is too polite to say, and no-one can remember how it began in the first place. I put my phone away; this is one I'd have to deal with alone.

The next day my alarm went off. My future acting career waited for me to leap out of bed but when I went to press the button I noticed my entire arm was missing. I could see the phone and blankets through it; shakily, I knew I had to do something. I needed to take action. I turned over and went back to sleep until four.

When I met him he smiled. He stuck his head around my paint-cracked door and admired my film collection. I hid my arm behind my back. "I'm Sam," he said. He was short and squat and he grinned like a wolf. "I'm making dinner, do you want some?" In his room the fire raged hotter than I could ever get mine. After wolfing down the beans and meat of the stew I felt warm, parented and safe. I kept my arm hidden but I was certain I could feel it gain a new solidity.

"It's nice to have a new face around here," he chatted amiably. I nodded, trying to think of a response but instead letting the silence grow to an embarrassing length. Each night that week I ate with him. He didn't notice my arm or, if he did, he didn't say. To my relief the fading seemed to have stopped, but I had become a helpless orphan, cheered only when Sam appeared at my door and offered me a meal. The rooms in the squat were so large and all I could hear of other life was the scrabbling of the mice and the occasional glimpse of another person. I sat back in my chair, full. "Living with the others is like living with pigs," said Sam, offering me more food which I turned down. "No-one clears up after themselves." I didn't disagree out loud, but to me they weren't pigs, they were ghosts.

"Christ knows what I'm supposed to do with my life now; I've no savings and I'm nearly forty."

I tried to think of something reassuring to say. "Erm…"

"It's alright," he rolled a cigarette; "I just need to figure out what I'm doing."

That night in my room I rang my boyfriend. "Is everything alright?" he asked, "are you settling in? Have you found somewhere proper to live?" I didn't know what else to say but yes.

That weekend the squat was overrun by visitors. They swarmed through the unlocked door and open window and partied loudly through the night. I joined them in the main barroom but didn't recognise anyone. "Do you want some cider?" offered one man with a half shaved face.

"Alright, thanks," I went to take it with the wrong hand and performed a strange dance while I darted the other out instead, had a sip and passed it back. Maybe, if I could convince them that I was normal, everything would be alright.

"What brings you here then?" asked a girl with dreadlocks. She seemed nice.

"I'm not really sure," I laughed. The truth escaped my brain under the scrutiny. From my lips the most exciting story would sound boring, but they accepted my non-explanation and I began to feel hopeful.

"Have some more cider," the man almost pushed it into my chest and, automatically, I reached out to grab it with both hands. I saw the look of discovery in his eyes and I retreated, leaving the bottle to splash over the floor. "Oh, dammit," he muttered.

Another man with a fashionable haircut and coat pointed at me. "Girl who lives here," he growled, "Get some tissues."

"No!" I yelled, surprising myself too, "you go get them." I ran to my room as if I was being chased, and all night I listened to the mice in my room, their little fingers scratching the woodwork.

"She's weird," they seemed to be whispering, "What sort of person acts that way?" When I checked my arm at dawn, I could see the sheets through my toes.

Enough was enough, I told myself later that day. Wrap up your missing limbs and visit a gallery, then check online for auditions coming up. Everything will be fine. I had an afternoon of contentment, feeling like a real person as I made my way around the Serpentine and navigated my way around the tubes. On the way back I sat between a young Asian man reading a book and an old white woman looking at her phone. I watched the black windows fly past until my neck got tired, and then I focused on my foot, certain I could feel it returning to normal. My thoughts were melting when the phone ringing snapped me back. "You impressed us at the audition but we need you to pop back for a second one, could you be here by 5?"

I checked my watch. "Um, I'm on my way home now I'm afraid."

"It won't take long. You are local after all, aren't you?"

"Yes, yes."

"Now arriving at London Bridge," announced the mechanised voice.

"Erm," I struggled to think, "I mean…I am here in London for a while, but I don't live here…"

"Not only are you a liar," said the director, "but a very bad one." I stared at the phone after he hung up. The eyes of the passengers around me were fixed straight ahead, as if to assure me they had heard nothing. The pursing of their lips told me otherwise. When I got home, my entire leg was missing.

I was about to set the alarm on my phone when I received a text from Sam. Just got back from work, he said, do you want to bring a film down? I pulled on my slippers and long sleeved jumper and padded downstairs. "Hello, come in," he grinned when he saw me. We sat on his bed, touching without touching. The gap between us was too wide for him, but I needed only his furtive glances to know that I was there, real and solid, that I wasn't disappearing. Halfway through the second film, however, the chasm closed in and he reached for me.

"I'm not…I mean…I've got this problem," I spluttered. He looked at me confused while I pulled back my sleeve and trouser leg. Part of me was hoping he'd tell me to get to a doctor, that there was a cure, to go and get some sleep. I didn't expect what happened next.

"Don't worry," he said, pulling off his sock to reveal nothing, "you can ignore it most of the time and if you don't panic, it doesn't spread."

I was so relieved I almost cried. I let him put his hands up my top, turned on by how much I didn't want him. He stripped me bare, invisible limbs mixing with solid, and I faced the wall while he entered me. I didn't look at him once.

When he leaned back against the pillows his eyes saw nothing. I leaned back beside him. "I'm very tired," he said, just those few words. Embarrassment flooded me and I leapt from the bed like it had an electrical charge, but it was too late. I could already feel myself disintegrating, fading, floating away from the rest of my body which drifted into the corners and melted into the woodwork, and here I stay, watching and waiting, hidden amongst the dust and the scrabbling mice.

CARE FOR A DANCE?

Helena dreamed of a castle in the sky, a kingdom in the clouds populated by giants. The next morning she awoke still in her white nightdress, her weave removed exposing afro hair, staring from a bed in a room she didn't recognise. A candle lantern glowed from the bedside table. The walls were beige and the carpets were soothing blue, though Helena was anything but soothed. Her head was heavy and her vision swirled like a black hole. "This isn't real," she decided, "it's one of those dreams that feels real, but isn't."

She shrieked when she noticed a pyjama clad man next to her looking just as confused. He was white with unremarkable brown hair and a face she'd seen a thousand times before. Desperately Helena pinched her thigh, expecting to wake up. She opened her mouth to speak but nothing came out. The man's blue eyes flicked to the window and then down, as though refusing to acknowledge what he had seen. Helena turned her head.

She screamed and sobbed, pinching her arm until red welts formed and tears coursed down her cheeks.

Two girls peered through the glass, smiling with teeth the size of pillows. Their appearance was ordinary, their dress simple and modern, yet they were enormous. "Who are you?" Helena shrieked, "Why am I here?" There was no response. She yelled again and one spoke to the other in a bizarre language of rolling tongue and guttural vowels. "Where are we?" she demanded of her male companion.

"I don't freakin' know!" he replied in a thick New York or Jersey accent.

"Well, who are you?"

"I'm no one," he shrugged, "I'm Robert, I work in a goddamn office, I go home – I'm nobody. You?"

"Well," Helena searched her mind. Picking specifics seemed impossible. "I'm Helena. I'm supposed to be travelling around Europe. I'm just saving money to go with my…" she paused. "James won't know where I am! He'll be waking up without me." She pushed against the beige walls and thick windows, all the while stared at by the couple who made 'aw, isn't that cute' faces. "Can't you help me? All we have to do is work things out logically. There must be a way out." She pressed the button on the TV for news, but nothing happened. It wasn't real. She picked up the candle lantern and turned it upside down – it was a bulb.

"Logically?" Robert snorted, "Look where we are, lady." He sauntered into a room next door. "Geez Louise, would you just look at this bathroom?"

"What?" said Helena, hoping he'd found a gap in the wall, anything.

"This is freakin' luxury," she heard him turn a tap and flush the toilet, "and the water really runs."

"Whoop de doo," she said, unable to express quite how annoyed she was at that moment.

Then the phone rang. Helena hadn't noticed it beside the bed, hanging from the wall – an old fashioned thing from the 40s. Robert entered the room, staring at it and then her, then it again. "Ain't you gonna answer it?" Helena reached for the ear piece with a shaking hand. "Oh, darlings, you're up at last," said a warbling female voice, "the drugs can knock one sideways, can't they? Still, you'll feel much better soon."

"Who is this?" Helena snapped, "what's going on?"

"I'm Christina, and nothing's going on," said the voice, "you've just found a new home. We'll be by in a minute – I've just seen my person fetch the carry case. Do keep an eye out for what Drusilla's wearing tonight. She described it to me on the phone, sounds hilarious. Don't tell her I said anything of course. See you in the ballroom."

The pair crept down the dark steps through an empty living room. The kitchen contained a working fridge of ready-made cold food in Tupperware and stubbornly useless cooking appliances. Helena flicked on the light in the hallway, turning back to Robert. His shoulders were hunched right over and he was nibbling at a handful of chick peas. He reminded her of something and she went cold. "One more room," she said loudly. A corridor with thick red carpet led to a single, white door at the far end. The red carpet was soft under Helena's bare feet as they stepped forwards in unison.

She turned the door knob. A hundred artificial lights from a chandelier and candle holders bathed a vast ballroom in a golden glow. The ceiling was adorned with rococo frills and the floor shone like freshly scrubbed wood, but felt plastic beneath their toes. Small tables covered in white cloths hugged a corner and on the largest was a punch bowl and tall glasses. The liquid inside was deep red. Beside the empty fire grate stood three figures apparently made of wood, two holding violins and the third on a stool with a cello. Their limbs moved jerkily across the instruments while the strains of classical music leaked from a miniature speaker in the wall behind them. They were automatons.

The pair turned sharply at the sound of scrabbling, the hairs at the back of Helena's neck rising. A small wooden door in the corner of the room creaked open. A woman in a ball gown, gold mask and tall hairdo emerged fluttering a fan. A man in an elaborate jacket followed her, and another couple in equally flouncy garb arrived soon after. "Who the hell are you?" said Robert, his voice wavering. The newcomers removed their masks to reveal smiling faces.

"I'm Christina," said the first woman, "remember me?" Dark make up contrasted with her powdered white skin. "We're here for this month's ball, silly. This," she indicated the woman beside her, an Indian woman with bright yellow eye shadow matching her dress, "is Drusilla. Doesn't she look divine?"

"Goodness, they're not ready," shrieked Drusilla.

"R-ready?" Helena said.

"Yes," shrieked Christina, "quickly, follow us before the others get here."

Upstairs the women fluttered about like annoying birds until she looked just as they did, squeezed into a corset and flowing skirts, wig piled high on her head. Robert was fussed over too and she would have laughed when she saw him if she hadn't wanted to cry so much. The faces peering in had multiplied and occupied several windows.

"Please," Helena said, "How do we get out? I have to get home."

"Home?" the women tittered together.

"Don't jinx this," snapped Robert.

"You are home," said Christina forcefully. "You look like..." she cast a disapproving eye over them, "new money, so you should count yourselves lucky to be in such a nice location."

"But hasn't anybody ever left?"

They thought for a moment. "Well," said Drusilla, "Misty's owners stopped feeding her when they went on holiday apparently. We never saw her again." Helena remained silent while she was led back to the ballroom.

"This is my husband Richard," said a new arrival, "well, husband since we've been here, anyway." The group guffawed and the women fluttered their fans. Helena took a hand offering a dance.

"You seem like a nice couple," said her dancing partner as he manoeuvred her through the now full room.

"Oh, we're not..."

"Sometimes this place can be like, drama, drama, drama!" he laughed, "so it'll be nice to have some sanity for once." Helena smiled weakly, her eyes searching for exit points.

"This used to be our place," Richard said when she returned. He beamed a relaxed smile which Robert tried to emulate. "They must have given it to you when we got the new place. Our new house is far too large," Richard leaned in conspiratorially, "I've no idea why they thought we'd need three swimming pools." Robert sighed in admiration. Helena was handed a goblet of wine and gulped it down, pretending to survey the room while she gathered her thoughts.

"Everyone, masks on, dance time!" Helena watched them swirl and lurch across the room to the crackling strains of the music, feeling her own stomach do the same as the wine seeped into her bloodstream.

"I'll be back in a minute," she whispered, picking up her skirts and launching herself through the door. The front room was almost pitch-black but through the windows her eyes met the enormous orbs of the giants. "Let me go," she shrieked, "Let me go!" She heard footsteps behind her and turned to see the others approach, their button and brooches sparkling in the darkness.

"Helena, calm down," said Robert soothingly. She paused. "Everyone's watching, honey." She stepped back from them, shaking her head. She span on her feet almost gracefully and threw herself into nothingness, the crash and smash of tinkling fake glass ringing in her ears. "I'm free now," thought Helena as she fell down deeper and deeper, "I'm free."

The kohl around Helena's eyes cracked when she prised open her lids. She was on a bed in a dark room. Was she home? Had she awoken? "Goodness," said Christina, leaning forwards, "we've been awfully worried. Lucky they caught you or Heavens knows where you'd be." Helena sat up and there they were, crowding in the bedroom.

"How are you feeling?" the third woman was sticking out her bottom lip in childish simulation of sadness.

"No," Helena whimpered.

"You had us worried there," said one of the men, "if you'd gone goodness knows what kind of person you'd be replaced with." The others, including Robert, tittered.

"Oh Samuel," said his husband, "You are naughty."

Robert took Helena's hand in his. "Care for a dance?"

DIMENSION LAKE

The lake is smaller than I thought it would be, but the crowd sitting on the benches surrounding it are chattering and red-faced with excitement. The benches reach right the way to the back of the field but we're at the front as my mum can't bear to be late for anything. We're situated a couple of metres back, in case anything that pops up has a long reach. People are pouring in and out of the ad hoc café set up after the discovery of the lake. On the journey over I'd played on my ipad even though mum had told me not to bring it, but I don't think I'll be looking at it much now. Next to me Tom is pinching my arm, annoying me because he doesn't know how else to release his energy. My parents laugh; they know what we're like. We put up with the school taunts of "Ooh, are you his girlfriend?" "Do you bum him on a Friday?" because otherwise we'd have to make friends with those people.

Mum offers me a sandwich but I can't eat, I'm chewing my nails looking at the expanse of water in front of us. I know the formation of reeds at its edge by heart. "Something's happening!" screeches one child. His mother shushes him but the noise around us goes up a notch.

"Look!" calls a woman. The gnarled grey head of a shark breaks the surface, but soon I see it's not normal. It gnashes three rows of teeth and the head rearing up is much larger than a regular great white.

"Daryl, stop it!" bellows the dad of a boy who's thrown his sandwich towards the monster. The prehistoric shark crashes towards the soggy bread, water drops landing at my feet. I tuck them under my seat; I feel a bit too close.

"Megalodon," sighs Tom in awe. He's brought his book of dinosaurs in case any show up today. Everyone at school tells him fourteen year olds aren't supposed to like dinosaurs anymore but he doesn't listen. I don't say anything; I'm just now noticing the lack of barriers. "Stop worrying," Tom complains - his favourite sentence when he speaks to me. "They can't leave the lake. Nothing can. It said it on the TV."

"TV isn't always right, you know," I muttered.

"Not always right?" exclaimed my dad. People turned to look. "She says the TV's not always right." Others around us begin tittering, possibly from nerves. My dad is the stocky kind. "It's OK love," he searches through the paper and cups on our table, "I'll show you." He finds what he's looking for, a piece of half chewed crust, and throws it into the water. Black beady fish eyes turn to stare at him.

"Jack," my mother hisses. She never has the courage to tell him off properly.

The Megalodon's jaws open frighteningly wide but then he sinks out of view. Bubbles ripple the surface and the nervous giggles grow louder. Tom and I glance at each other, white faced. The ripples widen to a worrying size and what emerges makes me stop breathing. Blue bodied, its long, muscular frame twists upwards and upwards endlessly until the sun is no longer in view. I grasp Tom's hand and the saucer eyes and mess of mandibles looks down at us. I'm shaking, and I check I haven't been to the toilet early.

"In other News tonight the Arron Galaxy has denied knowledge that the currency used when they visited Andromeda for a holiday would get up and run back to their ships as they were leaving. When questioned during a Press Conference, the Arron King shrugged and said, "Them's the breaks.""

Tom's shook his head in disbelief. "It's...a newsreader." I breathed out, my head feeling as though eggs had hatched inside.

"For a full update join us at ten. Now here's Naargblaarg with the weather."

Tom gets up, saying he needs water and that coke is too sticky. While he's gone he misses a couple of changes but nothing too impressive. "So," I turn to him on his return, "what do you most want to come out of there?"

Tom leans his head back, gazing at the sun even though he's always being told not to. His eyes are screwed up exaggeratedly. From this angle he looks like the marble statue of Caligula in my history text book. "Hank Williams," he says proudly.

"We've got all dimensions in the entire universe to choose from," I wrinkle my nose. Tom shrugs. "Why do you like him?" I sigh as I look back at the lake.

"Well, why do you like the Marx Brothers?"

I fold my arms, brows furrowed and lips pursed. "That's completely different."

For a while nothing appears and the audience gets restless. Tom and I begin a game of paper rock scissors while my parents resume an argument, her voice hidden behind clenched teeth and his loud and boisterous. Our game moves faster and faster as I grow in embarrassment and then Tom squeaks loudly and points to the water. Others are looking now too, except for one family who are more interested in shoving each other.

The ripples are small this time. A figure rises from the water and hovers, his feet skimming the surface, seemingly unaware that he's performing from a liquid stage when he launches into a country and western lament. I forget to cover my ears, so peculiar is the thing I'm seeing. My confusion is mirrored on the faces of the other onlookers. Tom is enraptured. After two songs he takes a bow and, to a ripple of uncertain applause, sinks back down. "Here, drink this," Tom shoves his water cup into my hand.

"What have you done to it?"

"Nothing," his face is intense, "just drink some and say what you'd like to appear."

"What if it doesn't exist?" I shrug.

"In the whole universe, which is infinite," Tom's hands are moving quickly now, "it's bound to exist somewhere. Unless it's really stupid I suppose."

I sip the water. "A pink glittery tiger." Tom looks at me in disgust. "I am allowed to be a girl sometimes, you know," I shove him not so gently.

We wait, and when the water ripples again I'm preparing my sceptical face. The sun is growing angry and no factor number can save me now, I'm almost ready to leave. Again, though, I'm held still by shock. A terrifying beast with sabre teeth emerges, paws floundering and grasping at land, unleashing its claws in frustration. It's a sabre tooth tiger, all furry rage and sharp aggression. It's also baby pink with hot pink stripes, and covered in glitter. I'm aware that my mouth is open and it's not an attractive look, but I can't help myself. I close my eyes, willing it to sink back down to its own planet, not wanting to watch it drown. Everyone around me is feeling it too.

"Shouldn't we do something?" I hear one person say.

"No, I'm sure it's all part of the thing," someone replies.

I stand up and stride to the water's edge. "Go away," I whisper. The creature continues to flounder. I vaguely hear my parents shouting behind me but I don't hear them. "Go away!" The tiger is sucked down and away and I lean back against the table, the tightness in my chest gone. The conversations around us largely involve going home, and we decide to do the same.

I try to involve Tom in a game of eye spy in the car but he's not taking much notice, which makes me weirdly angry. He's doing his thinking face - a kind of odd - tight expression, and we have an argument about him not joining in with things.

The next night I go to his house after dinner, feeling bad because I was a bit over the top when I got angry. His mum answers the door. "Oh, hello Sarah," she says brightly. When Tom and I were small both our parents thought we wouldn't have friends because we were too odd, so when we found each other they were very relieved. You can still see it in their expressions when they invite one of us in. "He's been very quiet in his room today," she says, standing aside so I can rush past her and go up the stairs.

"Thanks Mrs Jeffs." I open his bedroom door, remembering to knock only when it's partway open. Luckily he's not doing anything embarrassing and I sit on the bed which still has a batman duvet cover. He seems as though his mind is on other things which makes me slightly indignant. When I look at his eyes I see they're sparkling with something, probably mischief. "What?"

"That lake," his hands flutter in his lap as he searches for the right words, "when we drank water, we controlled what came up."

"Yeah, but," the sense of unease is back in my chest, "I nearly drowned something."

Tom looks annoyed at my lack of enthusiasm. "You did something wrong, it worked when I did it." I don't reply; anything I say will just cause another argument. "We have to test it out again. Can you imagine?" His eyes aren't seeing me anymore, "We won't have to live here anymore. No more Jenny or Mike, we won't have to listen to them going on about us having sex with our parents or being gay – even though you're a girl. We can go somewhere else." I want to say something - to say no - but I don't want to deflate his happiness. I haven't seen him like this in a long time, probably since we used to play with aquatic toys in a half filled bath when we were nine.

"Yes," I say quietly. He takes this as a cue and pulls me to my feet.

"Come on," he marches to the window, "we're going to the lake." I follow him like a simpleton with no voice, grappling onto the tree and following him down to the ground, not making much effort to be quiet when I almost slip. We've spent too long being good children, however, and Tom's mum doesn't come outside like I hope she will. We probably could have just told her we were going for a bike ride but somehow it seemed as though it should be like this. Tom takes his bike out of the garage and hands me his mum's, and we're off.

I'm out of breath halfway there and have to keep stopping. Also a stone is caught in my sock and I can't seem to find it. Tom waits not so patiently but I remind him I didn't bring my inhaler and that shuts him up. Keen as he is to escape, he doesn't want his plan to involve murder. After a while we set off again and with the wind in my face and nature around me I forget we have a secret plan and just enjoy myself.

This ends when we reach our destination and I get that feeling like I used to just before birthday parties when I'd get too excited and spend the entire time in the loo throwing up. The benches are empty and the café closed. The lake is doing what they do in poems; it surface is sparkling and shimmering in the evening sun. Sitting in a chair beside it is a security guard, which makes us pause until we hear his deep snoring. We creep closer. There are no ripples, nothing surges forwards, but I can't move any further. My feet won't shift from their position, but Tom is edging closer and closer. His face is pale and mine probably is too. He takes a bottle of water from his pocket and twists the lid. The liquid spurts up and outwards in a foamy fizz. "You brought sparkling," I say accusingly. He looks embarrassed.

"I didn't realise. I wanted to use mineral water just in case."

I sigh. "I'm going to see if they've got water at the café. If it's locked I'll smash a window or something."

"You'll get in trouble," says Tom, the fear of being told off seared into his face.

"Well, if we're going to another dimension it probably won't matter." I think of the new life me and Tom can begin, away from school and parents and bullies. I pull the café door handle but it doesn't give; I hadn't thought this far ahead. I look about me for something to use against the glass, but the only chair has the sleeping security guard on it. I could distract him by pretending to fall out of the tree over there and, when he's going that way to help I could run back and grab…something in the café catches my eye and interrupts my thoughts.

"Hank Williams," I hear Tom call.

"Tom hang on, don't," I gabble, "it's not going to work. They're suctioning water from the lake to sell in there," I point inside the café to demonstrate further but Tom is already wading in. He's drained what little of the water was left and thrown it over his shoulder, a rebellious act by a boy who had never been naughty in his life. The water bubbles and the security guard stirs, making a weird choking sound and gazing about him in sleepy confusion. "Tom!" I yell, "Whatever comes up, it won't be him." Tom hears the urgency in my voice and takes a few steps back; I slump to the ground in relief. But I was wrong - a human figure is emerging, rising upwards, toes skimming the surface with guitar in hand. Tom yelps in delight and bounds into the depths, swimming towards freedom.

Hank looks down at the boy rushing towards him. I know, suddenly, that things aren't right. I don't move though, the security guard and I call out to Tom but he can't hear us anymore. The singer licks his lips and opens a jaw wide as a baleen whale sucking in plankton. I scream as Tom's head is sucked in and an audible crunch attacks my ears. The creature opens his maw to get a better grip and Tom's body slides down as it lifts its head to the sky. He stops struggling when his feet are submerged, and we can do is watch. Eventually the creature's head disappears from view beneath the surface and everything is peaceful. The water bottle and the lake glint under the surface of the moon.

FEATHERS AND FAME

"Anne, are you ready?" Martin asks me, his eyes big and blue and earnest. All the suits at the table in the beige room are waiting for my reply.

"Uh, yeah."

It's all they can do to keep from clapping their hands, their faces registering almost obscene pleasure. I'm certain mine has paled. I hope it looks porcelain and stoically beautiful like the painting of the First Woman.

A year ago, before my first journey, I went to the Gallery of Brave Women to get myself in the mood. As always I bypassed the photos and clippings of the modern era and the sepia jazz age pictures of girls in flapper dresses and went straight to Her. There is always a small crowd around her but, as I had been chosen, they murmured amongst themselves and parted the way for me.

The Brave Woman's image is captured just before she goes on her first mission, a tradition dating back to the very first one. She wears only her bloomers and corset, a normally scandalous image for the time, but it is necessary to wear as little as possible for the journey. She looks so proud that you could never accuse her of indecency.

"Why do they always have to die?" asked a small boy. His mother glanced at me, horrified. I gave her that tight smile to show it's alright your little darling didn't offend me, when really they have.

"Come on, let's go look at last year's Brave Woman," she dragged him away.

"But they dooooo," he looked at me, outraged that no one will listen, desperate for backup. "They fly for a year and die on their last mission and everyone's sad and then there's a new one."

"Michael," the mother's tone was final and they were gone. All eyes avoided me and I scuttled to the next room where I laid down on the gilded mattress and looked up at the painting on the domed ceiling. The famous classical artist, Don Mercheado, captured with pinpoint detail, precise brushstrokes and endless patience the flight of the First Woman. It was a warm study of her soaring over the hills of the Terrible Unknown with terracotta wings on her back, the then much smaller city behind her surrounded by the iron fence. Below her in the grassy expanse were depictions of the children's toys that had, one day, come to life and started attacking: Squishables. Snapping their teeth and beaks were pink kittens, purple ducks, big eared rabbits and fuzzy pandas, while the crystal blue stream held tubby Narwhals, green turtles and octopi who waved their felt covered tentacles in the air, all straining to reach the figure miles above them. Since then avant-garde artists had done their own depictions of the scene, but to my ordered mind this is the best.

I said goodbye to the public gallery and moved into the ultra-secure Elite compound. From the window of my new chauffeur driven car I saw high class restaurants, vintage diners and sleek coffee shops. Nestled between them were shops to buy suits, tailors specialising in suits, shops to buy ties to go with suits, casual jacket shops and an evening dress multiplex. At the centre of it all, looming over every other building and pointing far up into the sky, was the 'Pulse Point,' the building all the most important people work in. The gates to the rest of the world closed behind me and I was taken to my new luxury apartment.

I was shaking the first time I removed my outer clothes. I held my hands in front of my underwear but the photographer kept telling me to look more relaxed, so eventually I complied just to get it over with. They had taken me in the lift up several flights of stairs to a tiny room like a clock tower, empty save for a pair of motorised purple wings. They hooked my arms through the leather straps and connected them with the one between my legs.

"This latest model is the most sophisticated yet," smiled the suit on the right. I smiled insipidly back and stood on the windowsill, feet together like I'd been shown. I pressed the button by my shoulder and the wings flapped slowly. With a shot of adrenaline I closed my eyes and tumbled forward – and I was flying. My limbs bobbed up and down on the wind, feeling almost like swimming but even more weightless. I soared over the city fence while people cheered below me and I couldn't help feeling like I wanted to cry with gratitude. Soon I was flying over the Terrible Unknown, the vast wilderness no longer inhabited by humans.

At first there were just a few dotted about the landscape, but those few began to cluster. I navigated my way over some particularly tall trees, the rush of air beneath the flapping wings making me feel like I've been shot into space. I spread my arms and legs out, stretching my digits as far as they'll go. Beneath me the clusters of Squishables collected into a mass, dog teeth gnashing and stumpy pig hands reaching up, and other animals that I don't even think truly exist. I could hear their demanding growls but there was nothing they could do about it.

I felt like singing or crying when I reached the supply compound in a new record time, landing on the other side of the fence to the now hysterical Squishables. Ruddy faces under hard hats looked me up and down and, for a moment, I wanted to cross my arms over my chest again. "Got a good one 'ere," one of them nudged his younger comrade, who shot me an apologetic glance.

"Here," said the younger as he guided me to a large crate and fed ropes through handles on either side. "These attach onto here," he looped the ropes through the straps of my wings. His overalls smelled like oil and sweat and soap. Again I was conscious of my lack of attire but this time in a different way. "Ok," he looked down awkwardly, "you're good to go."

I pressed the button on my back and this time the take-off wasn't so swift. I was conscious how ridiculous my flailing looked to those men behind me and I couldn't look back. To look back would have been to acknowledge that they could see me. After several minutes I was high enough to push forward and sail above the Squishables, who still wailed and moaned for my blood. As I crawled awkwardly across the sky I was certain I could make out a human skeleton half wedged underneath a bush. I kept my eyes resolutely on the distant point until the multi-coloured bricks of the city were visible.

I was shaking when I landed, partly from exertion but also elation. I struggled to keep my cool; the last thing I wanted was for them to think I enjoyed myself but what the Hell, I had. The lightness when the wings and crate were removed made me feel as though I was passing out and in a second I was guided to a chair and fussed over by the suits. "You should come to the party tonight," said a woman, Maria. I agreed to go but nothing made me want to throw up more. When I knew they were all back in their offices or getting ready, I snuck out. I just needed to breathe fresh air for a moment instead of that same expensive soap smell that permeated all the corridors. I wandered the shops and entertainment facilities of the compound, keeping my head down so the kids in the bowling alley and couples in restaurants didn't notice me. When I reached the cinema I dived into its quiet darkness, buying my ticket and hurrying through the turnstiles past the popcorn and candy floss vendors.

The room was empty. A short flashed across the big screen, a silver document of Woman 556 who stunned the world with her beauty before falling into drugs and dying of an overdose during her final mission. I stared at her large eyes and wraithlike figure during footage of her posing for photographs and signing autographs, not noticing the person approach until they flopped heavily into the seat beside me.

"Oops, sorry," she said, dispelling my fears that I'm about to be molested. She was dressed in a torn overcoat and her hair was a bird's nest that matched her hooked beak nose. I should have been disgusted but it was an odd relief to see her.

"That's OK," I smiled.

"Want some popcorn?" she offered me an overflowing cardboard bucket.

"Oh, no thanks," I said, "I have to watch my figure."

"Bollocks," she retorted, "a couple of handfuls won't make no difference." I had no answer for this so I scooped up a load and shoved the sweet, buttery morsels into my mouth. My tongue warmed pleasantly.

"There you are," said a sharp voice that made me yelp. Maria's hands were on her hips as if I'd been naughty. Which, I suppose, I had. "Come on, we've got to get you ready for that party." I turned to my companion who simply shrugged, and I followed Maria out into the light.

My mind ticked over the mistakes I'd made with my outfit and hair when I saw the well groomed folk at the smooth and shiny bar. In minutes though I felt as though I could have arrived nude and they would still squeal and flock and squawk at the sight of me. In fact they probably would have declared it 'edgy.' Daniel and Martin were by my side in an instant, leading me through the melee to the now empty bar. "Just a coke please," I said, and the disappointment in my choice radiated from them.

"You know Agara, or Woman 334, would drink an entire bottle of whiskey at parties. She did some hilarious things," Martin's eyes crinkled in Daniel's direction as they shared a memory, "she would get up on the bar and sing and, one night, she fell into that bucket of glass and had to be taken to hospital." They snuffled and snorted with laughter.

"Of course," Daniel said, "eventually it proved too much and it took over her life. She crashed into the Squishables after an all-night bender. She'll always be remembered, she burned so brightly." They lowered their solemn gazes in respect. I knew the woman they meant, my cousins and their friends still made regular pilgrimages to her 'grave' to pray for thanks. I tried not to fidget but I wondered how long I had to follow their example and if those sofas in the backroom were as comfortable as they looked. At last they collected my drink and led me to them.

The night was a hurricane of praise and laughter. Familiarity seeped into the caricatures buzzing at my side, showing me the warmth and humour beneath their veneers. I'd been so wrong about the elite and I felt ashamed of myself, but also deliriously happy. Martin and Daniel seemed almost as pleased. "You know," Martin leaned in closely, "you have what it takes. The others only lasted a year but you," he appraised her briefly; "you can go on forever. I saw you when you got back, those creatures don't frighten you. You give the people hope in a champion." I laughed somewhat louder than I meant to, feeling remarkably hot on the inside.

"You're tired," Daniel said, "let's get you back." I followed him like a contented sheep.

The months followed in a blur of photography and parties. Crowds still gathered whenever I dived from the balcony and I waved to them from above. I landed with a balletic flourish over the supplier's gate and grinned at the waiting men. The young man on my first visit was there again and he smiled before looking away, blushing. "Good to see you," I purred like Woman 165 and sidled up to him. He looked like a frightened animal and I secretly rejoiced at my power. The smell of his skin was just as good as before and I looked forward to the time when, no doubt, I would sample it.

I sashayed to the crate and allowed him to hook me up. I was aware of every pulse in his body.

The Squishables never learned that they couldn't catch me and I swooped lower, feeling the tips of their fingers brush against my stomach before pulling up again. The suits were delirious as always to see the bounty and I was informed of yet another party I was expected to attend. I picked out my clothes hours in advance.

I donned a sleek dress and purple Squishable fur-trimmed coat. The bar was packed and all faces turned to me. I felt breathless from the attention and made my way to the back room sofas, taking my place next to Daniel and Martin. We chatted briefly before Martin smiled awkwardly and disappeared into the crowd. "Where's he going?"

"Oh," Daniel flicked a hand "he has some people he needs to speak to. So tell me how this morning went." After a minute or two, however, he patted me on the shoulder. "Excuse me for a moment, won't you? I've got to see to something." He too disappeared and I swilled my vodka while I waited. Everyone else in the back room was involved in serious conversation so I gave up and joined the crowds in the non-VIP section, pleased that they at least were excited by my presence.

I awoke the next morning, wrapped in extra soft sheets and anxiety. I needed to do something, to ease something, but I wasn't not sure what or why. I dressed quickly in nondescript clothes and a hat and made my way to the cinema.

The feature was a full length colour biopic on Woman 771. I spotted my companion, already munching on sickly sweet smelling popcorn, and sat down next to her. Woman 771 wasn't as fascinating as the others but I didn't care, I was just grateful for the moving images. Known for her excessive body building, Woman 771 lasted a little less than her allotted year and famously announced that she would "never be executed like the others." Of course after her death when they searched her apartment all the evidence of a troubled mind was found. My companion offered me popcorn which I take greedily and, after a while, I had to admit that the actress playing Woman 771 was convincing enough to draw me in.

"You know," said my companion, "this lady might have been well rank but at least you remembered her." I nodded thoughtfully, my mind ticking as I stepped back into the sun. That afternoon I called Martin and told him to arrange a press conference.

Their eager faces stared up at me like baby birds. The cameras were poised and the pens of the reporters were waiting like beaks pointed down at their pads. I breathed deeply and steadied myself. "Thank you all so much for coming," I said, "I have an announcement to make." The only movement is the dust. "It is with regret that I inform you of my struggle with Lymphatic spasms." For a tenth of a second there was a silence so silent it pounded, and then the questions and flashes began. I reached out in shock and Martin was right there to tightly hold my hand.

"We don't know too much about it at this stage," he said, "only that Woman 997 is an inspiration to all and we are certain we can find a cure to this terrible affliction that blights her life." At this I bowed my head, willing the tear I had nurtured for the last ten minutes to fall down my cheek. It did, right on cue. Martin guided me through the crowds to the door, where I stepped into my car and was driven to my apartment. Before I got out Martin grabbed my hand. "Make sure you rest well." I was uncertain whether to reply honestly or in character so instead I just nodded.

I laid down on the bed and sleep came swiftly for once. It was dark when the telephone woke me. "Oh, Anna, they finally let me through."

"Hmm?"

"I've been trying to ring you all evening and the operator kept telling me you were sleeping. Well, I didn't want to wake you but I just had to know, you must understand."

"Mum," I shouted, "what is it?"

"Well," she paused, "it's all over the news, your illness, Lympho...er, what was it? I'm sorry I can't remember, I..."

"Mum," I was sweating with panic, "I'm fine, honestly, there's nothing wrong with me."

"Oh, you're so brave, but you don't have to be with me. I can put in for a visit? Surely they'd make an exception and let me in sooner than a week..."

"No, mum, honestly, it's only a small problem, honestly don't worry."

"Yes of course," she soothed, "you just get your rest."

I hung up and shivered, trying to dispel the icky crawling sensation. I switched on the TV and almost collapsed – headlines screamed on every channel: "Woman 997's brave battle with fatal disease." I slapped a hand to my mouth, I was shaking; this was a dream, a dream. I pinched my face but the press conference footage was still there, rolling captions declaring: "Woman 997 bravely pours some water and takes a sip," "Woman 997 heroically adjusts her chair." I dived for the telephone.

"Don't worry" said Martin, "this is just to keep their interest. Imagine how wild they'll go when you beat it. You'll be an inspiration to women everywhere." I replaced the handset, deciding I would just have to trust them.

Press conferences followed and leaked photos, all staged of course, of me in hospital beds waving bravely, followed by family pictures including the embarrassing one of me dancing in a bear outfit at the age of 7. When my mother phoned, however, the operators told her I was sleeping. I just couldn't deal with the guilt. When the next pick-up time arrived I was weirdly grateful. I wanted to show them how talented I was so they'd keep me on forever. I felt pure freedom as the wind rushed over my skin and prickled against my cheeks. I didn't even look down; I didn't want to spoil anything.

The compound loomed ahead and I smiled when I saw the young man. His older companion waved me down as if I didn't know how to do it myself, but for some reason that day I was touched, finally seeing it as the helpful gesture it was meant to be. I landed without flair and the crate was hooked up to me. I leaned into the young man but he seemed preoccupied, his eyes darting everywhere but at me. I leaned further, embarrassingly close to him, and felt my cheeks turn red when he pulled back.

I was set, ready to go, and they stood there watching me. I should have just pressed my button and pushed myself into the air, but for some reason it felt like my last chance. "Do you want to meet up sometime?" I asked with a voice hoarse from a closing throat.

"Uh, I kind of…I'm not really…"

"No, that's fine!" I blurted, climbing high into the air and not looking back. I couldn't let him see the mortification on my face. As soon as Martin and David removed my wings I dived past them and ran down the stairs. I could hear them call after me about press conferences and fake hospital appointments but I didn't answer, I just kept running. The security men at the ground floor door looked up in surprise, not expecting to have to catch the person they were protecting.

I ran aimlessly past the Sushi Takeaway and the Velvet Curtains shop until I was outside the cinema once again. As always in the afternoon only a scattering of people were watching the show; a biopic of girl 334, the jazz dancer with the petrol problem. I was relieved to spot my companion, briefly wondering if she ever did anything else. We exchanged smiles and I stuffed my mouth with as much popcorn as possible.

"You OK?" she whispered. I half shrugged, half shook my head. "You know, it helps to talk."

"I've been lied to, and now I have to do something I really don't want to." A kernel stuck in the back of my throat and my eyes began to water. Humiliatingly they turned into real tears.

"Oh shit," she rubbed my back hard with calloused hands but the thought was there, it was comforting. "Sometimes we've got to put up with things. Look at her," she indicated the woman portrayed on the screen, "she had problems, the audience loved her and she did what she was meant to. Would we still be watching her if she lived to be an old lady?" I shook my head, my thoughts glooping together like paint. "Course not. We need those women, where would we be without them? Depressed as fuck, that's where!" I was shaking violently and, when she went to speak again, I raised my hand to stop her. We watched the rest of the film in silence and at the end I got up without saying goodbye.

They lead me from the beige office up the stairs to the launching room. They clip the wings to me and Martin takes one hand and David takes the other and we look at each other with a strange detachment. We're sad, but we all just want to get on with it. I launch myself into the air and the concrete below fades into green. Every part of me shrieks but I remain silent until I've flown about halfway. I consider smacking my head into a tree to cushion it but I doubt it'll work, and I lower myself down, down, down until I feel their little hands grasp at my belly and thighs and shins. An extra hard tug on my ankle pulls me to the ground and I'm amongst them and they cover me and I can't breathe and their teeth and claws are tearing and yanking, and all I can think about is the office company logo I saw peeping from beneath my cinema companion's torn jacket.

GIRL IN THE PICTURE

The industrial building was filled with sweaty, curious people. I wanted to see the main attraction of course but, unwilling to appear a philistine, I wandered through the gallery as slowly as possible. When I finally reached the room upstairs, which was white and clean with pine floorboards, I could sense her. I hurried through the other exhibitions; past a clown weeping on a podium, party blower tooting before another burst of sobs, past a man covered in cobwebs sleeping on a bed, past two women endlessly breast feeding each other and then she was there, Girl In The Picture.

I joined the crowd, quietly resenting the idea that children should always go at the front. I'm short, why can't I? I felt momentarily grateful that those around me couldn't see into my mind. All of us were transfixed by the thing hanging from the wall: a large square golden frame surrounding a bare room containing a desk, a table and a chair. If you were to run to the other side of the thin wall to check behind it you would see nothing but a nude old man in a Marilyn Monroe wig.

In that little bare room, centre place, was a girl. Not a painting, not a video, a girl. Her scruffy black hair was mostly in bunches that stuck up in the air, the rest loose tendrils. She wore an old looking dark jacket that may have been smart once but was now covered in badges, and leggings. She was dancing but not the kind I do until embarrassment stops me or the aggressive grinding perpetrated by strippers. This was a dance you do when you're completely free of self-consciousness, although I still got the idea that she was entertaining us. She twirled and whirled happily, arms reaching out gracefully whenever she deemed it necessary. She was in her own world. She looked wonderful.

"She's a bad influence," said a Yorkshire lady whose arms resembled uncooked dough. "My sister went to see her last week and she were smashing that chair against the table and sticking her middle fingers up."

"Oh, no," said a second Yorkshire lady (I surmised they must be a tour group). "My children went to see her last Monday with their dad," she indicated the two girls in front of her, "and she were blowing bubbles through one of those things," she held her thumb and fore-finger up to indicate the stick. "They went all through the gallery, it sounded lovely."

"Well," the first lady sniffed, clearly put out, "I still think she looks scruffy."

"Oh, no," said an old woman leaning against a stick, "she's like them artistic ones in the building next to mine. Always bring me Garibaldis from the shop they do."

"Well, I agree with you," said a man to the now red faced and fuming woman, "friend of mine said she was swearing too. Violent benefit thieves the lot of 'em."

I tried to tune out the conversation but it was no good. I decided to go and come back before closing.

The natural light had disappeared and all that remained were the brutal strip lights on the ceiling. This time I forewent the show of looking at the rest of the pieces and went straight up the metal steps. The clown was still tooting and weeping and the man was still sleeping and the women were still suckling and there she was.

For a split second I couldn't see her but when I turned fully to face the bare room I saw her sitting serenely in the chair just waiting. She saw me and smiled. "Can…can you hear me?" I asked, feeling a bit daft.

"Yes, I can hear you," she said.

I was silent for a moment. I hadn't actually expected her to reply and now that she had I didn't know what to say. "Erm, is everything alright?"

She laughed a deep, free laugh. "Yes, I'm fine." But I caught something in her face, momentarily.

"What is it?"

"Well," she seemed uncomfortable, "I like being looked at, but sometimes it's very tiring." I nodded, wishing I could say something but finding nothing in my mind. "I look at all of you and I think about how nice it must be to do whatever you want and not worry about it."

I shrugged. "Well, why don't you try not worrying about it?" I realised how ridiculous my statement was and proceeded to turn bright red. "What I mean is, just do what you would be doing anyway."

She stood up, a dangerous gleam in her eyes. "Will you help me? To get out I mean?"

I scuffed my shoes. "Well, why me?"

Her beautiful face tipped to the side, tainted with sadness. "You're the first person who's actually spoken to me."

I could almost hear the groan I felt inside. "Ok," I said, "what should I do?" She gestured for me to come close, closer, closer. She reached a hand out and I did the same. Our fingertips touched and I felt a shiver, a jolt of something that made me want to ring, tweet and text everyone I knew.

"Take my hand," she said and I did. I gripped as hard as I could and she did the same and I found myself wondering what she would do when she was free, would she consider staying at mine, when she told me to pull. I pulled and pulled her arm as hard as I could, until sweat dotted my forehead and my grip became slippery. With a final desperate yank I tore her free and I yelped with excitement. I went to hug her, already planning how I would smuggle her past security. When I stepped forwards, though, there was nothing there. "Um," I said desperately, "hello?" I looked up and down the gallery, expecting any minute to be hauled away and arrested, but it was silent. She had gone. The room was now only a desk, a table and a chair. After about fifteen minutes of just staring I made my way back down the steps and, for lack of any other options, out of the front door.

I CAN SEE YOU

Her hand gripped the plastic chair. Her face ached from holding her smile but she held it like a true professional. Occasionally she wondered about the people passing the department store window, did they notice her? Did they wonder how awkward it was to hold the same position day in, day out? Were they tempted by the fake dining room she stood in, and what were the men thinking when they tried to peer up her dress? When these thoughts weren't running through her mind she reran her favourite music videos and films in her head to pass the time.

She didn't move at first when the store manager called her name, so ingrained was the company rules. "Julia," he said again, tapping her shoulder. She jumped, disproportionally shocked, which made him jump too. "Sorry to uh, startle you," he said, tugging at his grey beard, "but we'd like you to do something different today."

"Oh really?"

"Yes, please follow me." He handed her a change of clothes which she slipped into behind a changing stand. The new white lace dress covered more of her body than the previous outfit. Julia didn't like the chintzy frills on the edges but would never let on to the manager. "Marvellous," he said, "let's get you set up."

Julia spent the remainder of the afternoon in a kitchen, she and the appliances a frozen imitation of aspiration. The customers laughed and joked, checking which oven did what and how much space the cupboards held, the flush of promise on their cheeks. Julia stared into the middle distance, her hand poised proprietorially on the table. No men's eyes peered at her ankles, for that was now all that was visible. Despite this she put as much effort into keeping still as she always had.

"I like that cooker, by the old lady," announced a voice. Julia almost looked up and ruined the illusion, but caught herself in time. The words, though, reached into her most private hiding spaces.

She shut her front door at the end of the day, almost treading on the envelope on the mat. The whiteness of her flat and its furniture was hypnotic in its blankness. She took the envelope to the sofa in the front room and tore at it with shaking hands, her heart fizzing as if she were opening an invitation to a party. Two pictures fell into her lap; this was a new thing. She studied them, one of her in last week's window display with the parasol and one taken yesterday. On the back of both was written in neat biro: "I can see you." She picked up the letter that came with them: "I will cut you up." She held them all to her chest and sighed deeply, she could almost smell his cologne and her fingers must be touching the same places his had. She studied the handwriting again for any clues but, as always, she couldn't place it. She thought back to the shifts she had worked in the photograph, re-imagining them with the sensation of someone's gaze caressing her.

She was half watching television when the knock came at the door. Nervously, wondering if her man had come at last, she called through the letter box, "hello?"

"It's me, you plonker," said her sister's voice. Julia rolled her eyes as she let her in. "What took you so long?" said Sam.

Julia watched her ramble on about work and her friends who were apparently selfish because they didn't finish a report for her while she was off sick, delicate hands flicking up every two minutes to touch the ends of her short dark hair, and ended up missing her favourite programme. Eventually Julia steeled herself. "Why are you here?"

"Oh, that's nice, isn't it? Well, Jim's doing the decorating and there's paint fumes everywhere, I just can't deal with it so I thought, Julia always needs help with her life, she'll be happy to see me."

"Yes," Julia smiled tightly, "it's nice to see you."

"Speaking of which," Sam surveyed the white walls, "this place still looks like a bloody spaceship. Have you not redone it yet?"

Julia got up and headed upstairs, "spaceships are silver, and this is how I like it."

In bed, hidden by darkness, Julia thought of the letter and the pictures again. She imagined the man who sent them, thought of black tentacles oozing towards her home and smashing the windows just to get to her, wrapping themselves over her body and face, sliding up her nostrils and into her ears and eyes. She brought herself to climax just as she drew her last breath.

When she made her way down the stairs that morning she knew something was wrong. "What the hell is the meaning of this?" her sister fumed. Julia felt her face flame, what had she done and what could she say to limit the damage? When she saw the letters in her sister's hand she knew it was over.

"It's not…I haven't technically done anything or even met him…"

"Julia," Sam snapped, "I know you don't want to worry people but you can't just deal with something like this on your own."

"I…" Julia deflated, "I can't?"

"What have the police said?"

Julia shrugged. "I didn't think it was necessary." Why didn't she just lie?

"What?" Julia imagined Sam exploding. "When will you stop burying your head in the sand?"

"Oh, why don't you leave me alone?" Julia knew she sounded like an adolescent, or at least the younger sibling, but the compassion in her sister's eyes was worse than her scorn. Sam had always been the one wanted by men.

"Remember to behave," Sam would grin when Julia was dumbstruck by another boy. It seemed too intimate to just talk to them at parties. The few times she tried they stared at her hunched shoulders and lank hair with embarrassment, glancing wistfully at Sam. Instead Julia led them to a room upstairs where they soon forgot everyone else, if only for ten minutes. With pride she would watch their cheeks flush and their pupils dilate. But in the next minute they were already turning away.

When expensive wine glasses replaced ash filled beer cans a note of concern crept into Sam's warning, "Remember to behave." But Julia fell in love with each new man, a light switching on inside her. They fell in love with her too – if only for ten minutes.

Sam reached for the phone, handing it to her when a local officer appeared on the line.

The crowds in the department store were pushing and knocking against Julia but she stood absolutely, resolutely still, unlike the new girl in the main window who was smiling at a young man this morning. It was the lack of professionalism that upset Julia. She, on the other hand, could almost convince them she wasn't there and yet draw them in with a hand subtly placed against the product. It wasn't her job to be the customer's main focus. They weren't meant to be looking at her. The fact that they so rudely bashed against her whilst checking the appliances just meant she was doing it properly.

Huffing with relief Julia opened the front door to her home, hoping that another present might be waiting for her. Instead two policemen sat on her sofa, one with thick hair growing from his ears and nostrils and the other looking as though he couldn't even shave yet. They refused a cup of tea and Sam gestured for her to stop fussing and sit down. The one with sprouting hair looked pleased with himself. "We've had a breakthrough," he said. "Your sister here caught someone posting one of the inappropriate letters through the box today and called us. We know who he is and we've got officers looking for him right now to bring him in for questioning."

"Oh," Julia said, "that was rather quick." He sat back, waiting for her to thank him tearfully. She managed a weak smile.

"We looked right at each other," Sam shivered dramatically, "and he ran away. The message inside the envelope was just horrible."

"You read it?" shrieked Julia.

"I did, I just had to know," Sam looked as if she were finally getting the desired reaction from her sister.

"You...*bitch*! That was meant for me." Julia didn't care that tears sprang into her sister's eyes – she wanted to claw them out completely.

"No doubt you're exhausted by all this," the officers rose, "we'll let you get on with your evening."

"Yes, thank you officer," Sam stood with them, glaring at her sister as she opened the door and let them out. "You're obviously shaken," she said without much warmth, "maybe you'd better lie down?"

"Yes," Julia muttered. "Could you...would you lie with me? Just for a while?"

Sam took on a matronly role, "yes, come on, upstairs then."

Julia opened her eyes. Sam's breathing had softened into rhythm several hours ago and the window was black. Shadows skulked over the white room. The footsteps had led up to the house and she had heard the distinctive creak of a ladder being climbed. He had evaded the police. He was coming for her, she knew, and her heart could have leaked onto the sheets for joy. She turned to her sister; for once she would be made to understand things from her point of view. Once she experienced love the way Julia did she would understand at last.

Julia closed her eyes like an excited child waiting for a present. The smash of the window was enough to yank her sister from sleep but still Julia refused to open her eyes. Instead as the screams began she felt the black tentacles oozing from the broken glass, twitching their way towards the girls and coiling around them. 'At last,' thought Julia as they wound their sticky way up her body, finding and filling her mouth and nose and ears, 'I'll never be alone again.'

INVITE GHOSTS AND EARN POUNDS

"You did what?" I stand in our front room, staring down at Mike rolling another joint on the sofa.

"You're always getting onto me about getting a job, so I got one."

"I meant…" Fury fizzes my mind away like a bath bomb. "I meant…a job…not…"

"Look," he meets my eye with firm finality, "This gets me money and it means I can carry on writing. That's what you wanted, isn't it?" I have to admit this is true, though part of me wants him to experience the gruelling banality of rising at the same time every morning when your mind hasn't had enough time to dream and refuel, over and over again. Accepting ghosts into the house, however, is good enough for the time being. He shows me the newspaper ad: "do you wish you had company all the time? Short of money? Accept ghosts into your house and earn £££££."

It happens quickly after that. The house is checked over for suitability – enough rooms for psychics to wander through and plenty of cracks and loose panels for TV crews to shine torches into. A few days afterwards the handler arrives with several boxes. He's very attractive in a conventional sort of way, which isn't normally my thing, but I can't help getting depressed when I see him next to Mike's pale face and vacant eyes.

The front door is checked three times to be sure it's locked and the boxes are opened. Tiny beams of fluorescent light shoot from them; one settles under the loose floorboard in the front room and the others dart through the open longue door. "That's great," beams the handler, "they're finding a base. In a couple of days they'll be strong enough to make themselves known. The TV channels will be in touch as soon as." I shake his hand, holding onto it so long he begins to look nervous.

Several nights later Mike and I are sprawled over the sofa watching TV. "They're the COPS," roars the voiceover, "they don't take no shit from no-one, you better get out of their way." One of the beefy cops on screen is holding a taser and running after a crying shirtless man. When the door knocks I yelp disproportionately.

"Sorry," I grumble to Mike who looks up in surprise. "I've been a bit on edge."

I'm even more shocked when I open the front door to see a large camera crew and female presenter with smooth blonde hair. "Here we are," she says to the crew, "at number 53 Terrace Green and this is one of the residents. Tell me," she turns to me with ardent blue eyes, "have you heard knocking, or banging or groaning?" She stares at me, the crew waits, there is silence.

29

"Erm, yes."

"I'm sure that must have been terrifying," she barges inside followed by her entourage.

"Oh, it was," Mike rises from his seat, his eyes now wide with fear. "Some nights we've just considered leaving, but all our money has been sunk into this property."

I open my mouth to contradict him but something clicks. "Oh yes," I step forwards, unnerved by the cameras swinging my way. "Sometimes I'm too scared to go anywhere on my own."

"Yes, it must be awful," the presenter, Amanda Ballad I remember now, makes a sympathetic face. They film throughout the room before disappearing eagerly into the others, Amanda wittering about a history of witches and broken hearted housemaids who all met their fates in these very rooms. I'm shivering just thinking about it.

Mike and I sit back down on the sofa while heavy footsteps trample upstairs. Mike's nervous, I can tell. We've not had any visitations yet and who knows if the things even took? The floorboards could be damp or the walls might not have big enough gaps or…

I hear a moan and a quick glance at Mike tells me he heard it too. I grab his hand and hold it tightly and there's another moan. It's deep and basey and like something from the bowels of Hell. A finger pokes its way through the floorboard, followed by a hand and an entire arm that pulls a torso up to the middle of the room. Its head lolls to the side and its eyes are blank, unseeing. It knows we're there though, and it pulls itself by both hands towards us. I'm unable to repress the shriek of pure, abject terror as it gropes blindly for us and the camera crew thunder downstairs. "Oh my God!" Amanda is wailing and I'm shrieking and the thing is moaning and Mike's hands are up to his head and he seems to regret his decision when a short, pixie-like man steps forwards.

"Tell us why you are here, why do you mean to disturb us so?" he bellows.

The thing stops groping and remains still. "I must have my revenge," it groans.

"You will have no revenge here," says the pixie. I recognise him now, the famous psychic and ghost hunter Trey McRae. "Those who have wronged you are long gone. Leave these simple folk in peace."

Hyperventilating with relief I watch it return to its hole, the only sign it ever existed a small scratch on the wood. After ten minutes telling the camera how scared we all were the machines are switched off. "That's great," says Amanda "should be a good one, it looked very real. Pay 'em Gary." A tubby man in a grey t shirt and tracksuit bottoms searches through his pockets and produces a wad of notes. I take it shakily, my mind still processing what's just happened.

"That was amazing," I say to the pixie psychic, "how did you do it?"

"Huh?" he appraises me as though I appeared from thin air. "Do what? Oh, you mean that? Those things are stupid, they have no will of their own they'll do what you tell 'em. That one's 'programmed' to come up when he hears lots of people." I made a mental note to forewarn party visitors.

"Oh." We offer tea which, to my relief, they turn down. After waving goodbye I shut the door and Mike dances about the room clapping his hands. I laugh and embrace him tightly, almost cracking his ribs. That night we have sex and I don't even complain when I notice the eyeless figure standing in the corner.

The next morning is a Saturday and I make my way down the stairs, ignoring the face in the wall. Mike is already up making us beans on toast. "Ooh, royal treatment," I joke, taking my place on the sofa and flicking through the channels. We eat in contented silence and, when the plates are beside us on the floor (me glancing briefly at the scratched floorboard) I put my feet on Mike's lap. "So how's the book coming?"

"Oh, OK."

"What?"

"Nothing."

"Mike, what, you made a face?"

"No I didn't."

"Yes you did." I remove my feet and stare at him, but he remains fixed on the TV. He's doing it again, I know he is, and suddenly all the goodness is sucked out of the day. "Why aren't you finishing this one?"

He shrugs. "I don't know, I had a better idea yesterday which'll do much better, I don't know." His eyes remain ahead, as if turning to me will make his situation real.

I swallow my fury and try for reassurance. "But, Mike, its good, this one is really good."

"And the next one will be better."

"That's the fourth one in three years, why don't you just admit you don't want to fucking finish anything," I storm past him and slam my feet heavily into the steps. "Shut up," I grumble to the wrinkled face in the wall as it whispers for help, apparently set off by our argument. I shut myself away in our bedroom and read, and that's our entire Saturday ruined.

A tour group appears that night, their guide throwing out cynical humour and lowering his voice dramatically at particularly nasty bits. They draw in breath at the story of the maid who hung herself from the rafters and gasp at the highwayman buried under the stairs. Mike and I are sitting on the sofa when the familiar creak under the floorboard begins. We scream and howl theatrically when the creature approaches but I have to admit it still disturbs me. With one cry of "be gone, foul thing," from the guide, however, it sinks back down. That night Mike and I have make-up sex, but I can't rid my thoughts of the rolling head on its flimsy neck, or fully ignore the aimless wandering of the eyeless white figure in the bedroom.

The next day Mike begins work on his new novel and I'm somewhat soothed. I read what he's done and he's right, it is very good, although part of me thinks the others were too. Then I start thinking about how he could have had at least one book published already and I start getting cross, which I don't want to do so I lie on the bed. Mike settles himself next to me and wraps his arm around me, and I'm back to when we were in Halls at University and he did that for the first time. I was upset about something, I forget what, but I always remembered how much better I felt when he hugged me.

Another tour group comes that night, this time holding a séance downstairs. All the spirits are called to them and I can finally breathe when I have the room to myself for ten minutes. "So," I say, knowing it's time to pose the question I've been dreading, "are you thinking, do this for a year while you finish your book, then maybe have a think while you're sending it out?"

Mike stares off into the distance as there's no TV to ignore me with. "Yeah, I suppose."

"What do you mean, you suppose?" I'm picking at the scab but there's no return.

"I don't know," he says sulkily, "I might want to look at it in six months and see if it's the right one."

I lay back against the pillows as if I've been pushed. At that moment the eyeless spook wanders back into the room followed by a new one, a little worried looking girl. She must have taken longer to grow than the others.

"That's great," A technician with the séance group climbs the stairs to chat after the clients have left, "Billy and Dan are just going to install the night vision cameras and then we'll be off."

"Install the...?"

Mike looks at me as though I'm reacting in the same, annoying way he's used to. It makes me feel like his mother and I don't like it. "It's just for extra cash. They set up cameras for a live feed online. Not," he reads my expression, "in the toilet, just everywhere else."

I agree to it and watch it happen, doing nothing as always. Mike chatters with the men like he doesn't do with me anymore and everything's apparently fine and dandy as mini cams are set up overlooking our bedroom, the kitchen, the front room and the stairs. I watch the men downstairs finish setting up and make my way up the stairs. I can hear the conversation in the bedroom between the workman and Mike before anyone knows I'm there. "So, yeah man, don't forget to check out that site,

Girls frightened By Ghosts. Super hot. They, like, run out from the shower or bed and stuff."

"Will do," Mike chuckles softly. I burst into the room and smile with cold politeness.

"So, yeah, you're online and good to go," the workman leaves hastily. I just want to go to bed. I set my alarm for the morning and the mattress is so comfortable it's like a cloud, and I'm so content that I make a deal with myself to forget about everything for the time being and let Mike put his arm around me again.

I'm wide awake. I look at my alarm: it's 5 am; I have an hour before I need to get up. The strangeness and the darkness of the hour sends bugs crawling over my skin and I sit up, searching for whatever it is that's frightened me. The fluorescent figure of a man with a long beard and sunken eyes looms from the wall. He stares into nothing and his voice is droning on and on and I think I recognise it… "Perhaps the lady is a natural beauty, or perhaps she's using Sparkle Cutie." Over and over again it sings the jingle until I yell at it to shut up. It ignores me.

"Hmm…wha?" Mike opens his eyes and looks up at me.

"What is that thing doing?"

Mike rolls over and tells me to go back to sleep but I shake him awake. "I knew you'd get like this. We get extra money from advertisers if one of the spirits sings their jingle for five minutes. Just ignore it."

"Just ignore it?" I get out of bed and search for my clothes. I'll have to get changed in the toilet unless I want everyone to watch me, which no doubt would get us even more money. I emerge dressed and tired and look at Mike's sleeping figure. The ghost has stopped its monotone and simply stands there, staring down at him. "Goodbye Mike," I whisper, and leave for the office early. The next time I come back will be for my things.

MY OWN REAL DOLL

Jason heaved the monolithic box into his minimalist front room, decorated as such because he'd assumed that's how men's apartments were supposed to look. In truth he'd always preferred the clutter of his grandparent's knick knacks from their Indian homeland but had never had the courage to do the same.

His cock was hardening before he'd even opened the front flap and then there she was, Jessica. She was beautiful; long blue hair, pale skin, pretty yellow dress, exactly what he'd ordered. Faced with her, he felt suddenly shy. "Come on," she winked her butterfly wing lashes dirtily, "get in here and do me from behind."

Afterwards her almost real flesh lay against his on the grey carpet. She turned to him, holding out her hand. "Nice to meet you," she joked.

"Erm, yes, you too," he blushed as he took her slender digits in his. She laid her head against his chest. She smelled of cupcakes and bubble gum.

Over the next month he'd return from work depressed but she'd help him forget. They got through every position they could think of, used candle wax and leather boots. One evening, as the night thickened in the air, he collapsed onto the sofa. "You're so good," he sighed.

"I ought to be," she said, nestling beside him, "you bought a recycled model after all." Jason didn't reply, but the eczema on his elbow raged back into life.

She watched him set up the table from her position on the bed, her pretty chin resting on her hands. "There," Jason stood back proudly, "I'm going to teach you to play Pictionary. You can do it with two people I think."

"You can do something else with two people," said Jess, reaching out and sticking her fingertips beneath his waistband. "Why don't you pick out one of my outfits and take me to the woods?"

"No," Jason snapped, regretting it when she flinched. "Just...come here, I'll show you." The claustrophobia drained from Jason when he saw her brow wrinkle in concentration after picking a card. She drew a terrible picture for him to guess and they both laughed until his ribs hurt. 'This is alright,' he thought, 'this is working.' That night they slept companionably back to back, occasionally stirring to reach for the other before settling back into comfortable sleep.

When Jason returned from work the next evening, he knew without seeing her that something was different. Dark winter shadows lurked and tentatively he pressed the light switch. Jess was sitting on the sofa in a pair of his boxers and a t shirt. She was smiling and seemed somehow denser, more solid. Her eyes were deeper. "You upgraded." She nodded, biting her lip, suddenly unsure. "How did you afford-?"

"I sold all my sexy outfits and toys," she said. "I kept the gloves though," she added. Jason nodded his approval. "Does this mean I can come to the Christmas party with you on Friday?" She looked down at her hands as though embarrassed by such a simple reason to change. Jason sat beside her and hugged her tightly; she still smelled of cupcakes and bubble gum.

The grey industrial building stuck out in the street like a hangnail. Singing and drunken middle aged flirting leaked from the windows. Jason tightened his grip on Jess' hand and opened the door, where they were greeted with ecstatic cheers. They were pulled immediately into a circle linking arms and yowling to 'Last Christmas.'

"I hate George Michael," Jess whispered.

"Me too," replied Jason.

His co-workers, heels and ties removed, gathered around them in curiosity. "Well, where has Jason been keeping you?"

"I like your hair, very unusual."

"What say we go to the punch bowl, leave the boring gits to it?"

Jason watched Mike's lips move for more than an hour. He nodded during any gaps having given up trying to interject. It took a moment for him to awaken when Mike nodded to something behind him. "Well, well," Mike grinned widely, "Your lady friend is certainly the life and soul." Jason turned to see Jess – arms linked either side to two unattractive male colleagues – performing a wobbly folk dance. They and everyone around them shrieked with laughter and Jess laid her head against Sam's worryingly hairy chest. Jason smiled and continued to smile as Sam planted a bleary kiss on her cheek.

"What?" Jess kept snapping during the walk home, but Jason couldn't speak.

The next morning Jess was hungover. She demanded bacon sandwiches and cups of tea, which Jason dutifully made. That night he awoke to a tingle in his groin. He thought of the moment he opened Jess' box and the way she had winked at him. He rolled over to where her dark figure breathed rhythmically and shook her gently. Her eyes opened wide, almost fearful. "Let's have sex," he whispered.

"What?"

"Go on, I'm all aroused."

"Good for you." Jess turned her back to him, and this time there was nothing companionable about it. Jason watched her stiff figure for a few moments. He didn't want to say his next words but he couldn't stop himself.

"Did you say no to your other owners? There must have been quite a few." When Jess turned to him with wounded shock on her face he felt a needle of guilt. Much stronger, though, was a sense of delirious joy similar to when he scratched his eczema, which he did with abandon while she gathered her pillows and a blanket from the airing cupboard.

The next morning he crawled under her blanket on the sofa and embraced her, cold feet included. "I'm sorry," he said, and they stayed that way for a long time.

Several weeks later Jason was watching TV in his underpants, a deep gloom emanating from him and polluting the room. "You ought to leave that place, find something else," Jess said, her skin illuminated under the orange glow of the kitchen light.

"That's kind of easier said than done. Yes please," he said absently to her offer of tea. He glanced at her, turned back to the TV, then did a double take. Jess was holding a plastic mould of a penis – one of her previous owner's – and flicking her tongue over its tip before submerging the entire thing in her mouth. After blinking he saw her leaning against the cupboard doors, daydreaming and chewing on the teaspoon as she waited for the kettle to boil.

"What's wrong Bimble?" she asked.

"Oh nothing." He changed the channel.

He awoke before the alarm went off. Lying in darkness, he envied Jess' rhythmic breathing. His eyes flicked open. Her breath just then had sounded more like a sigh. Then it was definitely a groan. "Oh, Dave," she moaned. Jason sat sharply upright. Her back arched, she threw her head back and her cries became piercing. Jason covered his ears and closed his eyes. When he opened them again she was laying still, a gentle snore the only sound issuing from her. Jason lay back down, his mind racing. The cotton wool of sleep was just softening his brain when the alarm went off.

His day at work was just as confusing. His eyes still crusted with sleep he began to type up his reports, when a movement in the corner of the screen caught his eye. Enlarging the picture he heard the soft sigh of her orgasm and saw her nails dig into someone else's shoulder. While the man pounded away he reached forwards and yanked her blue hair...

"Hello?" Jess sounded irritated. It was his third call home that hour.

"I just – wondered what you were up to."

"I'm pulling the hair out of the plug hole. Would you like me to post it?"

"No, I'm sorry, I just miss you."

"Oh." There was a long pause. "Well, I miss you too."

Jason hung up, determined to concentrate on work. Another small box popped up in the corner of the screen. He tried to ignore the flickering movement but couldn't help clicking on it. His screen was flooded with the image of a woman sitting reverse cowgirl on a freakishly large and slimy erection thrusting in and out further and further inside her. Her head lolled back and forth while she wailed with pleasure, sending her blue hair tumbling every which way. Her eyes were half closed and her mouth formed an 'O,' her shaved vagina sucking him in like a hungry creature.

With a roar of outrage Jason swept the computer to the floor. To his disappointment there was no crackle and fizz, just a dull thud, and instead of restraining him the onlookers merely seemed embarrassed. "Mr Carol," his boss stood in his office doorway, "that will be coming out of your wages."

"That's fine," Jason stormed from the office.

On the walk home his thoughts formed sentences he could cling to, some specifics that could help him win an argument. Clearly it was all her fault; she didn't have to do everything her owners wanted her to. Christ, didn't she have any self-respect? She clearly didn't know how to be a real human. He flung the door open, envisioning the great battle he would win with words. But when he saw her he froze.

She was silent. She was motionless. Her eyes were clear and blue but completely unseeing. Her blue hair was the cheap kind you find in wig shops. Her mouth formed the 'O,' but this time she had no choice; her plastic face would form it forever. "What happened?" He shook her, nothing. "No," he choked, "I'm sorry." One of her arms lowered involuntarily. He climbed onto the sofa with her and hugged her tightly, but the smell of cupcakes and bubble gum was gone. She gazed back at him dispassionately, not another man's penis in sight.

ONE PHONE CALL AWAY

The headset bleeps in my ears. I grit my teeth; I can't afford for this to go badly. "Good morning, is this Mrs Gipper?"

"Yes, who is this?" says the ferocious reply.

"This is Sian calling from World Review; we need your opinion on the earth's rotation and whether you agree with it…"

"What are you selling?" Her rage is barely hidden now.

"Oh, we're not selling anything, but if you would like to know more about the earth and how many men it takes to push it around the sun we have a catalogue that explains…" The click is audible. The computer screen shows that she has hung up and is calculating another stored number to call. I moan audibly – my desk-mates ignore me, their backs hunched over, voices earnest and quietly desperate. Some of them have hardly any limbs left and Tony on the next table is just a head. One more bad call and he joins the ones on the ceiling.

Before the next call goes through the system I feel the tell-tale tingles in the one limb I have left – my right arm. I hold back tears as flesh and sinew loosen, and the body part that's been faithfully with me for almost twenty-two years slips painlessly away, leaving me nothing but a torso and a head. My one chance to earn myself back is a run of perfect calls and, once that's done, I'm getting out of here and never coming back.

The screen flashes before me and my stomach melts. I can't pronounce that name, which means they're understandably angry before I've begun. "Good morning," I begin cheerily, "is that Mr Xabiblee?"

"Mr Zaperbly," he corrects coldly. I shut my eyes and will myself to continue.

"I do apologise. How do you feel about termite's nests, Mr Zaperbly (show you can say his name correctly, the rapor battle is not yet lost.)? Were you aware that the majority have not sought planning permission?"

"They haven't?" he sounds genuinely shocked. My heart flutters.

"No, that's true, they just begin building wherever they feel like it (I'm improvising now, I know the script on wilted paper before me so well that I don't think this will do any harm).

"Bloody immigrants," he growls. I can almost hear his teeth gnashing. That's it, I think – you get angry at those immigrant termites.

"Yes, and we're releasing a pamphlet that explains just how you and your neighbours can…"

"A pamphlet?" The sharp note of doubt has invaded his voice. I know he'll be lost if I don't reel him back in.

"Oh yes, but you don't pay at first you see. No, what you do is…"

"I can't do that," he replies simply. He doesn't know what he can't do, but he can't do it. To be honest I don't blame him, I wouldn't do it either, in fact I would have told me to piss off, but the part of me that can see those on the ceiling and then looks down at my disappearing body is furious with him.

"Well it's not a decision that needs to be made now, you see, and that's the beauty…"

"No, I'm afraid I just can't," he cuts in, "and I think I can hear giant ants attacking next door's cat again. Bloody ants."

The click is the axe slicing my body away. I sit, a torso and a head, just waiting. It begins painfully slowly; whoever is making this happen is enjoying themselves. I catch the eye of one of the supervisors as they strut between the tables – they survived the calls, now they offer commiseration to those who watch themselves disappear. Some are genuinely troubled and others offer weak advice whilst trying not to laugh. The one who looks into my eyes now is one I've always trusted, there's nothing he can do to stop the process except pretend not to watch.

My body shivers as though it has the worst kind of flu. My teeth chatter and my muscles spasm. My head tips forward involuntarily, I can feel the tendons lose their grip on the rest of me. One long, intense shiver and my head falls onto the desk, alone and unprotected. My body slides to the floor with a heavy thud, where it's then removed by one of the supervisors. A single tear falls from my eye and I'm angry I've let them know how upset I am. The supervisor bends down to me, "do you need a break?"

"No," I say through gritted teeth, "I'm fine."

He looks uncertain but continues on past me holding the useless lump of meat. The computer has bleeped and it takes me a moment to react. The voice in my ear is already saying hello in an irritated manner. Good start, I think bitterly.

"Is this Mrs Lampen?"

"Yes, who is this?" I hope her voice is naturally shrill and not just hateful, so I launch into my script.

"Were you aware that when water evaporates from the sea it is absorbed by clouds?"

"Oh, my!" her surprise is a good sign.

"Yes, it isn't distributed amongst the poor in this country or even the tax payers, it's all taken and kept by clouds (again I'm improvising but I feel it's a point that can be layered on thickly). Now, we're issuing a pamphlet that raises awareness of such things and tells us how we can stop it."

"Oh, that's marvellous!" She's on my side! I'm ecstatic; if my head could do a dance it would. I've told her the bit that usually makes people angry and she's still interested.

"That's right, and we can have it sent on subscription if you just answer a few questions," I continue almost breathlessly. "Now, how much does a soul weigh?"

"Ooh," she thinks for a moment, "I think it's…21 grams?"

"Yes!" I shriek. Several red-rimmed eyes glare at me. They know the excited tone of a person who's getting a sale. "Right, now…"

"Who is this?" The person now speaking to me sounds like a big burly man.

"Where is Mrs Lampen? I need to speak to…"

"You need to bugger off!" he told me with absolute authority on the subject. "She's 95 and she gets 50 pamphlets sent here every day as it is now I wish you vultures would just piss off."

Before I can try to bring him onside I hear the deadly click. I hold my breath, but I'm not sure where it would go anyway since I no longer have lungs. I feel the tingling, this time in my brain. I look around at the others though I know it's useless, they'll all pretend they can't see me for fear of jeapordising their own positions.

The tingling becomes an unbearable fuzzing and I know I'm disappearing, I'm leaving my body. I feel a lightness - a weightlessness - and I wonder what all the fuss was about. I distantly notice the back of my head brush against the ceiling and I'm surrounded by other shadowy figures. "Excuse me, is that Mrs Jarren," the one nearest to me whispers. The others are repeating similar phrases over and over, shades of past phone calls endlessly whispering. I feel a mild interest in speaking to Mrs Lampen. "Excuse me, is that Mrs Lampen?" The supervisors are looking up at me. "Is that Mrs Lampen?"

"Should get rid of some of them," says one of the supervisors.

"Excuse me, is that Mrs Lampen?" I watch them fetch the hoover from the cupboard and wonder if Mrs Lampen will answer the phone.

SON, I'M AFRAID I'M A ZOMBIE

"Simon," his mother's voice was sharp, nervous. "Could you come in here before you change out of your uniform?" Both his parents were sitting in the front room facing the chair he was obviously expected to sit in, hands stiffly on their knees.

"Here it is," thought Simon, "the divorce talk." He took a seat, school blazer rustling.

"Simon," his father said, "your mother and I need to tell you something." He paused before taking a breath. "I'm afraid I'm a zombie."

A silence followed. "What?"

"I'm a zombie, Simon." Simon's mother grasped his father's hand tightly.

"A-are you sure?" he asked. "How do you know?"

"I read about the symptoms in a magazine," his father's eyes sank to the ground, "suddenly everything made sense." Simon's mother began sobbing. His father patted her back comfortingly.

"We'll get through this," she wailed through snot and tears. Simon pursed his lips and sighed.

Three days later Michael and Simon squealed as they played Eat My Kidney 7 on the Gamebox at Simon's after school, their fingers flicking over the controls like dancer's feet. "You stabbed me in the face!" Simon laughed. He turned sharply when he heard the thud. His father had pinned Michael down and clamped his mouth around his throat, and Michael's face had turned a worrying red. Simon grabbed a ceramic vase. "Dad, stop it! For Christ's sake you're not a zombie!" He smashed it down hard but not too hard, the thought of hurting a parent made him feel sick.

"Ow!" His father rubbed his head and stomped upstairs. "I thought you might be a little more understanding of my condition."

The next morning the school councillor looked down at Simon. Her smart suit and neat blonde hair didn't fool him, he knew she was aching to be in a woolly jumper and lamenting how no-one 'touched anymore.' "How does not sleeping make you feel?"

"Tired."

The councillor nodded. "Could you keep a diary of your thoughts?"

Simon clenched his fists, urging himself to speak. "What are you supposed to do about zombies?" he blurted. "I mean, there's ways of making them normal again, isn't there?"

"Oh, uh, that's great, Simon. Writing fiction is a good way of dealing with problems. But…I think with zombies you're supposed to cut the head off aren't you?"

"What if you're wrong and they weren't a zombie?"

"Sometimes," her eyes glittered frighteningly, "affirmative action is the only way."

Simon slumped back in his chair and closed his eyes till they hurt.

It was dinnertime. Simon set the table, the smell of his mother's curry almost calming him. He heard her taking the plates down from the cupboard as he straightened the last fork, and when the front door handle creaked open he glanced at the dark object under the sofa.

"Hello!" called his father as he placed his briefcase by the stairs like always.

"How was it?" his mother asked as she scurried from the kitchen to embrace him.

"Oh, they'll come around. I've a meeting with the boss tomorrow to go over sick pay contracts with a fine tooth comb. I mean," he leaned forward to remove papers from his briefcase, "no-one could predict this."

The spade smashed across the back of his head with a thud like an axe on wood. It took a few more cracks against his father's prostate neck for his blood splashed mother to start screaming, and even more to produce a noticeable wound. Alerted to the noise the neighbours gathered at the windows and banged on the door, their chatter and calls lost amidst the furore in the house. Simon paused as green slime oozed from the twitching, snarling body. "Look mum," he said, the police siren growing louder, "he wasn't making it up."

THE ANNUAL ESSEX MEDICAL CONVENTION

I was lying in bed when I first heard the growl. My head shot up and I stared at my belly; it was a rumble like one I'd never heard, the growl of a disgruntled but sleepy animal. I patted my stomach and it definitely felt harder than before. But what had it really felt like before? I tried to remember but couldn't. I sat up and spent several minutes prodding my belly – there was no way it hadn't changed. I decided I would go to the doctor the next morning.

After my morning shift my parents took me to lunch. "I had to tell a customer we'd stopped selling the fertilizer she liked," I said as I spooned potato into my mouth, "she told me I was the reason no-one trusted customer service anymore. Then she started crying."

"Oh well," my mother patted my hand, turning her head so that her fashionably short hair caught the light of the fire in the grate, "just think of the money." My dad grunted in agreement, his eyes on the pudding menu. My mother cast another disapproving eye over my ordinary brown ponytail and heavy jumper.

The growl that followed the digestion of the meal was like a tiger snarling over a carcass, announcing to anyone with ears that this morsel was his and his alone. I sat hunched over, too horrified to look at anyone's reaction though no one said a thing. My parents exchanged a tired look as if to say, "What is it this time?"

The next day I saw Dr Tamboli who sent me for a scan, which found nothing, and then a specialist who also found nothing. He seemed perplexed when I arrived back in his office, "We could try some neurological tests?"

"No, thank you," I got up and walked out. That afternoon I arranged another appointment with a doctor I'd never seen before, a Dr Merryhew. He had a reassuring brown beard and dark eyes, which smiled when I walked in, as much as eyes can really smile. "It's my stomach," I explained, "it feels like something's in it, and it growls." An odd light seeped into the doctor's face as he got me to hop up on the makeshift bed.

"Does this hurt? This?" He prodded viciously and the beast within made its dislike known. I nodded. "Yes, my God!" he yelled, his sudden outburst causing me and my new addition to jump. "You've a hobgoblin! It must have crawled down your throat while you were sleeping and made a nest. Oh no, calm down," he soothed when he saw my stricken face, "it won't do any damage, it just needs to hibernate."

"Hibernate? I don't care if it's tired or…" I tried to think of a witty finish but nothing came, "just get it out."

Dr Merryhew shifted uncomfortably from foot to foot. "Well, I can't really do that. You see, the Hobgoblins are an unforgiving race and if I were to disturb it in any way it would get quite cross and so would its friends." I sulked silently. When I looked back up at the doctor it was obvious by his red cheeks and madly glinting eyes that he was dying to say something else.

"What?"

"Well," he went maddeningly coy, looking at his toes like a 14 year old about to ask a girl out for the first time, "We have several medical meetings coming up and...er..."

"You want to display me like a freak show?" I sat bolt upright and zipped my jeans.

"Yes, er, no!" His eyes were pleading. "Just give one a go. If you don't like it we can stop. This really is quite a find you know." He put his hands together in a begging gesture. My shoulders slumped – to say no would be like kicking a kitten. "Wonderful! Make sure you pack for a short trip." He leapt back to his desk and picked up the phone, forgetting about me already. He was making plans with his colleagues as I saw myself out – but perhaps I misheard as it sounded like he was arranging a drinking competition.

A week later I was pushing open the door to a brick building where Merryhew waited for me in the sparse hallway, toes tapping on the dark carpet, black leather briefcase in his hand. He looked as though he was going to a wedding; a top hat was perched on his grey flecked head and a waistcoat of deep burgundy nestled under a grey jacket along with the chain of a pocket watch. We turned a corner and I felt suddenly nervous; candelabras lined the walls ominously. "Is this the right place?" He shushed me, pushing the small of my back through the candlelight towards two double doors.

"Wait here," he whispered, disappearing inside. I stood patiently for a long time, hearing the rumble of applause and the doctor's voice mumbling an introduction. After a while I sat on the pitch black carpet and watched the shadows of my knees stretching and shortening against the walls. The grumbling in my stomach caught me off guard. He'd been calm for days and now he sensed my concern. I lifted my jumper and inspected it. The belly had swollen further and the skin stretched as it stuck a foot outwards. I prodded it angrily, disgusted. The thing yelped and span round a few times making my innards lurch. Cold sweat dampened my armpits and forehead.

His voice came nearer and I stood hurriedly. His face and hand appeared, beckoning me inside. He stopped me near the door where I hid behind a white curtained medical stand. Only my tantalising shadow would be visible to the waiting crowd. "Ladies and gentlemen," said Dr Merryhew in a grand tone, "I bring you the bearer of the Hobgoblin. See how it growls and snarls." He reached out for my hand, leading me gently towards exposure, encouraging me to lift the material hiding my belly. The gasps and whispers from his audience seemed to nourish the doctor like a fine meal. The room was low-lit with gas lamps and stuffy and fragrant as an attic. The other medics – dressed in full Victorian regalia and seated on wooden chairs –chattered amongst themselves excitedly. One or two of the mutton-chopped men placed monocles over an eye and nodded approvingly.

"What is going on?" I whispered.

"It's the annual Essex medical convention," replied Dr Merryhew.

"But we've had electric light for several decades."

"Shush," the doctor's frown was cavernous with shadow, "you're ruining the role play."

I gazed about the room at the top hatted men and silk-gloved women, and past them at the shelves stacked with gas lamps and candles and murky specimen jars. A fine cobweb linked each item and I wondered how often the room was cleaned before I gazed a bit harder – it was fake cobweb, like the kind you buy at Halloween.

I stood dutifully silent while the good doctor continued his patter, much of it incomprehensible to me. "My dear fellow," said a woman, a tiny green hat to match her dress perched on the side of her head, "I trust you will permit close examination?"

"By all means." I sighed as my stomach was prodded and poked and patted, irritating the thing to a murderous rage.

"Oh my," they twittered excitedly as all four of its limbs tried to push its way through my flimsy skin. The beads of sweat became lakes. The doctor looked as though he would inflate with joy.

"I feel our good doctor," said one Faustian fellow with suitably pointed beard "is quite incorrect." He tapped my stomach, again encouraging molten fury. "Permit me, if you will, to conduct my own enquiry according to the teachings of the modern professor Freud. An understanding of our patient," he raised an eyebrow, "will assist us no end." The others scuttled hurriedly back to their seats but Dr Merryhew stood firm.

"This is my patient," he said, "found by me. I have diagnosed her and it's already done and Dr Bigelow is merely jealous that he has nothing to present."

The crowd dissented raucously and Dr Merryhew had no choice but to defer to his colleague, bowing into the shadows in the corner muttering dangerously. Dr Bigelow spent several minutes posturing before opening his briefcase, producing from it an ancient and enormous syringe.

"No, no no no," I babbled," but the doctor smiled.

"This is not for you, but for me. Freud," He said as he rolled up his sleeve, "encourages the use of cocaine to rid sufferers of morphine addiction." The onlookers nodded sagely.

"You're a junky," I shrieked, "and you still practice medicine?"

"Well, no, I-"

"That's it, I'm leaving." I turned to go and the muttering of the crowd was deafening. Dr Bigelow barred my way.

"It's just vitamins," he whispered, his brow creased pathetically. "Just play along, can't you?"

"You promise you'll help me at the end of this?"

"Yes," he almost begged, "yes of course."

I sighed. Dr Merryhew grinned from his corner. The audience leaned forwards, waiting. I lowered my voice, "alright, pretend you've overpowered me." Dr Bigelow grabbed me by the shoulders and led me, flailing dramatically, back to position. "No!" I cried, getting perhaps a little too enthusiastic. He resumed his former place where he directed the syringe into his arm, and calm was restored.

"I'm going to speak with you now about your childhood," he said hypnotically. "I want you to think back to a time when you were happy and with your parents."

"I'm in my room," I said, mustering a far-off expression.

"And what are you doing in your room?"

"I'm playing with my toys."

"Good. Can you tell me what you remember of the room and your toys?"

"My room is decorated with planes," I grin, surprised at my memory, "and I'm holding my favourite toy, Flying Ted. He's" – surely I can't remember all this – "a teddy dressed like a pilot."

"Marvellous," Dr Bigelow's eyes gleam devilishly, "and what else can you remember about your good friend Flying Ted?"

"He tells me stories," I grin, "stories about where he's been."

"And did you wish to go with him?"

"Yes, I was going to go to all the places he told me about."

"Fantastic, and did you?"

"No," I shifted uncomfortably, feeling like a child caught in a lie.

"You see?" Dr Bigelow reached out to the audience, "this is not an ailment of the body but a sickness of the mind."

"I am not making this up," I folded my arms defensively across my abdomen. To my relief Dr Merryhew lurched from his corner, stepping protectively between me and the interloper.

"Quite right," he said piously, "how can one dismiss this?" he prodded my stomach once again, provoking a howl of rage.

The audience seemed to agree and applauded, their claps still ringing in my head as we left through the back door and into the afternoon sun. We waited at a tiny train station I had never seen before, the sort you'd see in little country villages. Fog billowed over the platform and I pulled my coat across my chest, linking arms with Merryhew to prevent any accident. I coughed and held out my hand; I could barely see a meter in front of me. It was almost June, where had this fog come from? My questions were answered when I noticed a machine almost completely hidden behind a bush. I looked again at the train tracks in front of us, they were suspiciously small. My questions were answered when our transport arrived. It was a steam train, certainly, but its exhaust emitted the clouds of another fog machine, followed by only two carriages hardly big enough for adults. It strongly resembled the trains that wind their way through zoos and theme parks. We stepped on board and I prepared for a slow and boring journey.

So began my medical tour, sometimes in dark rooms, sometimes makeshift tents lit red by oil lamps while Merryhew twirled his moustache and promised his audience the "visual treat of a lifetime." Contortionists and sword swallowers and acrobats accompanied the showing of the freaks and the Essex doctors were having a wonderful time. I was considering just checking into hospital and having the damn thing removed. "Boiled sweet?" Merryhew shook a jar beneath my nose on the train. I turned away. "You could probably do with a tin of nervous pills," he grumbled, and on we continued in silence.

Two weeks into the journey I stood behind the medical stand in the centre of a dimly lit circular auditorium, wooden seats winding around the edge and growing higher as they reached the back. I dutifully trotted out when my condition was introduced and the audience was suitably aghast. The doctor was running through his now familiar patter while I held up my jumper, when a loud cough echoed about the walls. Merryhew continued but the cougher became a talker, and soon a portly gentleman with top hat and cane was making his way towards us.

"I beg your pardon, Giltbridge, but I believe your demonstration follows mine," said Merryhew tersely.

"Quite right, quite right," the interloper muttered, "but I'm wondering if I may be of assistance." The candy floss of daydream left me; at last something different was happening.

"Right," Merryhew had been completely pushed aside and this new figure and his assistant pushed a wooden chair with stirrups from the back of the room to the centre. "If I may ask you to…"

"Hang on!" I burst, "what are you doing? Who are you? What's going on?" Several members of the medical observers rushed forwards to restrain me, pulling my trousers off and strapping my limbs to the arms and legs of the seat. I wriggled and wept with frustration, terror seeming too small a word for what exploded inside me.

"Here you are," said a lady to the interloper, handing him a wooden stick which was placed between my teeth. Drool leaked from the corners of my lips. I tried to think of things, places that made me happy. My favourite song played in my head but got stuck on one line, repeating like a scratched record. An odd, sweet smell reached my nostrils and I looked down to see a plate of cupcakes placed on the ground at my feet.

"Come now," he called as though instructing a child, "a nice cupcake for your hungry tum." His assistant began to look familiar. Through my fear I recognised him somehow...

My stomach crashed. Whatever was in there had decided enough was enough and now was the time to emerge. "Oh my god ooooooh!" I wailed through the stick. The women spoke to me in soothing voices and the men mopped at the sweat on my brow with fashionable handkerchiefs. A surge of pain pushed downwards into my abdomen as though a metal pole had impaled me from womb to backside and I screamed again.

"That's it, almost there!" Dr Giltbridge and Dr Bigelow were jubilant. I almost relaxed until I realised it wasn't over. "Push," said Giltbridge.

"Push!" said the others. Even Dr Merryhew was chanting with them.

"Aaaaaaaaaah!" With a final wail he was free, the thing that had blighted my life for the last few weeks. I couldn't see him for the first few minutes while Giltbridge wrapped him in a blanket, but when I could I was ecstatic to see him. Proudly placed in my arms was Flying Teddy. His once missing ear was now restored, his patchy fur had grown back sleek as velvet and his wobbly eye looked new and firm and I hugged him tightly, promising things would be different.

THE BLUE SEASHELL

She loves to feel his mutated green skin on her fingertips – smooth and slippery as a fish. Their webbed digits cut through the water as they dive down and the pressure wraps around her head like a helmet. Hideous creatures populate their dark world, but to them its home.

She kisses Tony's pumping gills, knowing he'll shiver and pull away. He reaches for something in the sand, a blue seashell twisted and empty. Its single turret reminds her of palaces in stories she read a lifetime ago. He holds it to his lips and pretends to play it like a trumpet and she laughs like it's the funniest thing she's ever seen.

The silver watches on their wrists vibrate. She shakes her head no, to ignore it, but she knows they can't or the cramps will come. He links arms with her and guides her back to the light, and she resents him for not seeming as sad as she. She imagines living under the seabed with him, never moving, entwined together, a life of sand and his skin. But now, as he presses his lips against her neck and blows a raspberry, she laughs and forgets.

Above them the Meeting Bay surface sparkles and two hazy faces peer down at them. He kicks his legs harder and she feels him slip away. She races him to show she doesn't care. The two men, Sean and Dave, haul them on board. Sean has a reassuring smile, and Dave's beard reminds her of a father she once knew.

The speedboat hums across the sea, the temperature dropping when they reach the caves. Soon they're at the metal door. "Got some new ones in," Dave smiles, entering a number combination on the entrance keypad. "Some beauties too, like yourselves." She likes the look of her neon flesh under the fluorescent lights of the laboratory. The noxious chemical smell is familiar, soothing. The men get out and haul them into wheelchairs, pushing them past cages with faces she hasn't seen before. Winged women with tired looking breasts stare out at them, their cries for help long ceased. A half man attempts to stand on horse legs while someone in a lab coat scribbles notes. A wolf woman howls in lament and a bearlike couple clutch a furry child to them. Maria, leans back against her seat and closes her eyes to the lost, the lonely, the homeless and the runaways.

The questions begin once they're in the tank. "Did your gills work properly this time?"

"Could you feed sufficiently?"

"What improvements could be made?"

She answers them calmly, a layer of ice hiding a tempest, thinking of nothing but the moment when they could sink back down together again.

When the questions are complete, she lifts her arms for the straps that will assist her back to the ground.

"Tony," Sean says, "we've had a request to put you under the change again I'm afraid, we'll need you to come with us."

"What?" She wails as he's hoisted into a chair.

"Maria, we're so sorry," says Dave. "We wanted to tell you but the orders were to let you to continue as normal." He places a hand over her flipper and she looks away. They stand a moment, awkward, waiting to get back to work.

"Fine, its fine," she shrugs, shaking her head nonchalantly.

"I'll still be out there, we'll find each other," Tony yells as he's wheeled away. His bug eyes look even larger. She just wants him to go; she's closing her heart to him already. She wants to float over the seabed and feel the waves on her rubbery skin. "I'll get word to you," he calls, and he's disappeared. She feels nothing. On the journey back to the sea she avoids the pitying looks of the two men.

The seabed is smooth and the waves are gentle. She lets the current carry her to an inch of the invisible fence, imagining the thrill of the mini electric shock. She hunts fish, shooting through the water like a tornado. She makes a game of seeing how close she can get to sharks before darting under the seabed to safety. However everything changes the morning she finds the blue seashell; it glints and glimmers on the rock, a dapple of light rippling across its surface. She picks it up and turns it over and over. The stitches in her heart were rudimentary, temporary only, and now they burst open. Pressing her watch she heads for the surface where Sean and Dave are waiting already. They haul her onto the speedboat and she clutches the shell as though it's Tony's hand.

"What happened?" asks Sean, "are your gills OK? Can you find fish?" Embarrassed now, she says nothing. They notice the shell. "We know you're upset, but you can't call us just because you're having a bad day."

"I'm not upset," she raged. "I just…want you to change me again, make me like him." The men looked shocked.

"Maria," Dave says in a placating tone. She bristles but he continues, "every time we do it, it lessens your ability to recover. Why don't you just give it some time?"

"No," her skin prickles hotly, "Change me too or I'll…just find the next shark." The shock in their eyes is genuine and they ask her for a moment to confer with Head Office on their walkie-talkies. She splashes overboard and watches them gesticulate persuasively. She knows what they're saying without hearing it – they're debating with Head Office whether to go ahead with her request or just let her get eaten. After a time, Sean leans over the side and waves her up.

"We can go ahead with it on one condition."

"Anything!"

"Well," Dave's eyes dart about, "we have a scheduled change in a couple of weeks for Alyssa in pod 12, but we'll do the change on you instead."

Maria's laugh is tinged with hysteria, "fine, do whatever you want." She feels as though her head is inflating when they race to the laboratory and wheel her down a corridor.

At first the room is a blur. Voices discuss her pulse rate and blood pressure as if from a dream. Slowly faces come into focus and peer down at her. "You're doing very well," one assured. "We've injected some antibiotics, just rest now."

Each minute she spends in recovery is another minute away from him. Though they keep no mirrors in the lab she can see her long, clawed hands and the badly sewn fur on her body. A large scar runs down her middle and becomes infected, the yellow pus demanding more time locked away. She rages about her room, forcing her legs to walk more than they can bear, until the stitches feel as though they'll come apart. She tries to remember everything about him but things are cloudy, she sees him as though looking through a frosted mirror. It's all she can do not to drag her weak, mutilated body from the hospital wing to find him herself. She begs them to let her speak to him but a glance passes between them, a look she can't quite fathom. "It'll tamper with our results," they say, "He needs to settle into his surroundings." She sleeps with the shell next to her pillow.

When the night comes Sean and Dave escort her to a minivan. "We found a suitable empty building for him," says Sean, "it's very comfortable, there'll be plenty of room for both of you." She watches the moon, full and still above the moving scenery. The roads thin, becoming increasingly remote and winding. Motorways fade into fields and hills spread before them, the dips between them great dark chasms under the night sky. They pass a cluster of houses, their flickering lights whispering of families watching television and friends having parties. They drive through a wood and a castle looms amongst the trees. As they near she sees that the bricks are made of white plaster. She can't speak her heart is beating so fast. She pictures him embracing her, both of them weeping. She feels the shell in her pocket.

Her hands shake when they reach the arched wooden door. Sean knocks twice, then three times, then twice. After a click that makes Maria jump the door opens onto a darkened hallway, flame torches burning on the stone walls. A large, lumpy figure stands before them. Maria gasps when he steps into the moonlight; it's him. Patchy fur covers his body like an old teddy bear and his elongated fingers and toes are punctuated with claws. The pupils of his cat's eyes thin against the white light. He seems ambivalent to Sean and Dave's presence.

"Tony?" Maria steps towards him, "it's me." He looks her over, confused. Recognition drips slowly into his eyes.

"Maria." They stand awkwardly for a moment or two before she embraces him. He's stiff at first but softens, and Maria weeps. Tony pats her back as though she's a baby, and a stone of fear lodges in her stomach. "Come inside," he mumbles gruffly. They enter a great hall filled with dusty second hand furniture and bean bags. A fire sparks in the grate and more torches crackle on the walls. Tony settles himself in an armchair while Maria sits between Sean and Dave on a sofa. She wants him to ask her to sit beside him but he doesn't.

"We hope you understand about the electricity," says Sean, "we just can't afford for all our subjects to use it." Tony shrugs. Maria wants to tell them they don't care, that it doesn't matter now they're together. Tony just stares glumly at the flames. "And you've been keeping yourself hidden too?"

"I've not revealed myself to anyone, but I can't promise they haven't discovered me," Tony glares at them. "Little eyes are curious and little hands find ways of sneaking in." After an awkward pause, Tony huffs. "Never fear, the only eyes that have seen me belong to the delivery girl." Maria notices his cheeks flush.

Maria settles into bed after Sean and Dave leave. The candle has sputtered out on her bedside table but sleep evades her and she stares at the plaster bricks. She can still feel the tight goodbye hugs from the scientists, as though they would never see her again. She stretches out her limbs and still can't reach the edges of the mattress. It's as soft as a dream but she remains awake when the white dawn light turns golden. She thinks of Tony sleeping far away, of the moment he showed her to a separate room. It's a poisonous splinter under her skin.

The banging edges her into consciousness. She turns over and tries to slide back into sleep but the knocking continues. Maria waits a moment to see if anyone else stirs but there's silence. Sighing, she slips out of bed and wraps a robe around her, her feet freezing. The face that greets her has blue eyes like a lagoon and skin like fresh white sheets, all framed by thick red hair that matches her coat. "Is Tony here?" Maria doesn't like the way her eyes search the hallway and the fur on her hackles puff up.

"He's not awake yet."

The girl's bright confidence slips. "Oh, OK…well, I brought this," she indicates a basket with a blanket draped over its contents. Maria smiles ungraciously and takes it. "I'm…Rosemary," the girl says, catching Maria off guard.

"Oh, Maria." She waits for the slap of recognition, or even a glimmer, but the girl smiles with polite blankness.

"Rose!" Tony sweeps down the stairs with a vigour Maria had thought lost to him. She notices the colour in Rosemary's face, a charming glow worthy of her name.

"Why don't we take this into the kitchen?" Maria smiles brightly. She stomps as delicately as she can and sets the hamper on the table. She waits for the other two to join her, each second adding to her fury, while the scent of homemade bread and sweet jam tempts her nostrils. She waits, and waits, and finally with a sense of foreboding she retraces her steps. They were talking, Rosemary with her arms folded. Tony places a giant claw on her shoulder, explaining something urgently. After a few minutes Rosemary seems to accept what he says and softens. It was a subtle gesture, almost imperceptible, but unmistakeable. When they head for the kitchen she scuttles ahead.

"Rosemary will be joining us for lunch," says Tony briskly. He looked as though he could climb the tallest mountain. Rosemary holds her hand out to Maria.

"It's wonderful to meet you, Tony's mentioned you often." Maria accepted it, biting her lip.

Rosemary cuts bread, spreads jam and sets cakes out on plates. She knows where everything is. "I live in the cottage with my gran," she chattered nervously, "the nearest one on the hill. She's looked after me since I was five. I became a voluntary delivery girl about two years ago when this place was built." She gazes at Tony and he catches her eye. In that tiny second they communicate something to each other.

"What was that?" Maria springs to her feet. Tony charges to the Great Hall next door, where the scrabbling came from.

"You little bastard!" He roars. Rosemary and Maria run to him. "Goddamn kids always coming in here to stare at me," he growled. Rosemary flung her arms around him and he slowly calmed. "I'm sorry, let's have lunch."

When evening crawls into the castle Rosemary lights the fire in The Great Hall. She chatters endlessly, nervously. "And Mr Liggot says, 'Hold onto this sheep's head while I shave her will you, she won't stay still.' Well I end up lying in mud and sheep poo with this possessed thing trying to trample me." She and Tony laugh raucously, and Maria tries to joins in. She sips her glass of lemonade, forcing herself to feel happy. Then they hear the footsteps. Tony growls, a monster once more.

"Don't," Maria snaps.

"Let me just see who it is," Rosemary soothes.

She pushes the bolt across and the front door creaks open, the torchlight from inside the castle lighting up the villager's anxious faces. Tony and Maria watch from the safety of the shadows. An elderly man steps forward, leans against a cane and takes a deep breath. "We don't know who you are or where you've come from, but we have all decided," he pauses, "to welcome you to the town with open arms. We'll arrange regular deliveries of our produce to you, and anything else you need you can just let us know." The others nod proudly, pleased with their grand gesture.

Maria turns to Tony, sure now that all obstacles have melted away, but she stops abruptly. His arms are flung around Rosemary and hers around him, and a sweet cloud of bliss surrounds them. The prickling on Maria's skin returns. She grinds her teeth. Tony squeezed Rosemary even tighter and kisses the top of her head before resting his chin on it. Maria's knuckles twitch.

The audience are sprayed with blood so fast that they simply stare for several minutes. Rosemary's body comes apart in Maria's hands and teeth like overcooked meat. She tears limbs from ligaments and her head from the torso and the ground and walls are splashed with dark red sludge and greasy organs. Hearing the skin tear and joints pop is like scratching a scab or a mosquito bite and Maria doesn't stop until the girl is pulp. There's a short silence before a hideous wailing issues from the villagers...

The rain splashes over the hills but she's safe and warm in the darkness. Her search across the damp grass and fragrant wildflowers paid off; she found a shiny rock. She snapped up a few mice along the way, ignoring the kestrel hovering over them in the grey sky. A sheep brays loud and long, and others follow. This means the shepherd will pay a rare visit overhead. Perhaps she can steal another of his flock. He does nothing when she springs up from beneath the bridge to snatch a juicy one, he's too afraid of her; part human and part nightmare, all stitches and twisted face.

She drops the rock onto a pile beside her nest of straw where it sparkles satisfyingly. She has a number of favourites; a long abandoned bracelet from a camper, the thigh bone of a grouse, a jumper now more holes and mud than wool, but one stands out which she keeps pride of place at the front. She can't remember where she found it but she knows it's very important and strokes its chipped blue surface. She places it by her head as she closes her eyes imagining, for reasons of which she's uncertain, a rippling light dancing over its surface.

THE FILING CABINET OF DOOM

Elenor was playing a game – how long she could stare at Sam's charcoal grey skin and tight black curls before he sensed it and felt creeped out. She sat at a small table in the corner of the room, playing with the ends of her long black hair as Sam wiped surfaces, checked the till and opened the blinds of the Information Cafe. The morning sun shone each colour of the rainbow from deep black to bright white and all the greys in between. Intermittently she lost herself in the monthly tallies; 10 out of towners had visited on Monday 3rd and three of them had inward belly-buttons while the rest were outy. Overall in the entire month that made…

She pictured her ivory fingers reaching under Sam's shirt to pull gently at his chest hairs. His face leaned down to hers, their lips almost touching. "Could you help me with this? Someone put a tampon in one of the cups of orange juice and I just can't bring myself to touch it." His soundless words floated from his mouth, dissipating in the air. He pointed helplessly at one of the tables. Elenor removed the offending cup, tipping the contents into the kitchen bin.

"Thanks," said Sam, "I know you must be busy but…"

"That's ok," Elenor smiled. "Are you going to the carnival later?" She cringed as ornate flowers framed her words. She had never been able to hide her emotions. Since the posters had first appeared like a portal to a strange new world a week ago she had been planning the moment she would ask him. In her thoughts he had either crushed her to his bosom or flung himself away from her, wild-eyed with horror. The real Sam's reaction was predictably disappointing.

"Oh probably. My father would like to come too but there are always things that need doing."

Elenor nodded, "being Head Boss of the Entire World must be quite demanding I suppose. Well, good, perhaps I'll see you there."

"Sure, bye. Oh, wait!" Elenor span around eagerly, "would you like some free information? You did do a whole month's worth of bellybutton tallies in ten minutes after all." He pressed a button on the till and a thin script spewed forth. "Emperor penguins can stay underwater for twenty minutes."

"Wow, I didn't know that. Thanks, Sam."

She stepped out onto the dirt road of the high street lined with slanting shops. She breathed in deeply; summer had arrived and the fresh scent from the field and the woods beyond the town was invigorating. Not that anyone ventured into the woods; that would be foolish.

The next place on Elenor's list was Bill's Taxidermy. She waved to John and Mary the married Siamese twins (they had got around the legal issue by holding a Pagan ceremony) in the dry cleaners and said a quick hello to Milkman Mike as he wandered his route. She nodded to the girls as they entered the glitter palace of Bella's Burlesque House. Cherry Bomb and Midnight Noir argued the finer points of DIY while Mitzi the Obese carried the props. Mitzi's fat rolled like the sea and a tiny 'jingle, jangle' drifted from the feathered head dresses. Elenor caught a whiff of the attic smell from the costumes, which she found oddly comforting.

Lilly, the young girl in the ice-cream shop, was giving her full attention to a man Elenor hadn't seen before; a tall, gangly creature with unruly black hair who prodded a spoon into his bowl but didn't eat. Lilly chattered excitedly, apparently untroubled by his distracted air.

At the end of the road she was greeted by a charging rhino and a cat, curled up and sleeping, rotating ceaselessly on an old gramophone. In the far corner May the mechanic's grandma knitted in a rocking chair, waiting to be picked up to continue her motionless task in May's front room ad infinitum. Elenor pushed open the shop door. The dust smell of the Taxidermist's was always just the right side of unpleasant. Bill greeted her with dark circles under his eyes. "She's on holiday," was the curt response when Elenor asked after his wife, before glancing nervously at a static weeping clown.

"Oh, Ok... anywhere nice?"

"Just away," Mr Fraser said as he dashed into the back room.

"Oh, good, maybe she could say hello to my parents, they went there about ten years ago," Elenor called after him. "They still write every week." Silence followed. "I'll...just get on with the tallies." There was still no response. Elenor could have sworn that Mr Fraser had tears in his eyes, but it couldn't have been. He must miss his wife, she thought. Without Sam to break her concentration, the job was done in five minutes.

"Thank you very much," Bill said weakly when she had finished, "Would you like a free dancing squirrel?"

The field had changed so much on Carnival Day Elenor felt she was on a different planet. The sun shone bright white over the grey grass and the air was sickly sweet with popcorn and candy floss. Children and adults alike queued in front of penny arcades and rides while jugglers, acrobats, fire-breathers and contortionists entertained them. In the centre stood a makeshift stage with a small collection of caravans behind it, separated by a curtain stand. The caravans were guarded by several large men in suits. Most people's attention, however, was on a row of mysterious tents circling the field's perimeter, each laying claim to something more horrible than the others. "Come see the man with no face," the words soared from one Barker; "extra tuppence and he'll give you a kiss."

"Visit if you dare the woman with no body, her flesh chopped away from the top of the head down!"

Elenor noticed Martha Selwyn and her sister join the queue to win a balloon. Elenor waved but Martha responded with just a half nod. She hadn't been friendly since her cousin went on holiday a year ago. Folks said Martha's jealousy was immature but Elenor had a troubling feeling in her gut, something she couldn't place. She ordered a giant cup of Fizzy Happy Joy from the refreshment van and waited for Sam by the haunted bucket. An old man on stilts leaned down to offer her a razorblade cupcake from his collection, smiling gummily. She took it politely, binning it as soon as his back was turned. Trying to appear nonchalant, she leaned against the bucket's donation request sign, her fingers tapping an anxious tune. She had decided simple was best and worn a black jumper with a skirt, but now felt like somebody's grandmother.

"Come on Elenor, why are you waiting?" Aisha's words dissipated in the air.

Elenor twirled her hair and tried to think of an excuse.

"Oh, I said I might wait for my…uncle. He wants to come but you know what his legs are like."

"Yes," Aisha frowned, "he had them taken off last week. He has a wheelchair now."

"Well," Elenor put her hands on her hips – how could she have forgotten? "He has as much right as any to go to the carnival, doesn't he?"

"Of course," Aisha put her hands up defensively. "OK, I'll see you down there." She left with a suspicious backward glance.

The crowds dragged friends and relatives to the next ride or mystery. Elenor's feet itched to step inside one of the tents or tumble through the crooked house, but she stayed put.

"Elenor!" Strong, cheerful letters tapped her shoulder. It was Sam, his eyebrows neatly combed and his trousers pressed. "I'm so glad you're here, I thought you'd be down there already. Why don't we head to the coconut shy, or maybe the burlesque tent?" Sam held out his arm for her to take. Elenor was almost shaking as she accepted it.

"Why don't we get some food?" she suggested.

Sam turned to her on the way to the barbeque, "Elenor…" Elenor felt the mild panic she always did when someone looked serious, "would you, I don't know, want to go to Ron's burgers sometime with me, or maybe go on a bike ride?"

"Yes, yes I would definitely like to!"

Amongst the families devouring hot dogs and burgers one silver dreadlocked figure in a loose dress stood alone, attempting to fit both a hot dog and burger in her mouth at once. Her large, expressive eyes and tall slender body drew glances from those around her, but she was oblivious to all but the meat. "Hi Holly," Sam beamed a little too widely. Elenor felt hugely disappointed but couldn't say why.

"I thought the Children of the Sun didn't allow the 'devouring of flesh,'" she said.

"Fuck the Children of the Sun," Holly drew more glances. One lady huffily covered her child's eyes and led him away.

"You left them?" Elenor didn't like the way Sam's eyes glittered. Holly tore off another strip of burger.

"You know what? I hate direct sunlight and being happy all the time. In fact, most of the time I'm pretty pissed off and I'm perfectly fine with that." She stood straighter as though she needed more lung capacity to expel her dormant anger. "They had four hours of cuddle time a day, and this last week I deliberately didn't brush my teeth. This morning Charlie kept prodding me in the back with his bell end so I yanked it like he asked me to." She grinned privately. "He started crying. So here I am."

"Well, we'd probably better go," Elenor said, tugging at Sam's sleeve. He followed her meekly, casting a look back at Holly that spoke of walks in the rain and sepia tinted memories. "Oh look, Mr Wiggins brought his performing slugs. He spent hours training them down my street last week." They joined a throng surrounding a white haired man in a crumpled showman's jacket and trousers. His face was flushed a deep grey and Elenor's heart flailed when she saw the embarrassed onlookers. Lying squidgily before Mr Wiggins were four slugs almost as big as a human. They chewed the grass gently, masticating blank-eyed leviathans.

"Come on Simon," begged Mr Wiggins, tapping the nominal slug with a long stick. "Show these lovely people what we've been learning for hours and hours." Simon looked up briefly, eyeing the stick. The slug next to him squirmed its way to the edge of the crowd. "That's it," Mr Wiggins' eyes lit up, "now, stand! Stand!" The slug leaned towards a grinning young man, its lips twitching outwards until they connected with his hair.

"Oh, get it off," the man tried to pull away, but the slug's grip was strong.

"I've seen enough," grumbled Sam, pulling Elenor towards the main stage. 'Fydor the Forseer,' blazed across the sign at the back, 'Prophecies for young and old.'

The gathering crowd waited; the Town Mayor stroked his long, curling moustache with glee. Sam and Elenor pushed their way to a place near the front. She was relieved to see him looking excited, as though he had come back to her somehow. The chatter vanished when a man draped in a grey cloak swished into view. "Ladies and gentlemen," he announced in Bold, "I have for you a being most sinister, a creature so disturbing you will not believe your own eyes!" Elenor's head fizzed with excitement and she gripped Sam's hand. "Not only will he horrify and torment your dreams, but he will predict your future!" Gasps drifted upwards from the crowd.

"Yeah, right," muttered a man next to Elenor.

Everyone was still as a slender, hunched creature hobbled from behind the curtains. His elongated fingers cut through the air, his black hair curled upwards and his skin was pure white. Elenor had the odd feeling she had seen him before. "Fydor," boomed the barker, "tell the good people their future." The onlookers strained forwards.

"Very soon," his letters scratched themselves into the space before him, "the world will end." He bowed low and edged towards the stage exit. The crowd remained silent, waiting for more.

"The world," said the barker with a flourish "will end. Today's prediction," he continued as he followed the psychic, "was for entertainment purposes only, and as such we are not responsible for any consequences." They disappeared behind the curtains.

"But..." some said.

"What?" the others said.

Within seconds, chaos erupted. "What did he mean?" The people begged, "Why did he say that?" Those nearest the stage tried to scramble onto it and those at the side tried to sneak behind the curtains to get to the caravans. The hefty guards skulked forwards.

"Who were they? How can they just come here and tell us this?" fumed Elenor. Sam's skin had faded from dark grey to light.

The Mayor took centre stage, his moustache drooping and eyes enlarged. "Uh...ladies and gentlemen, we still have a fun-packed show to delight and amaze. Please, please, calm yourselves!" His words eventually took effect, the townsfolk eager for reassurance. Having now got their attention, the Mayor straightened his jacket. "It is vital we stick together until we receive further explanation. Think of our children, we must carry on as normal."

"Yes," the crowd asserted, "for the children." Sam and Elenor watched in shock as parents herded weeping offspring to sideshow booths or to watch the acrobats.

"Timmy," shrieked one mother as she pushed her child down the helter-skelter, "I'm doing this for you, will you please smile."

"This is madness," said Sam. "We should find out." They snuck towards the caravans where the security guards eyed them menacingly. "Sir," Sam began, "perhaps we could have a discussion..."

Elenor saw the rage rising from tiptoe to forehead in the large men and knew she had to do something. Pointing into the distance she cried, "Someone over there is committing a hate crime."

"Really?" said one. "Quick, George, Tim, Mark, let's go and join in." They hurried away and Elenor flung one of the caravan doors open.

"Oh!" yelped the twisted figure, standing decidedly straight and peeling off false fingers. A pillow fell from the back of his jumper to the ground, seeming to blow a taunting raspberry at the couple.

"You're not a hideous monster?" Sam sounded more like a child who had been lied to than an angry man.

"No," the creature said, "My name's Alan, I…"

"You were in the ice cream shop this morning," said Elenor.

"Yes," he looked down at his feet, "I like ice-cream."

"Get out there and tell them the world isn't ending," said Sam.

"No, no," Alan held his palms out in appeal, "I was just following orders. I was told if I didn't make the announcement I'd be arrested."

Elenor folded her arms. "Who told you that?" Alan's eyes fixed on his toes and he shuffled uncomfortably. "It was in a letter addressed from the council. They knew I'd been trying to raise the dead without a permit." Sam lunged forwards but Elenor held him back.

"No," Sam's yell was so large it almost knocked Alan over, "he's obviously lying. Why would the council tell him to do something like that?"

"You have to tell everyone it's not true," Elenor pleaded.

Alan shook his head, face aghast. "Oh no," he said, "It stated very clearly, any dispute would have to go through the proper channels or else."

Alan searched through his drawers, pulling out a crumpled piece of paper. "He's right," said Elenor, "It's got the Council's heading at the top of the sheet." The official document politely but firmly informed the recipient that if he did not adhere to the instructions provided he would be forced to go on holiday. It then apologised for any inconvenience.

"I really had no choice," shrugged Alan. His thin frame slumped pathetically.

"Perhaps," said Elenor quietly to Sam, "we ought to speak to your dad. Where's the nearest Council Office?"

"Lindon Lane," growled Sam, "I could just give him a ring and get this sorted now."

"No," Elenor couldn't explain her feelings of misgivings, "this is too important, we ought to go personally."

"You're probably right," Sam shoved the letter into his pocket. They placed a paper bag over Alan's head and led him out onto the field. Parents still dragged their children from exhibit to ride, their offspring's tears glistening like silver diamonds. The older generation laughed manically to encourage their charges, succeeding only in frightening them with their wild eyes and clawed hands. The trio crept past them, heads down, narrowly avoiding an angry elephant as it surged away from parents holding their wailing offspring in its face. "We need to go down here," Sam pointed to an opening in the woods. "Oh, Holly!" Elenor rolled her eyes as Sam eagerly outlined their plan to her. Inevitably, she was enthralled.

"Wow, I wish I was going with you."

"Why don't you?" asked Sam. Elenor smiled politely.

"Oh, can I? I can't really be arsed with waiting for the world to end. I imagine it's better to be busy. I'll bring some meat."

"Oof!" Elenor turned to see Alan fall to the ground. In her desperation to keep moving her hand had lost his grip and he'd wandered into a laughing parent. He struggled like a writhing worm to get up and the bag fell from his head. Elenor rushed to put it back on but a little boy was already pointing.

"Mummy, it's the man who told us we were all going to end."

His mother knelt beside him. "What was that Stephen; you're having a wonderful time?" Her eyes caught Alan's and widened in terror. "It's him," she whispered, rising slowly to her feet. "It's him!" Her shriek ballooned upwards, the letters stretching across the clouds. There was a stampede and Alan curled into a ball. Sam grabbed Elenor and Holly, who cast a longing look at the barbeque.

Elenor turned back to see thousands of hands reach for the cowering figure before pushing herself through the wall of woodland after Sam and Holly. They fought through a wall of spikes and thorns which tore at their clothes and scratched their faces. Elenor pushed blindly forwards until the branches softened into tickling tendrils. A light appeared before them and they followed it, finally falling into a clearing. All natural light was concealed by the branches, the only source being a lantern sprouting from a tree. Sam leaned against it and Elenor fell to her knees in the undergrowth. Holly fanned herself with her hand, her cheeks shining with sweat. "Well," Sam straightened himself, "first thing's first, we need to call my father and get this sorted." He made to stride further into the forest but Holly threw herself in his path.

"No! Don't you both know?" She looked from him to Elenor beseechingly.

"Know what?" Sam shrugged.

"Your father is the problem," Holly said, "He's the one who ordered The End. He owns this town and everyone in it and gets rid of whoever he feels like." Sam looked outraged.

"Oh, that's just hippie rumours," said Elenor, but a tumour of doubt formed in her chest.

"Well, that's as may be," Holly was indignant, "but if we go straight to him we'll be sent to The Burning Room, you included."

Sam snorted with laughter. "The Burning Room?" Elenor wanted to weep and vomit but did neither.

"Yes," Holly held her hands up to quieten Sam, checking over her shoulders.

"How about this," Elenor stood up, earning her a look of surprise from the others, "we go in secret to Head Office and find out what we can. If it turns out we're wrong, we'll go right to your father."

"Turns out we're…" Sam was studying her as though she were a kettle barnacle.

"Yes," said Elenor gently, "we're probably wrong, but why don't we just try this in case?"

"Well alright," Sam shook his head, "but I honestly think you two are being very dramatic. My father could get this sorted in five minutes."

"Oh, we don't need your sodding father," yelled Holly impatiently, sticking two fingers up at the air, "balls to all of them. Come on, I'm sure it's this way." Elenor followed meekly, feeling that she and Sam now stood on different planets.

They emerged in a clearing surrounding by black trees. Lighting the way was a single glowing bush, the sign next to it reading "Those who do not pick up their dog's mess will be fined." Sam stepped forward first, almost tipping onto his face.

"Oh," he said, "It's all weird." Holly strode forwards and shrieked as she fell to her knees. Elenor gingerly placed one foot in front of her. The spongy ground rolled and swayed beneath their feet. They grabbed each other and clung on, falling like drunkards until they reached the other side. "Right," Sam straightened himself angrily, "this way."

They brushed aside sharp twigs and scratchy leaves. "The other two think you're annoying, you know," Elenor saw a tiny whisper. "They wish you weren't here. And that weird face you do when you laugh, they can't stand it. They said it looks like a fish. We know because we saw."

"Did you see that?" shrieked Elenor. The other two looked at her blankly. "That voice saying, um, things?"

"What things?" Holly asked.

"Never mind, nothing." They pushed on silently through the narrow foliage path, Elenor glancing at the leaves for signs of trouble. The trees stood passively, innocent.

They were scratched from head to foot and sporting new branch headdresses when they reached the edge of the woods. The sun was setting over a vast horizon of flat fields and more woods waited in the distance to the right. A single farmhouse stood against the heavy wind and clouds, surrounded by tracks of hoed earth and a few clumps of trees. All three stomachs growled in unison. "We could just go and see who lives there?" Holly said pleadingly. They trudged across the grass and arrived on the path. Cabbages grew in rows nearby, but something about them seemed strange. As they trudged up the steps onto the porch Elenor realised why.

"They're toes," she whispered, suddenly wanting to go home.

"And they're arms," Sam pointed at the strange branches sprouting from tree trunks. Peeking from the back of the house were hedges, until a closer look showed them to be clusters of fingers. Holly squealed. "I'm sure the farmer's a reasonable man, there has to be an explanation for this," said Sam. They linked arms as they knocked on the door. Elenor held her breath.

"Well, hello there," said a bearded, ruddy-faced man in dungarees. Tom launched into a speech about being lost and hungry and terribly sorry to disturb while Elenor tried not to look at anything. "Y'all must be hungry," the farmer stepped aside, "Why not come in for a bite?" The three stepped in, thanking him profusely, imagining plates of stew or roast meat. "Three more for dinner Mama," he said to an equally stout woman in a floral apron.

"Oh wonderful," she beamed, "we've got the finest powdered weight shakes in the area. Make yourselves comfortable and I'll pour you some." Reluctantly they sat at the oak table, watching her mix neon powder with milk into tall glasses. "Here y'are, that ought to fill those bellies." She placed a tray of them onto the table and they stared at the thick mixture. Sam picked up his glass and sipped. His expression was blank as he placed it back, a thick moustache now on his top lip.

"What the..." said Holly before she was sharply elbowed by Elenor.

"Yummy huh?" The farmer chuckled. "This here's what's known as a Parts Farm," he said, taking a seat at the table and draining half a glass of Weight Shake. "All those drones who work on the machines and filing rooms at the bureau need to get parts from somewhere, so we grow them in places like this. Speaking of the bureau," he eyed them, "I hear you folks are in a little bit of trouble, interfering in their business and what not." All three glanced sharply up. "Now, now," the farmer held up his hand, "I ain't gonna shop ya, but ya can't stay here or I'll be in a heap of trouble and Lord knows what'll happen." Elenor felt herself shaking.

"What say we only spend one night, and disappear as soon as day breaks?" asked Holly, batting her moth wing eyelashes. "You've already been so generous and we'll pay you back any way we can." Elenor caught the grind of Sam's teeth.

"Well, since you ask so nicely," grinned the farmer, "I guess one night ain't gonna hurt."

They settled into the double bed, Sam's feet nestling between the girl's heads. In happier times they would have attacked him with tickles, but in the flickering candlelight they merely stared into the middle distance. Presently Sam and Holly's breathing became rhythmic and Elenor watched the Zs drift from their motionless bodies, dissipating against the ceiling. She closed her eyes tightly, trying to match her breathing to theirs. The Zs floated towards her, tickling her face and arms. She scratched irritably and they tangled in her hair. A large Z bumped against her eyelids and she sat abruptly, brushing desperately at her head. The letters grew larger and sharper until Elenor tiptoed from the room, closing the door gently behind her.

She licked her dry lips and, gripping the bannister, carefully descended the shadowy steps. She stopped abruptly when her feet made a visible creak, but when no movement occurred she continued slowly. On reaching the bottom she released her breath and crept towards the kitchen. Sipping at a glass of water, some words outside in the distance caught her eye. Though she knew she should go back to bed, she opened the back door to see more clearly. The finger bushes in the distance reached up towards the moon, their tips painted in silver light. The insistent voice rose above them, its source hidden. The grass underfoot was damp but Elenor barely noticed – though she couldn't make out what the words said there seemed to be some distress behind them. She broke into a run, searching the perimeter of the clammy bushes for an entrance to the middle. Finally she squeezed her way through and stopped still, her hand slapping against her mouth.

"I knew it!" crowed a voice from behind her. Elenor turned to see the Farmer's wife, her face twisted in grotesque fury. The farmer, from his place amongst a special patch in the centre of the bushes, dove to his feet and scrabbled at his pyjama bottoms. "Invite this girly here to join you eh?" shrieked his wife. The farmer protested his innocence as Elenor ran back to the house, the image searing her eyes. She scrambled up to Holly and Sam, shaking them violently.

"I'm sure it was a misunderstanding," Sam mumbled, rolling over. Holly saw the desperation in Elenor's eyes and kicked him in the back.

"Move it," she threw his clothes at him, flinging on her own dress. They piled downstairs, past the kitchen where the farmer's wife clung to the phone.

"Yes," she wept, "they're here and they threatened us with swearing. It was awful!"

The trio snuck out the back door past rows of toes and noses and ears. "What happened?" asked Holly.

"I'll tell you later," said Elenor, unwilling to let her mind travel back to the centre of the finger bushes, to the special patch with their throbbing heads and thick veins and the farmer's cookie dough behind as he squatted over them. "We have to call town, make sure everything's OK."

They ran and ran, always on the verge of falling but somehow pressing on, until they reached the woods. "There must be a phone box around here," he muttered, checking each tree trunk until he eventually paused. "Here we are." He picked up an oval, bark-camouflaged handset with a mirror above the numbers and dialled furiously, his face glowing in the neon light. "Oh God," he moaned, "I think someone's pissed on this one. Hello mum?" Sam hunched forwards to read her words in the glass. Elenor and Holly exchanged a look of horror. "No, stop worrying," he said, "I'm fine. I'll be home as soon as I can." He stepped away from the other two and lowered his voice. "I doubt I'll want dinner tonight. No, I know Tandoori's my favourite. No, I-I don't need picking up. I don't know where I am. No, I don't, stop asking." Elenor and Holly tugged on a sleeve each and something seemed to sink in. "Look, I've got to go, I'll see you soon." His face had turned a strange grey as he replaced the handset and wiped his hands on the trunk. "Alan," he seemed to remember the plight of the fortune teller and picked up the handset once more. "Hello? Yes, please…do not harm Alan. Alan! Oh for God's sake, do not harm Fydor the Foreseer. No, I don't have time to speak to him. No, wait…" The girls hopped up and down. Sam blinked furiously while he waited – an act Elenor had never seen him do.

"Fydor – I mean Alan, you're alive. Eh? Yes, erm, well I think we're in the Wild Woods. The farmer's wife rang the Bureau but just… tell everyone to sit tight, we won't give up." He hung up and stared at his feet for a good few seconds. "Right, I think we should follow the dark trees. This way," his bravado now looked more like a security blanket.

"Look," Holly pointed ahead, "the trees are moving, that one used to stand over there." They stopped still and, sure, enough, through the shadows and darkness one tree shuffled slowly to a different resting spot.

"Shit," said Elenor.

"We're not lost," Sam shouted, "I know exactly where we are." He rubbed at his temples furiously.

"Sam, we are definitely lost," said Holly after walking an undetermined length of time in near blackness. She stopped and folded her arms; Sam looked physically winded and sat on a tree stump. Elenor tried to think of something reassuring to say but each word stuck to the roof of her mouth. "Are we going to stand here long?" asked Holly. Elenor glared at her but the other girl didn't notice.

"Look at that," said Sam.

"What?" said Elenor, worried she would have to deal with a psychiatric breakdown along with everything else.

"That." Sam pointed through the trees and Elenor noticed tiny words. Most popped almost immediately like bubbles but she caught the sentence 'overdue parking bill.'

Holly gripped Elenor's sleeve. "Do you think they might help?" Before the other two could stop her she crashed towards the origin of the voices. Elenor grabbed Sam's hand and pulled him after her, picturing the furious farmer's wife impaling a bloody dagger into Holly's chest. She wasn't so distracted that she didn't notice the way Sam's fingers gripped hers as though she were an anchor to reality.

Through the leaves was a clearing. A tall fire raged in the centre surrounded by a group of singing people. Elenor tried to make out the words of their song, but it largely seemed to be gibberish. Loose, natural material flowed about their undulating bodies; fleece wraps or leafy skirts and faces streaked with mud. A small group beat rhythmically on drums nearby. Everyone's skin was speckled with deep lines and crevices under the dancing firelight. "Look at them," Sam muttered, "they're all old." Elenor noticed the wrinkles and sagging skin, the claw-like hands and stooping backs.

"My God, whispered Holly, "we could take bets on who's left alive at the end of the night."

"Have we wandered into an OAP meeting? Do they just live out here?" said Sam.

"We ought to go," said Elenor.

"Nonsense," said Sam, "it's not often you come across something like this. We ought to study them for a while, maybe draw some pictures. Our findings could be important."

"Yes," replied Elenor, "while you're making jam and finger painting with them I shall get on with finding Head Office before the world ends."

"Elenor," said Holly, "you need to calm down, there's no need to be so uptight."

Elenor was about to sputter with disbelief when she felt eyes staring at her. Looking up she saw almost the entire party leaning over their hiding bush. "What do we do, what do we do?" Holly was backing away.

"Run?" said Elenor. But her body refused to move. They noticed movement behind them – they were surrounded. One of the men reached a wrinkle-mapped hand out to them.

"But why are you afraid?" asked a woman in a feather headdress. Despite her outlandish garb she looked like the kind of old lady you might see offering mints at a bus stop. "We only wanted to know if you'd like to join us." The trio silently followed them back to the fire, terrified to speak in case they offended their strange hosts.

"Here," said another old lady as she handed them piles of paper, "take these and, when the great one speaks, cast them into the fire." The aging tribe began a slow and creaking shimmy around the lapping flames. They copied them stiffly at first but when the tempo quickened Holly flailed her arms and leapt to a tune of her own, attracting worried looks.

"Prepare to make the offerings!" the feathered woman's wispy voice almost sank into the crackling logs. Elenor glanced down at the pages she held.

"Dear Mr Parker," said the top sheet, "it has come to our attention that you have failed to keep up with your ground rent charges." She flipped through them as inconspicuously as she could whilst hopping ungainly in circles. "Dear Mrs Masterson," read another, "if we do not receive the first instalment of your parking fine by October the 5th we shall be forced to notify the courts." Elenor pressed the paper to her chest.

"Everybody cast the offerings!" There followed a frenzy of shrieking and tearing of paper, and the fire leapt into the air as it lapped up years of fines and pension amendments.

The drums pounded louder. "Oh Gods," shrieked the leader, followed by wails and whoops, "hear our prayer. "We follow only the leader and reject all earthly ways!" The dancing loosened and became more instinctive. Aging hips rolled and cracked and the drums beat faster. Elenor cast Sam a frightened glance. Fur and feathers were shed and sagging skin glistened under the firelight and the moon. "Come on," squawked an old lady, breasts swinging like pendulums, "free yourselves; be at one with the music." The lady pulled at Elenor's top. Elenor recoiled, batting the crinkly hand away. "I'm trying to free you," the lady retorted, fury in her watery eyes. Elenor shielded herself as more hands pawed her clothes. She felt Sam's hand on her shoulder. He backed them away slowly but it was too late, shaky fingers pointed in their direction.

"Bureaucrats!"

"Oh God, where's Holly?" said Sam through clenched teeth. The tribe shuffled towards them, arms outstretched and dentures gnashing. Holly still danced wildly by the fire, swinging her dress over her head. Sam scooped her up and they dashed through the bushes, Elenor feeling a twinge of jealously at Sam's grip on Holly despite the adrenaline punching her veins. They reached another clearing and hid behind the trees, hunched and shaking, until the moaning crowd shuffled past.

"Sorry," said Holly, "I think I was having flashbacks." She pulled her dress back on and Elenor watched Sam pretending not to watch Holly. Even Elenor couldn't resist a few glimpses at her silver skin.

"Well, the good news is I remember where we are," said Sam, former assertiveness restored. "I imagine we'll need to enter the back way."

"Well, yes," said Elenor, "we can't just stride through the front door."

"Alright," Sam strode through the trees, "we'll do as you suggest but as soon as I speak to my father the whole horrible mess will be cleared up immediately." Elenor and Holly glanced at each other, open mouthed with frustration. Elenor knew she had to speak.

"Sam," she said sharply. "What are your memories of visiting him at work?"

Sam's brow creased. "Well, there was the day we went to visit the drones underground. Everyone spoke in song and laughed the whole time."

Elenor folded her arms. "Go on."

"Uh, there was the day we went to the complaints department. Someone had made a complaint by accident but they withdrew it straight away when we went to see them. Father said he'd shown great initiative and he was sent off to be promoted."

Elenor raised an eyebrow. "And...has he ever let you wander around on your own? Speak to the staff alone? Even come to his work that often?" Sam shook his head, a hunted look in his eyes.

"Jesus, Sam," Holly snorted, "Are you an idiot? Your dad's having people killed." Sam looked outraged and Elenor went to his side.

"It's just that we, perhaps, suspect him of being one of those rulers who's...more of an Iron Fist type." Sam deflated, searching his memories for evidence to the contrary.

Holly shrugged. "Well, I suppose if we don't find solid evidence and you still think the same way, you can do what you like – go to him and tell him everything if needs be." Elenor was about to protest but something in Holly's expression told her to keep quiet.

Sam shrugged. "OK, but a man who gets his son a personally made pony-dog for Christmas can't be a bad person."

They trudged along the dark path, breathless and tired. Elenor noticed the outline of a human in the foetal position on the ground amongst the bushes, covered by the leaves and fur of the undergrowth. She trotted slightly to catch up with the other two.

"There it is," Sam pointed to a monolithic black door. "I'll call Alan to let him know everything's in hand."

Elenor froze; she realised she had never actually expected to find it; she had assumed they would wander around, try for a while and give up assuring each other they had done their best. An unfamiliar sensation crawled over her, a pleasant feeling she supposed successful people had all the time and barely even noticed. "Come on," she yelled, rushing forwards excitedly. She didn't see the other two calling after her.

Alan lay sprawled on the ground, inhaling an unpleasantly long blade of grass but unwilling to attract further attention by moving. Unsure of what to do once they had reached him, the crowd settled for relentless prodding and poking. His waiting strategy paid off eventually with some of them. "Look at that squirrel!" yelled a man, and several people ran into the trees. Alan went to crawl away but enough hands remained to pin him down. Their faces were primal with anger and fear.

A wiry woman with a beehive stood authoritatively in front of them. Her face conjured images of oily overalls. It was the mechanic, May. "We're supposed to burn people like this," she sneered. Her face glowed with excitement, her beauty marred by her apparent to desire to have Alan killed. The crowd turned to her.

"People like what?"

"Well," May squirmed, looking less certain, "people who predict the future. Unpleasant, magical futures," she added, dispelling any comebacks.

"You mean witches," grinned an old man with a face like a gnarled foot, his teeth slanting like a pile of collapsed beach chairs. The crowd appreciated his input and roared in letters a foot high, pulling him to his feet. Tomorrow the rough fingers would leave bruises – if he was still alive. What worried him more was a familiar itch on his elbow. He tried not to think about it, which caused him to think about it even more. His fingers clawed in his attempt not to scratch.

"How do we burn him?" asked a second woman. May blinked.

"Well, we'll probably have to build a pile of wood or something." Alan could barely see their words through the 'Thump, thump thump,' of his heart.

"That'll take ages," whined a small boy, earning himself a rumble of assent. May's eyes flicked from face to face hoping someone else might make a suggestion.

"I suppose," she shrugged, "we'll have to chop down trees and make a log pile." A hush befell the crowd before they burst into action, dragging Alan behind them. Simon the slug was released from his cage into the wild and Alan felt a hundred hands push him into the slime-soaked enclosure. He folded his long body as much as he could, pulling his knees to his chin and slumping his back against the low ceiling.

"Sorry it's a bit small," said May.

"Oh, think nothing of it," fumed Alan.

"We just need you to wait there for a while," she continued, "We promise it won't be long." She skipped off to join the others, leaving Alan to focus on the pain in the small of his back and the itch he was trying to forget. The sky darkened along with Alan's optimism.

He was nudged awake and promptly hit his head on the metal roof. "There's someone for you," May said sheepishly, holding a white phone. The wire led to his trailer and a mad glare of hope flared inside him as he took the handset. Sam stared back at him from the glass above the dialling numbers.

"Hello?" He turned to hide his words from the watchers.

"Fydor – I mean Alan, you're alive!"

"For now."

"Eh? Yes, erm, well I think we're in the Wild Woods. The farmer's wife rang the Bureau but just… tell everyone to sit tight, we won't give up."

"Farmer's…? OK, I'll try to pass the message on." Alan pressed the off-switch and felt hundreds of eyes staring at him. "Er…" he swallowed hard. "That was my mum. She says my dinner's getting cold."

"Tell us what The Big Boss said," yelled an old man with a face like a melted candle.

"The Big Boss? Oh! He said, er, don't worry, lay low and everything will be fine." The onlookers muttered amongst themselves.

May flung her arms into the air in rapture. "We will build the underground fortress for you, My Lord!"

"What-"

"The underground fortress you have requested – and we will save the sacrifice for when it is complete."

Alan's head fell to his knees.

"We have no shovels," whispered a woman.

Eyes turned back to May. "Oh no, that's right, all the shovels were buried in the Great Cleansing. Well, doesn't rain erode rocks? Maybe if we all cried onto the ground it would collapse."

Excitement poured in a torrent through the townsfolk. They fell to their knees, holding their faces close to the ground.

"Nothing's happening," said the same woman.

"OK," May bit her nails, "I'll tell a sad story. Um, there was a kitten."

A chorus of 'awww,' drifted into the air.

"But – it died." Shocked silence. May shifted from one foot to the other. "It, uh, was given to a small girl for Christmas, but it had a rare heart condition." A few snuffles rose upwards. May visibly relaxed. "So her parents got her a rabbit and the little girl cuddled it every day. But... the neighbour's cat ate it." The snuffles became whimpers, and the whimpers became sobs. Alan watched in disbelief while the entire town wept uncontrollably onto the cold ground. He noticed the girl from the ice cream parlour that had been so nice to him that morning. Now her tears sparkled and her worry shadows were deep crevices as she sat huddled on the grass.

"Excuse me," he whispered, and May tiptoed towards him. "This could take some time. Any chance I could slip off? I'll have a chat with the Boss and have this all sorted out."

"No," said May wildly, clinging to the bars on Alan's cage. She checked behind her and lowered her voice. "I promise I won't let them hurt you." She paused. "I'll try. I just need you to stay here a while longer." As soon as she turned back to her subjects her demeanour changed and she sashayed through the hunched figures, her hands clasped gleefully. Alan scratched his shoulder, inspecting beneath his jumper collar. It was the thing he dreaded. The itch became a burn and he tried to think of other things.

"I just wanted to thank you," the words surprised him.

"Thank me?"

"Yes," May took hold of the bars, "The others are finally paying attention to me. Do you know how long it's taken?" She shook her head, a haunted expression on her face. "I've been in every amateur dramatic performance since I was five and still I don't get noticed. Now look at them!"

Alan noticed for the first time a strange look in her eyes. "I'm – happy for you?"

"It's all thanks to you, you know." Alan felt an involuntary twinge of sympathy and smiled back. His guard down, he again scratched his arm. May frowned. "Why do you keep doing that?"

"It's nothing," Alan barked, "everything's fine." A cloud rolled over the moon and a shadowy May re-joined the others.

A nudge dragged Alan from the safety of sleep back into discomfort. It was daylight. "What?"

"The Big Boss," said several awed voices in unison. Alan tried to straighten his leg, catching his ankle bone on a bar. He took the handset, turning his back to study Sam's crackly image and barely decipherable words. They had reached the building and, for the first time in hours, Alan felt hopeful. He switched off the phone and turned to the waiting crowd.

"Er, everyone stay calm. Just do what I say and all will be well." Expecting a flurry of activity he was surprised when they continued staring at him in open mouthed silence. May looked increasingly uncomfortable until she flung herself prostate on the grass.

"Forgive us, Oh Lord!" The others followed suit.

"Right," muttered Alan, "Its fine. I'll be off then."

"No! You can't leave us," the fear in their eyes was intense.

"I-I can't?"

"What do we do now?"

All eyes were on May and her shoulders slumped under the weight. "Doesn't anyone else have any suggestions?"

One man stepped forwards. "We could always ask the Wise One." The crowd buzzed.

"Oh yes, she'll know what to do!"

"Let's ask her!"

"Why didn't you ask her before?" said Alan.

All eyes looked down at their feet. "She doesn't actually like us," said May. The man stroked his chin.

"Yes, that's true. She doesn't really like speaking to anyone."

"Well," May shrugged, "just not to us." She pointed towards the woods at a row of thick hedges shielding twisted, unfriendly looking trees strangled by vines. "She's through there."

"Well," shrugged Alan, "looks like you haven't got much choice." May gestured to a heavy set man with eyes like a rabid vole. He clicked the cage door open and stood aside while Alan found his balance. He cringed when the bones in his knees and elbows cracked, but at least the burning itch had dampened. The goon stood so closely beside Alan he was momentarily afraid of a sexual advance, until May took her place on his other side, watching him for signs of escape. "Nice," he grumbled, "let's just get this over with."

He pushed his hand into the scratchy leaves of the hedge. He stepped forwards, his body encased in a constricted dark tunnel. The other two followed in single file. "What's that noise I can see?" he asked faintly.

"It's the hedge," said May, "I think its hearts is beating. I have to get out." Alan reached behind him and grabbed her hand, pulling her steadily forwards. She squeezed gratefully and soon her pulse was as regular as the ominous thud surrounding them.

Alan flopped onto the ground followed by the other two. Alan's thoughts were just pulling themselves together when the bushes nearby rustled. Four men tumbled before them. Where their mouths should have been was a smooth surface. The man in the middle leapt onto the shoulders of the one next to him, and the other two vaulted sideways and outwards, clinging onto their companions, forming a cross. The gap in the centre of this new shape puckered. "And who might you be?"

"We are on our way to see the Wise One," May tried to appear assertive.

"She sees no-one," the creature stepped forwards, side legs thrusting like tentacles. Alan ran for the path between the trees but a heavy boot to the back of the head sent him landing on his chin. His brain shook and a hand gripped his arm. He tried to pull away before noticing May.

"Go," she hissed. Alan looked back and saw the creature charge at her goon, who ran blindly in another direction. Alan and May dashed ahead, thorns pulling at their clothes. A shriek snaked past them; the goon was dead and the thing was following them now. Alan pushed his legs harder until he felt they would fall off – he knew they couldn't outrun it.

They burst into another clearing. Behind them the thing stopped and the men disbanded, stomping away. The vegetation was luscious and fertile. In the centre of the clearing was a pearl white seashell, tall enough to reach Alan's chest. Hanging from the tree branches were tiny party bags and Alan reached for one. May tried to stop him but he'd already plucked it from the boughs and peeked inside.

"Not much in here," he said, "just a fun sized whiskey and some nail varnish. What?" He looked up to see why May was shouting furiously at him. The shell was twitching and opening slowly, only it wasn't a shell but two clasped hands, the bent fingertips of top one slithering and shuddering upwards. On the bottom palm laid a snow white figure, its slender back the only visible part. They stepped forwards to inspect. Its legs were so thin they surely couldn't support the skeletal body. It turned, slowly and delicately, until facing them was a wizened old man. His skin was like stretched raw pastry and a thick silver beard wound around his torso, hiding his shame. Alan suppressed a shudder at the sight of all the sinew.

"You did well to pass the Guardian of the Gates," said the old man, his words faint. "How will you do, though, when faced with pure logic?" He cackled maniacally, revealing several missing teeth. "Answer me this, who has four legs in the morning, two in the afternoon and three at night?" His eyes widened and his hands clenched with glee.

"Well, man," May put her hands on her hips.

"What?"

She rolled her eyes. "Man. Everyone knows that one; first a baby, then a grown-up then an old man with a walking stick. It's been around since the Dawn of bloody time. Haven't you got a more difficult one?" Alan tried to shush her but it was too late, the old man was already thinking.

"Alright, um, what about this one: What goes around the world but stays in a corner?"

"Oh!" Alan hopped up and down, "a stamp!"

"Damn!" fumed the old man. "Very well, you'll not have heard this: I can run, but never walk. I have a mouth but cannot talk. I have a bed but never sleep..."

"River," Alan and May chanted as one.

The old man reared up like a viper, his weak pulse visible in his chest. "Curse you. You must sit there until I think of one." He turned his back once more. The pair did as they were told, leaning against a hillock and watching a spider ballroom dance with a beetle. Eventually the spider grew tired of his friend, mandibles smacking with pleasure. Alan and May looked away quickly and tried to focus on nothing. The sun was fading when the old man jerked up once more. "I've got one! Right: I can run but cannot walk. Wherever I go, thought follows close behind. What am I?"

They leaned their heads together and whispered. "What happens if we don't get it right?" May asked him.

"You're looking at it!" The old man shrieked with laughter again before collapsing into shuddering coughs. May approached him gently, as though she were about to whisper to a horse.

"You're tired, aren't you," she said softly.

"Well," the old man looked confused, "it's not really time for my nap."

"No," Alan stepped forward, "but you did a lot of thinking. It's worn you out, hasn't it?"

The old man's face wrinkled like aged paper. "I could lie down just for a moment I suppose. Oh!" his eyes were wide, alert, "But you won't go anywhere, will you? You must face your fate."

May placed a gentle hand on his shoulder. "Yes, we'll be here. Now just have a bit of a lie down and we'll deal with it when you wake up." The old man's eyes fell gratefully and he sank into the cupped hand. May reached up and nudged the pale fingers above her. The fingertips touched together once more and the pair tiptoed past, into the forest.

They barely noticed the snagging twigs as they trudged endlessly on. Both froze when they noticed voices, hunching down and creeping forwards until they saw chattering and laughter. The way was blocked by thick, soft tree trunks and they found peep holes where they could. A thatched cottage nestled in a wide clearing framed by mushrooms – some tiny, some the size of a tall man and others as big as a tree. Alan and May looked at the dark, soft trunks they leaned on and pulled their hands away.

A long table stood beside the cottage. Surrounding it were several people in grey suits, their eyes and hair wild, passing a teapot to one another. At the head of the table an ancient lady surveyed her guests, watching their giggles and shouts but not interacting. Cake stands lined the centre stacked with sparkling cupcakes. The pair's stomachs growled. "Stop," whispered May. Alan hadn't realised he'd started crawling into the open. It was too late; the crone's eyes were on him.

"Oh look, gentlemen," she said in a joyless sing-song, "Our guests have arrived. Won't you come out, my little slices of pepperoni?" The people at the table shrieked with laughter. Alan and May made their way over, shaking. "Oh, don't look so worried," the crone reached for the teapot, "I only want to offer you a nice breakfast. My cupcakes are the best in the land, you know."

"We're not hungry," said May, a growl from her stomach winding its way around the teacups. Alan tried not to breathe in the scent of freshly baked dough.

"Oh no?" said the crone. "Your friend seems to be enjoying himself." Alan gave a start when he saw May's goon, alive and well and stuffing a whole cake into his mouth, his lips already encrusted with icing sugar. He chased it down with an entire cup of tea, little finger pointing daintily in the air. Alan reached for a cake but May grabbed his hand.

"No," she said through gritted teeth, pointing. The goon, never the brightest of men, seemed blanker than before. Now Alan saw the terrible truth. Sprouting from the back of his head was the quivering tendril of a mushroom root. Its tip shuddered and trembled, waiting for the moment when it would grow long enough to reach the ground and take root, bringing the unfortunate body of the henchman with it.

"Oh, gross," Alan wrinkled his nose. "Why do you do this?"

"Because I get tired of questions all the time! Constant, endless bloody questions." Her eyes took on a hunted look, "my crops won't grow, my baby won't feed, the price of lemons has gone up, what do we do, what do we do – all the time." She turned to them with desperation in her eyes.

"Yes, I've met them and I know how you feel, but isn't this…" Alan indicated the other guests, "a bit extreme?"

She cackled. "Oh it's not for them, just people like your dear friend. The others are here to bring me very interesting news indeed." She paused, apparently hoping they would beg for the answer, but instead they waited. She sighed. "That's Derek and Giles," she indicated one with drool on the side of his mouth and another with hair splayed upwards, both with eyes as big as teacups, "They're from Data Entry. These three," the men she indicated were in a similar state as the first two, "are in Accounts and this is Jess and Delaney from Payroll." The final two, both women, screeched with maniacal laughter and grabbed fistfuls of cake, stuffing it messily into their mouths. "They're immune – from Head Office, you see."

Alan saw May stiffen beside him; they were from Head Office, they must know how the world would end. "Calm yourselves!" The crone boomed when both gibbered and gesticulated at once.

"We're sorry," said Alan, "it's just, well – you can understand why we're a bit worried. Can't you?"

Unhinged laughter broke out across the table, except for the goon who continued to graze. Cake was thrown into the air and tea sloshed onto the grass. "The world will end," said the crone, "and that's all there is to it. Nothing you can do will change that."

"No!" May and Alan wailed. May went to grab her shoulders but Jess and Delaney were either side of them in a blink.

"It's just one of those things," the crone said patiently. "I know it's inconvenient but we can't have everything our own way."

May wept gently. "So what was the point in coming here?"

"Absolutely none," the crone gnashed her gums together, "and we certainly can't have everyone thinking they can do the same."

The other office workers rose to their feet, lanky bodies bending madly to and fro and eyes rolling, incessant giggling stretching to the top of the trees. Alan and May were dragged into a back room in the cottage where one of the Data Entry workers opened a hatch in the floorboards and stuffed the pair inside the tiny space. Dust reeking of death and bowel movements spurted into their faces and they coughed and spluttered. Their captors found this hilarious. "Time for cake?" squealed one of them, and they disappeared back to the mushroom garden. Alan pushed at the hatch entrance but it wouldn't budge.

"Oh God, more tiny spaces," May choked. Alan put an arm around her shoulders.

"There must be…" he crawled forwards like an angry worm, occasionally pushing up at the floorboards.

"There's no weak points," May sobbed, "this is it; we're stuck here, forever!"

"That's not the attitude," chided Alan. He shuffled forwards with renewed energy and bumped into something. The scent of old meat was cloying but Alan was determined not to gag for May's sake. "Looks like we might have found where she dumps the rubbish, there must be another hatch around here." He put a hand up towards the ceiling but it connected with the object, knocking it into a visible position. Its wasted face was contorted in a yell and its eyes had melted into paste. Alan covered May's mouth so her wild screams wouldn't bring them more attention.

Once she calmed she followed him meekly, shuffling on their stomachs into the dark, their way lit only by a stray beam illuminating beetles and dust. "There's..." Alan thumped the ground with increasing vigour until he disappeared from view, sliding headfirst into falling earth.

"Oh, my jaw!" Elenor yelped when she fell on a sharp object. She pushed away the offending filing cabinet and rubbed her aching face. Holly and Sam tumbled after her, landing in similarly ungainly poses.

"Can I help you?" The words made Elenor shriek, earning her a look of alarm from everybody.

"Sorry," she mumbled, "I seem to be quite highly strung at the moment."

"Quite," said the man with a white beard from behind a desk. He wore a Hawaiian shirt and ripped grey shorts. Behind him was a painted scenery of a desert island, whose palm trees swayed realistically in the non-existent breeze while sea lapped against the wainscoting.

"This is certainly very nice," said Sam. The old man eyed them scornfully.

"Nice? I suppose it is if you aren't stuck here. Lost my bloody retirement papers, haven't they? 'Don't worry Norman,' they told me, you just stay in the postal department stamping envelopes while we find the form and you'll be out in no time. It's practically retirement down there anyway.' How long ago was that?" the old man asked rhetorically. "I'll tell you: ten years. Ten years I've been down here. I'm starting to think they've forgotten me. I tried to telephone Top Floor once but it was one of those multiple choice things. I never could get on with them." Elenor shuffled awkwardly, eyeing the door to the far right. "I expect you're after the way out eh," said Norman. "What brings you here anyway?"

"We're looking for some files or information," said Sam before Elenor could make something up. Holly groaned and Norman's eyes narrowed.

"I see. Know where you're going, do you?"

"Is that real sand?" Holly asked desperately, prodding the wall.

"Well, no, but it's very realistic don't you think?" replied Norman. Holly dipped her toe in the sea, leaning forward in a manner that was meant to be provocative and distracting but had more of a late night drunken quality.

"Yes we do!" shrieked Elenor. "We know exactly where we're going and we've been invited, so no need to tell anyone we're here." She marched to the door followed by Holly. Sam stayed put.

"We could use your help for directions," he said, sitting on a nearby chair.

"No!" said Elenor firmly, "we'll be fine."

"Yes, Norman," Holly draped herself disturbingly over Norman's shoulders, "we'll just be on our way."

"Oh come on," said Sam, "Norman here's been working here for years, he knows where everything is. We can trust you, can't we Norman?"

"Oh, but of course." Norman leaned forwards, widening his eyes and holding his hands up. "In fact it was the filing manager who sent me down here. I can reach her assistant on this," he pointed to a button on his phone. "If I told her you'd arrived she'd probably send for you right away."

"Wait," said Elenor, "can you just tell the secretary we want to speak to her alone?"

Norman grinned with jagged teeth. "Consider it done."

"You better be telling the truth, or we'll electrocute you with the company Vapor Ray," Holly glared, all traces of a heavily medicated femme fatale gone.

"Oh, no, I wouldn't dream of lying," Norman broke into an immediate sweat.

Elenor raised an eyebrow. "How come you can't just ask them to send you another form then?"

"It's got to come from the Dreams and Wishes department, and signed for in person" Norman slumped down again. He perked up, "but now I have you to do it for me."

"Of course we will," beamed Sam, "it's the least we can do for a friend."

"As long as it doesn't take too long," muttered Holly.

"Prove it," said Elenor, surprising herself. "Press it and speak to the secretary."

Norman's hand hovered shakily over the button. Perspiration beaded his forehead as he reached down and the three watchers drew in their breath. He pushed the button and Elenor's fists bunched by her sides. A beep trailed from the machine. The three leaned over the desk as the bead on his head grew into a tiny raging river. "Filing, how can I help you, Norman?" said an ornate, sparkling voice.

"Oh, nothing, sorry to trouble you," Norman replied, and the other line went dead. "You see," he leaned back triumphantly until his back clicked. Elenor admitted defeat, making a note of the needed form and ushering the other two from the door. "Bless you," Norman waved a white handkerchief as they stepped out into the dark, slanting corridor, "best of luck!"

A light shone in the distance and they headed blindly towards it. They passed a small room where, beyond the door, an entire eco system of forest trees and bushes grew. Holly pointed towards one of the odd, angular plants. "Biros," she said, "and look – bushes of staplers." From the tip of a high tree branch a tiny seed, mewling contentedly, twisted through the air until it plopped on the soft earthy ground beside others in various stages of sprouting stationary. They moved on until they reached another monolithic black door, bright light gleaming from its edges. They reached out as one and pushed, blinded by whiteness. When they stepped forwards everything became clear.

Black and white floor tiles stretched across the uneven ground. A coffee table in the corner was surrounded by comfortable seats on the wall and clouds floated past a giant window at the front of the room. Two doors stood at either end and a lady sat behind a desk, her body so plump it was almost circular. Her lips stretched far beyond the compass of her face, the corners pointing into mid-air. She hummed as she shuffled paper from one pile to another, her hat leaning forward in a jaunty manner on top of which was curled a sleeping kitten. Sam leaned on the desk. "Excuse me ma'am," he smiled, "We're after the department of Dreams and Wishes. By the way I do like your hat."

"Oh, do you?" the lady simpered, her smile enlarging further, "yes its rather fetching isn't it? It's straight from the runways of Glarn you know. It's a special breed of cat that stays tiny and sleeps most of the day. All it wants is feeding and then it curls right back up. Go on, give it a pet." They hesitantly stroked the tiny animal. It curled into a tighter ball and raised its chin slightly, emitting a row of purrs. "The Department of Dreams and Wishes? Hmm…" The lady stroked her own chin and flicked through some pages. "Well it's not listed in any of the departments above this one, so I imagine it's connected with Hopes and Complaints on the Ground floor. Ask someone there and they should know."

"Is it down in the basement, ma'am?" asked Sam.

The woman's eyes widened, cracking her eyeliner. "Oh no, nothing's in the basement but tortured souls and those waiting forever in limbo. It's where they hand out the," she checked around her and leaned forward, "Temp Jobs." She regained her composure. "Nobody goes in there and comes out again." Sam saluted her as they made to leave. "You know," she called after them, "the Wig Wall is just upstairs, in case any of you," she eyed Holly pointedly, "feels the need to look more respectable. You could always have a wash in one of the luxury bathrooms if the need takes you."

"Yes, thanks, great," said Sam and Elenor, each restraining one of Holly's balled fists as they led her away.

The lift carried them smoothly downwards, the muzak from the speakers punctuated by gentle sobbing. Elenor glanced at the other two to see if they'd noticed. The doors opened onto an industrious call centre, uniformly light grey and neatly carpeted, the call takers seated in pods of four or five. Their legs were in various stages of melting, some only had a few drips like a new candle while others sat in jelly. Thick glass on the black wall displayed an aquarium of mermaids, kraken, octopi and tiny glowing crabs. The other walls were covered in posters assuring, "Every complaint dealt with brings a happy customer," or "a cheerful smile shows in a phone call." Beside the lift was an enormous picture of the Big Boss, each tooth in his grin the size of a head, one hand in a thumbs up and a diamond shaped jewel lodged in his eye for a permanent twinkle. "The End is your Beginning," he claimed in a hopeful font.

"Well," said Sam, "I suppose we ought to…er…"

"Grab someone and force them to talk," said Holly, cracking her knuckles.

"Or," said Elenor, "we could just start talking to one of the staff, see what they know?"

"Surely we should just find whoever's in charge and get proper directions," Sam frowned, striding towards a man sitting alone at a desk, his concertina body dipping from one pile of paper to the next. Elenor tried to catch up with him while Holly eyed the call takers threateningly.

"Can I help you?" asked the concertina man, his eyes enlarged behind his glasses. "Ah, you're here to make the checks, aren't you?"

"Er, yes," said Elenor, "and then we've got to get to the Department of Dreams and Wishes."

"Dreams and Wishes, you say. You'll want to see to it that someone fixes that printer once and for all; bloody thing's been off for ages. I'll have to phone up to Head Office to have you authorised you know."

"Oh, we're authorised, its fine," said Holly, "We've been sent to do checks." She leaned over his desk, allowing her breasts to fall forwards.

"Marvellous," he purred, staring ungraciously down their cleft, "I was wondering when you'd get here. Didn't realise there'd be more than one but follow me, I'll show you how it all works."

He boinged between the tables of chattering workers. "These are the people employed for phone calls. They assist those ringing up and call them back with our sales pitch. The Leads are everything to them," he guffawed, then leaned in closely. "They've exhausted all other professional avenues and lost all their friends, so essentially they belong to us." He grinned charmingly. "Each time they make a mistake or lose a sale it's logged into the system and they accrue what's known as 'payback time,'" he formed apostrophes with his fingers, "where they handle calls until they make it up to the company. Genius, eh?"

"Oh yes," they agreed. "What then?" asked Elenor. The manager slapped the shoulder of a worker who had just finished a call.

"Where do you go when your duty here is done?" he asked gruffly, a drill sergeant quizzing his private.

"To the retirement village, to sit on the comfortable sofas and watch television forever, sir," the worker replied efficiently. He turned back to his computer and the manager led them further on.

"It's a fool proof system," he whispered gleefully.

"Absolutely," agreed Sam, "and very thoughtful of the company to add a retirement room."

The manager gawped at him before breaking into unsettling laughter. "Oh right, yes, very thoughtful. A real retirement room ha!" He jabbed Sam with his elbow and wiped at an imaginary tear.

"Yes, marvellous, everything seems to be running smoothly," said Elenor, "you've earned yourself a tick there. And, uh, what about the place in relation to other departments, which ones do you work closely with?"

He thought for a moment, a frown denting his forehead which eased when he glanced at the aquatic creatures. A mermaid swam up to the glass and placed a hand against it, her eyes pleading for something. The manager watched her, his expression serene. "Departments?" He said eventually, as though asked a question during sleep. "Well, we send our information up to the Department of Paper, then it gets shifted onto the Department of Corrections and Suggestions who then send it to Human Managing who deals with the caller's issues personally, via robot."

"And the Department of Hopes and Dreams is nearby?" she asked.

The manager nodded. "It's on the 400th floor." The mermaid swam away, her expression one of resignation. Sense crept back into the manager's eyes. "I'll have to buzz you up, let them know you're coming. I won't be a moment."

"No!" shrieked Holly. He gazed at her, confused. "I-don't want you to leave. I find you devastatingly attractive." She ran a finger over the lapel of his jacket, pulling her body closer to his. Elenor caught Sam's scowl. "Why don't we plug in an extra set of earphones and listen to the complaints over lunch? It'll be a laugh." The manager's face turned a deep grey and he placed his hands on her shoulders.

"But of course my dear," his words slithered, "we can do that as soon as I buzz you in to let them know you'll be coming." Holly pressed her lips against his. He pulled away, shell-shocked and bobbing furiously but smiling. "My dear," he assured, "I won't be gone a second. Control yourself." He swaggered through the call pods as the three exchanged desperate glances.

"Perhaps we ought to explain the situation?" suggested Sam.

"I think we need to run," said Elenor. The other two followed without hesitation. The manager called after them, at first confused and then furious, calling for security when he pressed the intercom.

"Stop!" he called, the words enlarging, multiplying and crashing before them. Elenor tried to push them aside but they were too heavy and the doorway was barred. The manager's shouts jutted into Sam's back and he sprawled onto the floor. Holly swung her arms viciously in all directions and Elenor ducked down onto her front. The words zoomed over the top of her head and she crawled, commando-style, towards the manager's desk, not knowing what she would do when she got there but knowing she had to stop him. The boss was focused on barring the doorway and didn't notice her hand grasping on the desktop, locating a pile of papers. She pulled them towards her while a vein throbbed in the back of her neck. Forcing herself to breathe evenly she stood, avoiding the words as they buffeted her face and shoulders. She waved the pages madly.

"Everyone!" She screamed, "They've hidden the good leads! Come and get them!" All eyes turned to her and gleamed with desperation. Headphones were pulled from ears and hands reached out like babies grasping for a bottle. They pulled themselves from their seats and shuffled towards her, tripping and falling. The ones without legs pulled themselves along the ground leaving trails of slime, their eyes unseeing to all but the paper in Elenor's hand.

"Leads," they burbled, "leads." Elenor shuddered and flung the documents at them, sprinkling confetti of scrap paper and junk mail over the room. They scrabbled at the ground and The Manager turned his attention to restoring order, first by shouting and then soothing, before losing his patience and wailing helplessly. By the time Elenor, Sam and Holly and dived through the door he was singing lullabies to no effect.

"In here," called Holly, dragging them into a broom cupboard in the corridor. She placed a hand over Sam's mouth and, in minutes, a tirade of footsteps passed and Security stormed into the Call Centre. All was silent for several minutes save for the trio's terrified breathing.

Elenor pushed the cupboard door open hesitantly. She and Holly tumbled out and waited for Sam to join them, but all was still. Holly stuck her head in. "I can't see a thing. Oh wait," she reached in a hand and led Sam out as though she were assisting a pensioner.

"Sam?" said Elenor. He raised his head, his eyes like a frightened deer. Elenor realised something was very wrong.

"Sam, what the Hell's your problem?" said Holly.

"He tried to hurt us," said Sam. "He didn't even offer a map or give directions." Holly shook him hard. The familiar worry-tumour settled in Elenor's stomach.

"Get back in there, keep him safe," said Elenor. She darted off before any questions could be asked, tiptoeing down the corridor until she found a back entry to the stairs. A man burst from one of the side rooms and she froze, but he merely tipped his bowler hat and rolled like a ball past her. Elenor pulled open the door to the stairwell and ascended with her head down, imagining herself invisible. Voices bounced down the steps and Elenor reached a plateau between floors where a man and a woman stood, he with limbs like a spring toy and she with the compact body of a beetle. They were involved in an intense discussion and Elenor snuck past them. She had almost reached the bottom step of the next flight when the man caught her attention.

"Excuse me," he said. Elenor half turned. "What do you think of office romances?"

"Er, nothing?"

"Well you must think something," the lady snuffled.

"Um, probably a bad idea?" Elenor eyed the top of the stairs like it led to Heaven.

"I knew it," the beetle lady sobbed.

"No, no, she didn't know, it doesn't matter what she thinks, she's obviously an idiot," the man comforted her with his spring arms.

"Right yes," Elenor reached out to pat her on the arm, "I am a massive idiot."

"Maybe you'd just better go," the man fumed, turning his back on her. Elenor didn't need further encouragement and sprinted up and up, until the air thinned and the clouds spiralled and whirled outside. She reached the floor above reception and panted outside the doorway, peeking through the small window onto the corridor and there it was. True to its name it spread right across the far wall, a carpet of soft black hair.

Elenor's fingers gripped the door handle when a troupe of black clad men and women wearing visors and carrying guns jogged past like an angry caterpillar. She ducked down until there was silence, finally emerging like a frightened rabbit and dashing to The Wall of Hair. Elenor ran her fingers through it, wishing she could lean against it and fall asleep. She checked about her before stuffing her pockets full, avoiding eye contact as she scurried back down the stairs. After descending for what felt like hours she arrived back at the cupboard and handed the prize to the other two. The stems rooted into their heads until all three had uniformly slick black quiffs.

"Oh God," Holly grumbled, "There's gel in it."

They ran past an office where a woman typed speedily at a computer. She wore a miniature hot air balloon as a hat. "Oh hello," she grinned, her large eyes blinking, "Can I help you?"

"We've been told there's a problem with the printer in the Dreams and Wishes Department," said Elenor, "could you perhaps give us directions?"

"Certainly!" the woman smiled. She floated slowly upwards from her seat and reached upwards, pressing a tiny button on the balloon. Air was released with a hiss and she sank back down into her seat. "Third floor first on the left. Don't forget to fill in the survey afterwards, the Line Manager gets very upset with people who don't."

The weeping from the lift intercom had progressed to uncontrollable sobbing. The girls tried to distract Sam but he stared resolutely into the middle distance. By the time they arrived on the third floor his shoulders had slumped so much he looked as though he was melting. The doors slid open to reveal a factory space filled with mountainous stacks of paper. Workmen in overalls leaned ladders against them, shifting pages from one pile to another while cranes lifted whole loads in one go. Artificial light burned over everyone's faces. The trio tried to look inconspicuous, marching efficiently towards the door on the other side of the room. Elenor noticed a tiny sign pointing to Dreams and Wishes, ignoring the look of suspicion in the workman's eye as they hurried through the door.

The room was a dusty office space; the sun poured from a wall length window and the other looked onto another glass zoo. Instead of water creatures, manticores bared human teeth and swiped their lion claws, scorpion tails flicking. Beside them chewing lazily at piles of hay was a small herd of bored looking unicorns. About their feet scurried Hobgoblins and, leaning against the hay stacks, Satyrs glugged at horns of wine and stamped their goat hooves, the sounds of their revelry muffled by the glass.

"Thank goodness you've come," a voice rolled listlessly in front of them, "It's the printer." They turned to see a man staring at them, his skin literally sagging to the floor. He stood hunched, his eyes as droopy as a Basset Hound's. Holly pulled at her wig irritably.

"I'll show you the way," he sighed as he trudged past desks of workers. Many were weeping and one endlessly wrapped sellotape around his head in an enormous ball. Nobody attempted to dissuade him or even seemed to notice.

"Well, hello ladies," a paper-thin man snaked through the air towards them, large eyes rolling up and down, "it's certainly a breath of fresh air to see such beauty.

Holly put her hand to her quiff and giggled, "Why thank you." Elenor tutted privately. "We've misplaced a form, we don't suppose you'd know where we could get another one, do you?"

"Ladies," he placed flimsy hands on their shoulders. Elenor blushed at the closeness – he smelled of fresh ink, "I am the man to ask. My name's Joffler, anything you like I can find. I've got any form you care to mention."

"Oh, wonderful," Holly beamed, "maybe once this boring job is out the way," she indicated the sagging man who waited patiently.

"But of course." He folded himself forwards to kiss their hands. Elenor kept her face neutral but her insides were a gymnastics tournament. She didn't watch him glide back to his desk but she sensed every moment.

The sagging man pushed aside the swinging legs of a hanged man in the doorway of a side room. "Excuse him," he muttered, "the cleaners haven't been doing their job properly." They entered a cramped space with paper stacked shelves and overflowing filing cabinets. A grey machine, almost completely smooth save for one red button, stared at them from a corner. "We appreciate your arriving so swiftly. We have plenty of customer suggestions to sift through and the company values our time." He shuffled out of the room so slowly that Holly tapped her foot. Elenor closed the door behind him and sat Sam in the corner, away from the blotched face of the suicide victim.

"Right," Elenor paced the floor, "this has to be done right or security will be here in a second."

Holly shrugged, "it's pretty obvious what we need to do." She went to press the red button but Elenor shrieked and restrained her. "What?"

"What do you mean what?" Elenor hissed, "What the Hell is wrong with you?" Holly jerked back, shocked. "Why don't you try using your brain instead of being a slag all the time?" Elenor was aware that she had jogged merrily past the line and waved it goodbye.

"Right," the other girl said in a cold fury. "So the fact that it says 'in case of emergency please press red button' had nothing to do with it?" Elenor gaped as Holly pressed it and the machine fired into life, printing a backlog of files. The girls stared at each other for a moment that lasted a little too long.

"Erm…"

"It's fine," Holly looked away.

"No, it really, I'm really…"

"Just leave it." Holly stormed to the door, calling the others in. They cheered and clapped, their strange bodies twisting and turning and rolling in celebration.

"You just pressed the red button?" they applauded. "We never thought of it, it just seemed too obvious." Holly and Elenor rolled eyes at one another. Joffler coiled himself around them both.

"Fantastic work," he said. "I trust you'll both join me for dinner tonight?" Elenor felt as though she had been placed in a small oven but Holly just raised an eyebrow.

"Elenor will," she patted his hand, "I've got to look after him," she indicated Sam, who rocked back and forth gently. Elenor felt a small pang.

"Shame," Joffler focused his attention on Elenor, "but I'm sure it'll be fun."

The restaurant was inside a giant ice cave on floor 17. Glaciers and icicles twinkled and a man in a polar bear outfit with a missing ear skated between tables in a lacklustre way singing an off-key aria. Couples looked lovingly into each other's eyes or at sparkling silver and white menus while moustachioed, clockwork waiters skated between them on wheels. Joffler ordered the Melanoma Platter soaked in the tears of drones. Despite his insubstantial appearance he ate well enough. "Of course I rarely get the time to relax," he said, "me and the guys are just so damned busy."

The waiter reappeared. "Is everything alright with your meals?"

"It's the fuck's nuts," said Joffler, snickering like a schoolboy. The waiter's lips tightened in a smile. Elenor felt her insides shrivel.

"It's lovely thank you," she squeaked at the disappearing figure.

"Me and the boys at the office are edgy, you're probably not used to that out in the country," Joffler prodded the dark sponge on his plate. "At night we all head into town and spray paint the walls. The Penniless Monks from the city keep getting arrested and burnt for it but really… it's us," he snickered gleefully. Elenor knew she should demand the form as soon as she could and leave but something clouded her thoughts. At that moment he put his hand on hers, looking serious. "I like you," he said. His eyes were several shades of black at once. The disgusted part of her brain was overwritten by the giggling half.

"I like you too," she replied. He seemed to be studying her as though looking at a beautiful piece of architecture or marble statue.

"You'd look much better with different make-up." He stabbed his fork into the sponge and chewed slowly.

"Oh, OK." She touched her cheek, wishing she was someone else.

"So what form was it you lost? Jason from complaints did one of the secretaries from the Temp Department just to see the flame forms, it was sick."

Elenor's ears pricked up. "Flame forms?"

"Yeah," Joffler's lip curled as though he'd realised he was talking to a simpleton. "The orders for the burning room, everyone knows about it."

"Really?" Elenor stroked his fingers. "Wow, you're so clever. Why don't you tell me more?"

Joffler regarded her for a moment, wondering whether to divulge any more information. Another hefty swig of Drone's Blood settled the matter. He leaned forward and spoke quietly. "Yeah, The Little Cabinet on the Temp floor, all the good stuff's in there."

"Really?" said Elenor, "even stuff about…The Great End?"

He tapped his nose with a finger. "Need to know basis, love," he slurred, "only those in a need-to-know position are in the know." He winked blearily and placed a hand over hers. "So, coming back to my place?"

"No!" screamed her brain, "get the form another way."

"Yes!" said her mouth.

His sleeping pod was smooth and white. "It's very conveniently situated," he slurred as he removed her top. Elenor sighed as a response, her skin alight. "I got it on the cheap too, the person here before hung himself at work or something," he continued as he removed her trousers. Elenor felt exposed, as though her flesh took over the whole room. He bent her over the bed before removing his own trousers and entered her smoothly, and it didn't feel paper thin. Elenor knew she shouldn't be doing this on a first date but his skin was hot against hers.

"Oh yeah, bitch," he groaned loudly, flipping her onto her front. Elenor yelped with surprise, relieved when he entered her again. "Oh yeah you like that don't you," he yelled as he removed himself and lay down, pulling her on top. The meal sat on Elenor's digestive system worryingly. "Well?" he said, "you're not making enough noise."

"Oh right," said Elenor, "Um, ooh yes, that's quite pleasant."

"Yeah, you coming?" he roared as he pushed her onto her back and pulled her legs over her head. "You coming?"

"Yes!" Elenor yelled, wishing he would shut up. The initial sensations of pleasure subsided as he yanked her into several more positions. His face turned a deep grey as he finally shuddered and he fell on top of her, breathing deeply. Elenor wasn't sure what to do and patted his shoulder.

"God, that was amazing, wasn't it," he sighed, falling onto his back. Elenor went to lean against him. "Oh, I uh, I'm really tired."

"Oh right," Elenor rose abruptly, wanting nothing more than to crawl into a dark space and assess her faults. As she pulled her clothes on she noticed the sparkle from the key, thrown carelessly onto a pile of forms. He had already turned to his side, his sleep a pretence as no-one could reach the netherworlds that quickly. She scuttled out the room and rounded the corner, waiting and waiting for any hint of noise. After the first hour she allowed herself to breathe normally again and tiptoed closer to the door to listen for signs of life. The snoring issuing underneath was gentle and rhythmic, the snores of genuine slumber.

Elenor put the key to the lock when Joffler snuffled. Her hands snapped behind her back, ready to look innocent if he opened the door. More snores followed however, and she slid the key back in, her sweaty fingers almost sliding from the metal. She cringed at the clank of the mechanism and the creak of the opening hinge, staring as the words floated towards Joffler's sleeping figure and nudged him gently. Joffler raised a delicate hand and shooed them away, turning from the wall to face Elenor. His lids flickered – and then the snoring began again.

Elenor slid his bedside drawers open. The blemish-free surfaces belied a childish habit of stuffing anything and everything into the same place.

Amongst tax returns she found a crayon drawing of two stick figures, one small and one larger than the house beside them. "Me and my daddy," it said. 'Son of a bitch,' thought Elenor, 'he's married?' A glance at the bottom of the drawing changed things: "by Joffler, aged three." She looked up at the sleeping face and felt a gloopy mix of emotions before continuing her search. On the third drawer she found a bunch of forms that made a tingle travel from her fingertips upwards, 'Retirement Devision.' She searched the other files for ones bearing his signature and, locating a pen, did her closest approximation on the top one. She bit her lip to keep from laughing and snuck back out of the room.

Holly and Sam were waiting at the end of the corridor. "Well, did you distract him?" asked Holly wryly. Elenor held up the form and they danced dementedly. Sam looked up, frowned in confusion and looked down again.

"Right," Elenor pointed down the warren of hallways, "it was down the stairs and turn left."

"No, right," said Holly, pulling Sam in the other direction.

"It was definitely left," Elenor tugged at Sam's other hand.

"Aah!" shrieked Sam. "Both of you stop it! I'm not a bag of meat." He paused, catching his breath. "It's this way," he pointed ahead and round a corner. "Let's just get to Norman and get this over with." They followed him as he calmly retraced their steps to the old man's office and pushed open the heavy door. The crashing waves soothed them and they could almost smell the sand and salty water. Norman looked up at them with liquid eyes.

"Here," Elenor handed over the form.

He grabbed it with a shaking hand and knobbly fingers, raising it above his head triumphantly. "All this time," he said quietly. "All this time!" His legs found new flexibility as he scurried to the fax machine. "No more office! No more phone calls to secretaries!"

"That's wonderful Norman," said Elenor, "But, uh, what about us?"

Norman paused. "Ah, I think there might be a problem."

"A problem?" whimpered Sam.

Norman took a deep breath. "I may have…exaggerated my closeness to The Filers. But," he continued, balking at the horror on their faces, "You don't understand how long I've been kept down here! Always excuse after excuse: 'yes, don't worry Norman we'll get you the form after you do my work for me. We'll help you after you wax my bum hairs Norman. No longer!" He pressed a button on the intercom. When asked for the code he read smugly, "ZXDQ88," and a door of bright light appeared at the far end of the room. No-one spoke as he stepped like a ghost towards it and shadows lurked in the corner of the room. Light poured into the room as Norman stepped through. His silhouette faded and the door disappeared, leaving them with the gently crashing waves.

"Oh," said Sam.

"What a cunt," said Holly.

They watched the wall for several minutes but it refused to do anything exciting. Holly slumped to the ground. "Well, that's it then. We can't do anything else." Sam put his head in his hands and began to sob.

Elenor cleared her throat. "Actually, um, there is something we can try."

The lift's weeping took on a new urgency as it lowered into the basement, and the three joined clammy hands as they stared at the numbers counting down to zero. They reached the ground with a thud and the doors shuddered open onto a long corridor stretching out into darkness. To the right a stone staircase lined with flaming torches led even further down into the depths of the building. The sign above read in spiked letters "At your peril." The three exchanged looks until Holly took the first step forward. A howl writhed up towards them and they joined hands once more, stepping onto the staircase as one. Elenor yelped when one of the torches burst up to the ceiling in a rush of fury, and Holly squeaked with relief when they arrived at a large wooden door at the bottom. Above it, written in flames, were the words "This way to Temp HQ."

Just beyond the door was a neat office space where people leaned eagerly over their computers. Two women on the front desk chatted into mirror phones. One was plump with breasts that rolled over the desk, dangling almost to the floor, and eyelashes that brushed against the ceiling. The other was all sharp angles and grotesquely stretched limbs, her elbows jutting almost to the walls. Her nails were talons that scratched the computer screen as she typed. Elenor prayed for the former to notice them first but, of course, she didn't. "Leads?" the plump lady said into the mirror phone. "Well, give them leads if that's what they want. You can't have run out! Well how do they know if they're decent leads or not? No, we don't keep anything like that on this floor…"

"Yes," shrieked the woman, her catlike pupils shrinking.

"Uh, we need…some temp work?"

"Doing what?" Elenor wanted to cover her eyes against the shrillness.

"Whatever," Holly shrugged.

"Oh, data entry or something," said Sam.

"Just a moment," she held up a picture, glancing from it to them in quick succession. Elenor saw with a crash what was on it, a surveillance shot of them before the wigs. She clutched the sleeves of the other two, ready to drag them away if needs be. "Very well," the woman threw her head back and cackled at length. The trio waited. Holly sighed wearily and the other woman shot them an apologetic glance. Eventually the skeletal woman faced them once more. "Before you do anything you must face one of four dangers. You must choose: Fire, ice, water or earth."

Sam leaned over her desk and smiled charmingly. "I'm sure we can discuss…"

"Fire, ice, water or earth."

"Oh, for God's sake," said Holly, "ice." The other two gawped in disbelief but she just shrugged. "Well, I hate the earth and I can't swim – and who would choose fire?"

The wall beside them shuddered until a door appeared. They zipped up regulation hooded coats handed to them by the women until only their eyes were visible and stepped out into the frozen tundra. The last thing they saw from the Temp office was a phone ringing and the skeletal woman shrieking, "They've done what in the Call Centre?"

The wind and snow bit and scratched them like a savage drunk woman and Elenor wanted to turn back, but the door had disappeared. Sam gestured to something in the distance; through the blizzard they saw a glorious ice palace. As they neared the gates Holly grabbed Elenor's shoulder. "What was that?" Elenor saw it too; a low, mournful howl coming from the cliffs in the distance.

They jogged clumsily on until they arrived at the ornately sculpted gates of the palace. Turrets pointed into the sky and glowing icy windows promised shelter. As they crossed the threshold of the grounds two circular figures as large as the courtyard gates rolled from the side of the palace and clunked together, barring the way. They glared down, an intricate suit of arms glinting on their icy fronts. The trio unzipped their hoods. "Who goes there?" said the guard on the left.

"We are travellers looking for warmth," said Sam.

"We have signs up," said the guard on the right, "we will not open our doors to you sales people. We rang the number – we said we didn't want them to come anymore."

Sam looked at Elenor, lost. Holly pulled her lighter from her pocket. Elenor stepped forwards quickly. "We have been sent on request of the King to assist them in this trying time." She ignored the looks from the other two. The guards regarded her with renewed interest.

"The Queen has been dressing as a man again? Good Lord, there'll be another cover up. Very well noble knights," the pair rolled aside and the gates slid open, "may good fortune follow your quest."

Their footsteps ricocheted off expansive walls as they stepped through the keep to the courtyard. Icicles hung from the ceilings and pointed up from the floor. Sculptures stood about the grounds; men and women, bears, great stags and does, all watching them with unseeing eyes. Elenor shivered. "This is weird," muttered Holly.

"That it is," said Elenor. "Wait, did you see that?"

"See what?" said Sam, preparing to snap off an icicle and wield it.

"That stag's eyes moved. Oh my God, that bear just put its paw down!" They huddled together, all attempts at bravery melting away. The statues shuffled towards them; the stags lowered their antlers and the men pointed axes and broadswords chipped from ice, a group of maidens joined hands and skipped in circles to the tune of a lute, hair glittering about their shoulders.

"What is the meaning of this?" A masked knight pressed his sword into Sam's chest.

"Calm yourself, Sir Jeffrey," said a gracious voice decorated with snowflakes. "They have merely come to our aid."

"Ma'am," Sir Jeffrey bowed deeply and the other subjects followed suit. Elenor, Sam and Holly did the same, their eyes flicking upwards to catch a glimpse of the elegant, robed figure as she glided towards them. Her features were as delicate as the carving on her dress and her hair was arranged in an elaborate bun.

"Do not blame him," she addressed them, "Sir Jeffrey has risked melting and worse to defend me and is extremely loyal. I believe you are the ones the prophecy spoke of?"

Elenor wanted to declare herself free of responsibility and live in a cave. Sam stepped forwards. "Prophecy? What prophecy?"

"I'm not slaying any dragons, and I'm not rescuing any princesses," said Holly.

"Dragons? Princesses?" The queen furrowed her pretty brow. "We've no time for such frivolity. The era of darkness is upon us. It has been written that ones such as yourselves shall right the Great Wrong."

"Well," Holly looked exhausted, "what Great Wrong are we talking about exactly?"

The sculptures lowered their heads as though the Great Wrong weighed heavy on their shoulders. The queen wept tiny frozen tear jewels, though her face remained stoical. "A great and noble knight, Sir Kismet, journeyed far to search for the powder of the royal robes. All in the kingdom were to benefit from the soft suds of cleanliness, but alas the powder retrieved was the one known as Biological, instead of Non-Biological. Henceforth the time of The Great Rash was upon us. Mothers and babies, great and noble knights, princes and merchants alike were afflicted. T'was a dark time and the land has had but a short time to recover. Wash Night is upon us once more and the scholars chanced upon a passage in the Book of Prophecies which spoke of three gallant heroes to deliver us from the cloud over our land, and retrieve the vial of Non-Biological powder." An eerie hush followed.

"You get rashes?" said Holly.

"We'll do it," said Elenor.

"Yes, we'll do it," said Sam. A cheer echoed through the palace.

"Where shall – er, where must we travel?" said Elenor.

The queen pointed her hand into the horizon, "past the snowbound mountains, beyond the ice-capped peaks and beside the frozen lake. You must use our trusty steeds and sturdiest sled." The stable-hands pushed the sled into the courtyard and led several disgruntled people in snow suits from the stables towards it. Elenor watched the spectacle with the growing sensation of things again being amiss. The stable-hands fixed long snow-shoes to the people's feet and attached them in two rows to the reins. They didn't put up a fight, merely waiting for instruction.

"Sam?" said Elenor.

"I know," he replied, exasperated, "I see it."

Holly shook her head and stomped towards it. "Well," she said, "we don't have time to worry about it now. Come on."

"Wait," called the queen, "we must warn you before you leave."

"I'd rather you didn't," said Holly.

"No," said Sam, "I'm sure it's nothing we can't handle."

The sculptures surrounded them, faces filled with terror. "Something awaits you out there. Something terrible," said the queen. Elenor noticed for the first time the sparkling snowflakes lining the hem and twinkling from her eyelashes. "His name is Mr Charles." Eyes lowered at the mention of his name. "He was once in Middle Management and got wonderful results from his team. They were the best, pulling in sales and organising shipments the world over. But soon he became so great he could not be contained. Eventually he was cast out here, into the wilderness where he could do no more damage, and there he stays, a warped, twisted being."

A knight looked up urgently, "They say he can freeze your tears just by scratching his knee."

A maiden rushed forwards, "They say he can make a child cry just by blinking."

A knick knack merchant shivered, "They say he can boil a kettle just by pressing the switch."

"So you see," said the queen, urgency in her face, "you must take care."

Before Holly could chuck the reins and get them going, Elenor had to know, "and these people? Who are they?"

"We are the ones who failed the task," they said in monotonous unison. Elenor's blood dropped several degrees and she hopped between Sam and Holly on the sled. They zipped their coats back up.

"Go, go!" Holly screamed. Elenor saw the other girl's hands shaking before they were catapulted forwards at an impossible speed. Elenor gripped the fur-lined sled front and the ice gates rolled open once more, pouring the blizzard onto their faces. The trio gasped against the sudden cold, the coats no match against the ceaseless howls and whistles of the empty expanse.

"There," Sam pointed towards a vague shape in the distance, an outline of a tall cliff against the rushing, swirling snow. All conversation ceased and preservation of their body temperature became the only goal as they hurled forwards. There was another low howl.

The cliffs gradually morphed into a solid structure. The sled glided across the smooth whiteness and the puller's arms pumped back and forth in unison with their skating feet. Elenor kept her focus on the distance. They arrived at the cliffs and a howl raged up to the sky. Holly gripped the reins and her face was grimly determined. "We can outrun it," said Sam, reassuring himself as much as the other two. Holly chucked the reins again and the pullers thrust forwards at almost sonic speed. Elenor and Sam jerked backwards. Elenor's hood fell and the snow bit her nose and cheeks viscously.

"We're going to make it," she whispered. The sled passed the dark caves and the frozen lake was in view. A dark figure shot across the snow from behind the cave, reaching them before they knew what was happening. "Oh God its Mr Charles!" Elenor shrieked. Her brain rattled as his body slammed into the side of them. Elenor was thrown into the snow, too breathless to cry out. It took a moment before her thoughts returned and she sat up to look for the others. Mr Charles was chomping on one of the pullers, dark blood pooling over the white surface. His misshapen body and once human face was hunched over the broken figure, a severed leg in his mouth and various parts strewn around him. His eyes glinted in the dark, sensing something, and rested on Elenor.

Elenor blacked away but this seemed to pique his interest. Eyes fixed, he lowered himself into a hunting posture. Elenor felt an immediate urge to use the toilet and clamped her muscles tightly. Mr Charles' haunches wriggled from side to side as he prepared to launch himself when a shadow rose above him, thumping him on the head. It was Holly, her face full of rage, with a ski boot in her hand. The thump did nothing but enrage him and, bellowing, he turned and pinned her to the ground. His malformed head leaned closer to hers until a line of drool touched her chin.

"Sir!" Sam yelled, "Please can you give me some pointers on my performance?" Mr Charles paused, regarding Sam with confusion. "I – I'm new to the company and I heard you were the best. So, uh, can you give me some feedback please?" Mr Charles rose on his hind legs to full height, a head higher than Sam, who was lost in his shadow. Drool still dangled from Charles' lip.

"Help?" he said, his letters ragged. Sam nodded and stepped closer. "I – don't know how." Mr Charles fell back down on all fours.

"Go on," Sam put his hand on the other's shoulder. Mr Charles' lips drew apart in what must have been a grotesque grin, his teeth grimy with meat. It took Elenor a few seconds to realise it wasn't a friendly grin, but by then Mr Charles had turned his head onto Sam's arm and shook it like an angry wolf. Sam's wail loosened the snow at the top of the cliffs and Elenor grabbed an icicle. Holly gripped his head with both arms and Mr Charles released Sam and turned to snap at her. It was all Elenor needed and she lurched forwards, sinking the icicle into the soft tissue of his eyeball. The girls retched as stagnant water spurted outwards and Mr Charles roared loudly enough to dislodge the snow above them completely.

"On the sled!" yelled Holly, and they grabbed a limp Sam and propped him up between them. The surviving pullers tore away, dragging their dead comrades beside them. Elenor risked a glance back and wished she hadn't; Mr Charles flailed blindly and furiously behind.

Elenor spied a glittering surface, "the river." Elenor closed her eyes tightly. They were still tight shut when the wind no longer bit her face and the force from the pulling runners ceased. She risked opening an eye, then opened the other in astonishment.

***

May called after Alan but there was silence. She peered down the black hole, her heart thumping visibly, and after a few moments Alan's voice travelled weakly upwards. "May, come down, you have to come down."

"What? Oh, Christ." She leaned forwards, oozing towards the cavern like a grub tunnelling into a cow. Holding her breath she tipped forwards, the blood sliding from her feet to her head. When she finally plummeted she wailed loudly, trying to slow her fall by gripping onto the sides, landing on something solid and angular.

"Ow!"

"Well, you should have moved out the way." May stood up and dusted herself off. Huge machines lined the walls of tunnels that veered in all directions like the inside of an anthill. Operating them were men and women with passive expressions and jerky, robotic movements. All wore overalls and had similar pudgy faces and rounded fingers. "Drones," May folded her arms across herself, as though frightened one of them would grope her. They exchanged looks, both expecting the other to make the first move.

"Well...I suppose we ought to go to their headquarters and find out how to get out of here."

"I agree," said May, and they set off through the tunnel.

They stood in a canteen where several drones sat on long benches. Others wandered in and out, presumably coming to the end of a shift or just beginning one. A poster of The Head Boss covered one wall, his charcoal grey face benevolently smiling down at his subjects. It was a face you could trust and, indeed, some of the drones had drawn love-hearts on the picture. Alan squinted. "Are those lip stains?" They spotted a drone that looked particularly helpful. Those around him ate quietly, sang songs about machines or the Great One while others replaced parts with screwdrivers. Alan explained their predicament and he turned to them with unblinking eyes.

"You're from up top?"

Alan began to get a bad feeling. "Yes."

"Oh," the drone rose to his feet shakily, "Great One! You have come to save us!"

"Oh, for the love of…" Alan kept his smiled fixed as a crowd gathered around them, some literally dropping their food trays and sliding through unpleasant looking gruel. More than a couple had nosebleeds from slipping and hitting the floor.

"Erm," Alan began, "I think there's been some sort of mistake…"

"What he means is, he's more than happy to help you to overthrow the Big Boss!" boomed May. The drones blinked. Alan put his head in his hands.

"Overthrow the…?" They shared looks of confusion.

"Oh, no I meant lead you to live over ground. Why should they get all the sun?"

The drone's shock mutated into horror. "Live over ground?" they muttered, shaking their heads. May conceded defeat.

"Alright, what exactly do you want?"

One drone went to speak but lost confidence. The others nudged him, assuring him that nobody would tell. "Well, we'd quite like to get some sort of pay. And maybe some sort of group that makes sure you get looked after you know, like a…a…"

"A union," said Alan. The drones agreed and closed their eyes as if imagining the most beautiful kingdom in the sky. "You want a union. You don't even get paid?" He was horrified.

"Shush, we're not complaining!" The drones checked about them in terror, "we like the way things are run, we really do. It's just Ted," one of the drones wailed softly, evidently Ted was tired of being an example, "he went over ground, like, just to see if the plants grew the other way like we'd heard – they don't – and he heard someone talk about…" again he paused, looking as though he were about to say something offensive, "a day off." Again the drones clasped the idea to their chests, smiling at a private dream.

"Well," May shrugged, "that seems possible. We will help you!" Her words were greeted by a wave of cheers. Her cheeks were flushed as though she had drunk a glass of warm mulled wine.

"Um, excuse me," Alan pulled her by the arm to a corner. "This has to be handled very carefully, the Big Boss made them to be value for money.

If you go charging off demanding a union he'll just destroy them and make more. We need to think about a proper strategy."

May searched Alan's face for an answer. When none came she gave a small shrug. "Well, I suppose they'll be too dead to be cross with us." Alan stepped back, unable to process what he'd heard. "Oh, don't look like that," May grumpily folded her arms, "fine, we'll contact the Big Boss and negotiate rationally. As if that could ever happen."

Alan turned to the drones. "How do you communicate with the outside world if anything goes wrong with the machines? No, no!" he said when they gasped in terror, "nothing's wrong with the machines, but we need to speak to someone above."

A drone disappeared, returning with a small, flute like object. "This goes to the Drone Liaison Officer."

Alan took the bubble messenger and retreated to a corner with May. "It's something of a longshot. We've got nothing to negotiate with. When they get this message they'll be down here straight away though I'm sure, and as long as we seem confident we'll get things sorted."

May shook her head. "You don't get it, do you? As long as it looks like we're doing our best, they can't get cross if we don't manage it. Either way we're fine."

Alan wanted to punch her beautiful face. He sat cross legged on one of the long tables and raised the Messenger to his lips. He blew gently and a bubble formed at the end, enlarging and gorging and ultimately breaking away from the flute, drifting gently in the air before Alan. "Uh," Alan panicked, "this is the drones. Well, I'm not a drone, but I speak on behalf of them." From the corner of his eye he saw May roll her eyes. "Listen, we need to have a chat about conditions. This isn't the way to run things and when you're ready to discuss it, we'll be here. Over." The bubble drifted over their heads, the drone's eyes wide as it glided up to the ceiling and passed through it.

"Good luck," whispered a drone, and Alan silently wished the same.

"Marvellous!" An old drone clapped his hands, bringing everyone sharply back to the room. "Now you can celebrate with us."

May was jubilant. "Great, what do you do for fun around here?"

"We play a game...while we work." The drones charged out of the canteen emitting cries of "Ooh, let's do fastest button presser," or "Switch Machines." Alan caught May's eye as they followed, unable to restrain a smug grin.

"Shut your face," she growled as she found a position at one of the monoliths.

Time stretched onwards. With the lack of windows it could have been a day and a night or half an hour, but eventually the bell clanged throughout the tunnels. Alan and May were led to a series of chambers lined with plain bunk beds, the same regimented white sheets tucked in like the quarters of an army platoon. "You can sleep here," one drone pointed to a chamber with six beds, three unclaimed by workers, "Jim, Ted and Mick exploded last week." Alan thanked him, stretching out on the rock hard mattress. He felt the outer edges of his thoughts grow woolly when he was woken by a voice prodding his head.

"Ghost story!" one drone sat up excitedly.

"Yes, ghost story!" the others chorused. Alan turned to face the wall, trying to block them out. May above him sighed with frustration.

"Right," the first drone sat upright, cross legged, eyes gleaming. "Once there was a drone who worked the late shift on the Ginks Flacellator and he ignored the warning signs that it needed to be emptied. The top button went amber, then red, and when he tried to release the steam at the top, it didn't work. The machine had broken and no one could fix it." He sat back, waiting with pride for the reaction.

"Oh my God!"

"Aaah, that's it we're not telling anymore." They checked about them for imaginary machines that could stop working at any moment. Alan sat up.

"Is work all you think about? OK, listen to this; I'm going to tell a real ghost story." He took a deep breath and surveyed the expectant round faces. "A drone was working the late shift alone. He thought he heard a noise but put it down to tiredness. He carried on, but felt someone watching him. He could see breathing creeping from the corner, but nobody was there." Alan paused for effect, pleased to see the drones waiting in anticipation. "He turned once again to the machine but this time a footstep caught his eye. Again, nobody was there. He was getting worried but carried on, and the footsteps came closer and closer. Eventually he felt a cold hand on his shoulder and yelled out. When the other drones came to assist him, all they saw was his dead body – mouth contorted in a scream." Alan was very pleased with himself. He had never had such a rapt audience and, for a few seconds afterwards, there was a satisfying silence.

"What about the machine?"

"Yes," said another drone, "did they get to it in time to release the gas?"

Alan sighed. "Look, it doesn't matter about the gas. The drone had been murdered by a ghost. Alright!" he yelled when he saw more questions forming on their lips, "yes, he managed to release the gas just before he was murdered."

"Oh, well," the drones snuggled into their beds, "everything was fine then." Within seconds they were asleep, but Alan was left staring up at the top bunk. A giggle from May's bed floated down. He considered kicking the lump above but decided against it.

Alan rose the next morning momentarily unable to figure out where he was. The other beds were empty and he hopped up, expecting May to be there. She wasn't. Alan had a bad feeling no matter how much he told himself he was just confused. Shoelaces untied, he hurried to the canteen where the drones surrounded May, their misguided messiah at the centre. Alan's bad feeling was at once justified and he clambered onto a table to get a better view. "Oh Alan!" May looked at once delighted and embarrassed, like a child caught drawing a mean picture.

"What are you doing?"

"Well," May regained her defiant composure, "the drones weren't convinced your way would work, so I told them what I thought best and they agree with me."

"What's best?" Alan's fear deepened.

"They're going on strike."

Alan stepped backwards. She couldn't be serious. He looked at the drones gathered around her and knew at once that they trusted her implicitly. "But...the Big Boss, he'll..."

"He'll be unable to keep things going if everyone stops working at once."

"May, I need to have a word with you."

"No," May snapped, "this starts now and that means not listening to you talking us out of it. I know you'd rather everyone sat around twiddling their thumbs but this is a time for action."

Alan's face burned. He wanted to tell the drones that their best interest was not in her heart, he wanted to tell them that the Big Boss would destroy them all in an instant but, when he looked at their hopeful faces he knew they wouldn't listen. "I just really hope you understand what you're doing," he said through gritted teeth.

"The first person is trying to hold us back," roared May. "Everyone remember what I said!" The drones linked arms and chanted a droning monotone about nothing stopping them and having strength from each other. Alan glared at May, who shrugged and turned back to her adoring minions. "Right, it's time to let everyone know our position. How do you propose we do this?" Alan folded his arms and waited.

"Well, we could carry on standing here, chanting," one drone said nervously. The others looked around at each other, nodding half-heartedly.

"Yes, or," May clasped her hands together "we could go over ground and chant at everyone up there." This suggestion was met with enthusiastic approval.

"Have you ever actually been up there?" said Alan.

"They don't need to worry, they're with me."

"Wait," said one of the drones, "we need to decide who will go and who will work on the machines."

"Now, we discussed this," May said through gritted teeth, "we need to leave the machines, or nobody will notice we've gone." Her suggestion was met with fearful faces. "Look," May was losing patience, "what's the point of stopping work to demand rights if things are carrying on as normal?"

"Oh, yes...Ok..." They followed her obediently into the tunnels, chanting once again.

"Wait!" Alan loped after them, "let's just wait today for the message to get through! Stop!" His words faded into the floor uselessly. He paused, willing himself to think of something, when one of the machines caught his eye. He groaned and hurried after the disappearing mob.

May threw open the outside door. The drones lined up behind her, blinking at the bright sky with eagerness on their rounded faces. "We have to get noticed," May boomed, "the Big Boss needs to be scared, he needs to know we mean it." She nodded at the cheer that followed. "We have to hit him where it hurts and that means no one," she pointed in the air to show how much she meant it, "no one goes to the machines no matter what happens." Again she basked in the applause, feeling her body expand to take over the world.

May led the drones through the trees but nobody was around to hear their chants. In fact, Alan tuned in carefully, what were their chants? "We want decent pay, rubbish pay no way!"

"Stop!" Alan called. The drones did unthinkingly as they were told. May turned to him, eyes flashing violence. "The gas machine, whatever it's called, it's started leaking. There's smoke everywhere, it's going to explode!" The drones panicked, arms flailing.

"No!" yelled May, "this is what we want. The Big Boss is sure to respond now. This is good," she soothed, but the drones didn't look too sure. "We need to go somewhere more public, our voices must be heard." She ordered them to continue, winding a path through the forest while Alan followed.

"Well, I don't see this lasting," muttered a voice behind them.

"People just do whatever they want these days, no respect," said another. Alan turned sharply but saw only a pair of man-sized flowers. They stood innocently, but when Alan continued his way muffled laughter prodded him in the back.

On and on they wandered until the trees thinned onto a small, pretty town square devoid of activity save for an otter water feature vomiting and ingesting crystal liquid in a perpetual cycle. Public houses and bistros nestled between the buildings, some fashioned as medieval establishments and others geometric with modernity, their shining surfaces reflected against the street cobbles. Rows of houses slanted crazily and a caw above caught their attention; the birds were flying backwards. Alan noticed movement by his feet and picked up a worm; it was mumbling predictions on the stock exchange.

"What the Hell is this place?" he muttered.

"This," said the worm crossly, "is Commuterville. You will experience no finer beverage establishments or housing prices anywhere." Alan placed him back on the ground where he promptly burrowed to safety.

"Perfect," May rubbed her hands gleefully, "we'll set up camp somewhere that'll annoy the shit out of them."

They tramped over the cobbled stones until she reached a spot she deemed suitable – the train tracks leading through a thin forest path from Head Office to the town entrance.

"Perfect!" she shrieked, the odd look in her eye edging close to derangement. The drones looked as though they were on their first holiday. Alan watched helplessly as the group sat, and sat, and sat on the path. Their chanting and singing travelled only to the ears of indifferent public house owners, street sweepers and proprietors of suit emporiums. The sky darkened.

"Look, I can see something!" squealed a drone.

"Ok everyone, huddle together and sing your loudest," said May.

The group was a single entity ready to face down its foe. Their song flew up to the sky as the first commuters, the cyclists, arrived. Men and women with elongated limbs sat inside giant clear orbs, feet pedalling the sphere towards the waiting protestors. "Good Lord!" cried one as his bubble was thrown violently off course, "What the devil are you thinking?" Another spun towards the water feature, her bowler hat swirling around the perimeter of the ball and her feet pedalling like a toddler.

In the distance, through the trees, the train chuffed its way towards Commuterville. At first only a black dot on the horizon, it soon became a moving vehicle. Closer and closer it roared until they saw each moving part was formed from dozens and dozens of commuters. Some had long and winding limbs, some looked like slugs, some writhed like snakes and others had legs like springs. Men and women in black and white suits stood in two straight lines, arms bent sideways making a rowing motion. Beneath them others acted as wheels. A single figure stood on the foremost commuter's shoulders, shrieking violently when he saw the obstruction. Alan edged further to safety. "Um, May?" He was ignored. "May!" Still the group sat on the tracks. Closer and closer the train came and larger and larger was the whistle man's shriek. Alan threw himself as far as he could and landed beneath the otter. Still the group sang as the train consumed them.

"Now look here," said a disgruntled commuter, "that was damned dangerous. Are you trying to get us all fired?"

Alan looked up. The commuters lay in a pile beside the cross-legged drones, all shaking heads and tut-tutting. "That's right," said another from the bottom of the pile, "I've only just been promoted. Dashed if I'm going to let some flipperty-jippet and her friends get in the way of things."

"Flipperty-jippet?" May stood up. "We are holding this town hostage until our demands are met."

They snorted with laughter until she produced a wrench from her back pocket. "Good Lord," they said in unison.

"That's it," May herded them towards one of the buildings, "into the Post Office, quickly and no one will get hurt. Drones, tie them up once we're in there." The drones obeyed, but Alan noticed they were more hesitant than before. His eyes flicked towards the path leading back into the forest, if he could just get to…

"You too," May's voice was sharp and her stare alone could have killed him. Alan gritted his teeth and followed the commuters inside. The drones grabbed a pile of CVs and tore and twisted them into ropes, tying their captive's hands behind their backs. A low murmur from the restraints babbled beneath the hostage's protests, "I work well alone but also enjoy being part of a team," or, "I have had vast experience with Photoshop as part of my course." The drones sat Alan in a chair and pulled his hands behind him. He threw May his best 'I will get you back,' face. The drone tying his wrists together, however, only secured them in a loose knot. Alan caught his eye before May ordered her followers back outside, hoping he could sense his gratitude. The group trouped back out to the quaint street and Alan watched them continue singing and chanting to an empty courtyard through the glass door.

"OK," said Alan, "everyone listen to me. They mustn't know anything's wrong so still act frightened." On cue a horrendous wailing and begging for help filled the room. "Very good but do it quieter," snapped Alan. "That's better. Right, I'm going to untie each of you, but we need to be brave and stay where we are until we can make a run for it." All of them wept and one man died outright, his body slumping unhelpfully down in the chair. Keeping his gaze firmly on May, Alan worked at the knot at his wrists. He froze whenever May glanced in but eventually the rope dropped onto the floor whilst assuring its leadership qualities wouldn't hinder its ability to follow instructions.

Alan untied his ankles and snuck towards the nearest commuter, whose rope dropped to the ground as it recited its grades. They tried to keep the scurry of activity low key but a good few were still bound as May's glances became more frequent. "Stop," whispered Alan, "she knows something's not right." They froze – the same look of barely repressed fear matched in every face.

A woman cried out, "the Vice President of the Company! If he sees me here like this he'll never listen to my plans for a committee overhaul." She, too, died where she sat.

"Everyone untie the last few calmly, we'll get out of this," Alan whispered. The Vice President, so Alan presumed him to be, was sauntering towards May and her group in an expensive suit and pair of sunglasses. "What a wanker," Alan whispered, checking the commuters hadn't heard. "Right, he's distracted by May, while they're talking we sneak past them and make a run for it through the trees to the nearest payphone."

"But what about all my stuff? I've just bought a new TV." A murmur of agreement rippled through the group.

"You'll be back, we just need to run for help and…and…everything will be fine." He tiptoed to the door, keeping out of sight, trying to catch the words flying between them. It was hazy but he saw "Big Boss," "Disappointed," and "arrangement."

"Goddammit," he muttered, "the Boss can't be giving her a job, surely." The VP's hand reached into his back pocket as though he were trying to find something. The Commuters watched Alan. He knew he had to do something, but what? He gestured to them to be ready, but just as he went to open the door something terrible happened.

The attractive cobbled town centre of Commuterville became the scene of bloody horror and scattered limbs. The VP opened his jacket and released a blinding thunder clap, destroying almost half the drones. The rest piled together in panic while May stood white-faced in the middle. Alan couldn't catch what he said to them but it had the required effect, and the drones wept over the dead with great howls that stained the sky.

Alan clenched his fists. "Get him!" he roared as he charged out of the building, the electricity of his heroic moment marred when he realised the Commuters were still standing in the post office. He narrowly avoided a second clap of thunder and tore the man's jacket from him. May stared uselessly, mouth open in shock. "Get him, for Christ's sake!" Alan tried again, and this time the others launched into action, bundling him into a chair in the Post Office and securing his wrists and ankles.

"Oh God," they wept and wrung their hands, "I'll never lead that project now."

"I'll never get that promotion."

"Look," Alan snapped, "you can say May and I forced you into it."

"They'd never believe that," said one woman, "look how many there are of us compared to you."

Alan was quite sure Head Office would believe any level of their idiocy. "Say we forced you at gunpoint," he said.

"Oh, yes!" they murmured to each other excitedly, "we'll say you beat us to a pulp."

"Yes, that'd be fine."

"And that you sodomized us."

"Erm," Alan searched for a suitable answer, "if…if it helps, I suppose."

"Oh, brilliant!" some of them clapped their hands while others hugged. Alan looked over at May who looked as perplexed as he. The drones commiserated outside. "So," asked a commuter, "what now?"

"Now," said May, pushing in front of Alan, "we let everyone know we've got a hostage."

The word made them look at the VP afresh. "Yes," they muttered, "a hostage."

"Here," said a young man, his hair coiffured to a meter above his head, "I'm in the communications department and I've got a mirror." He reached into a tiny bag strapped to his chest.

"That's nice," said Alan.

The commuters tittered amongst themselves in disbelief. "No, look, we get him to talk into it and it broadcasts over all the screens in Head Office."

"Of course, great," May ushered him before the struggling VP. "OK, listen you – say these things and we'll let you go."

"Never!" he shrieked.

"You don't have many options," she snapped.

"Yeah," said the coiffured man needlessly.

The VP glowered. "You'll never get away with this."

"No, probably not," said Alan, "but let's just do this OK?"

The VP looked into the mirror bleakly. When the glass glowed to announce recording, he spoke evenly. "Please, someone help. I'm being held captive…"

"And so are we," a woman's neck snaked into shot, "the commuters, we are too."

"We're in Commuterville. They want rights for Drones or something. For the love of God they're mad!" May switched the mirror off and the VP wailed and pulled at the rope, which insisted it was the best person to lead a team under pressure due to the week it had spent at God camp when one of the children had a breakdown and threatened the others with a hot sausage. Eventually, tired and drained, he slumped forward, a long line of drool and snot hanging to his knee.

"May and I need to discuss our plan of action," said Alan, "We can trust you with him, right?" The commuters assented, an odd expression on their faces. Alan sat on a bench beside the splurging water feature away from the still weeping drones. "We can't win here, we're going to die. The drones have to get back to work before anything else happens. If things are going to change for them they need us to think sensibly."

"They won't help them now," said May coolly, "they'll wipe them out and replace them with new ones."

Alan moaned helplessly, his hands tugging at hair which was wilder than ever. "Why do these things happen when you're around?"

May shrugged. "I dunno. Always has." Alan wished he could run naked through the woods until he was taken somewhere and looked after. "Look," May put her hand gently on his shoulder, "everything will be fine." Alan sighed but had no choice other than to follow her back in.

"What are you doing?" he cried.

The commuters were crowded around the helpless VP, their arms a mass of tentacles and twitching fingers reaching for his most ticklish spots. A gag had been forced into his mouth, his face was a dark grey and his eyes bulged like a squeezed hamster. Before him stood the coiffured man, reading from a small book in monotonous text, the Health and Safety Manual for New Employees.

Alan found a seat at the back of the room. "We have to sort this out somehow," he mumbled, a good idea lurking unreachable at the tip of his thoughts.

"Well, I don't know how you'll feel about this, but I've had some thoughts," said a woman, her skinny snake-like body twisting in impossible angles.

"Really?" said Alan.

"Oh yes," she said, "it would really show some initiative if we moved all this furniture towards the back of the room, stripped the floor back to its original wood and repainted the walls with a simple cream. It's vintage, it's in. They'll love it."

"Oh, good idea," said another.

"Brilliant, I'll get onto my people in the next town, get them to bring supplies."

"No!" shrieked Alan, "we can't leave town, no-one can know about this locally. This can't go on."

"He's right," said May, and Alan felt a crazy warmth towards her. "Just use supplies around here. Well," she shrugged at a horrified Alan, "it can't hurt to let them have something to do."

"Oh fantastic," the snake-lady coiled herself in knots, "a challenge, only use what you can find!" Alan shared a look of exasperation with the VP.

A couple of hours passed with a flurry of furniture rearrangement and snipping stencils out of paper. Alan remained sullenly in the corner while May twirled giddily through the workers. Outside the drones still wept over their dead, but no-one inside seemed to notice. Alan scratched at his left shoulder and jolted when a burning tore through it; he'd almost forgotten The Problem. He pulled his sleeve down further.

The first Commuter to notice the newcomers in the square let out a screech that almost filled the room. Alan leapt to the glass door followed by May. The drones dashed into the bushes and the commuters cowered in a dark corner. An airship hovered overhead and figures in tailored suits parachuted to the ground, one holding a loudspeaker. All sported designer shades and serious scowls. Behind them the VP laughed. "It's over," he growled, "insurance are here."

"Oh God, no," the commuters flung themselves to the ground, "that's it, I'll never pay off that debt now."

"Oh, come on," May turned to them, furious, "are we just going to give up? The drones need someone to stand up for them." The commuters shrugged. "Alright, then, don't forget you're still our prisoners and aren't responsible for any of this." The commuters sprang up like jack-in-the boxes, clapping with excitement.

"Oh wonderful!" said the snake-woman, "now, I've been thinking cornflower blue for the walls, do we have any of that?"

The loudspeaker voice crushed all others. "Please, do not harm the Vice President. Let us know your demands and maybe we can arrange a deal." Alan and May stared at each other, panic-stricken. "Please," he continued, "think of little Sally, who'll end up without a mother."

Alan squinted at the weeping little girl in a bow-ridden dress next to the negotiator. "Oh, for the love of..."

Several commuters rushed to the mirror held by quiff boy. "We need some tins of Morning Sunshine yellow, some MDF and Jared you wanted newspapers for Paper Mache, didn't you?"

"Oh, and can we have some silver paper to make stencils," called a voice from the back.

"Right, we'll get right on that," said the negotiator. "Just, please, don't do anything stupid or Sally will be all alone in the world," at this the child's wailing grew larger, "and think of the forms you'll have to fill in." The Negotiator placed a comforting hand around Sally's shoulders.

"Who does that child actually belong to?" asked Alan. No-one replied.

By nightfall the commuters had worked themselves into deep sleep. Sheets of sparkling paper, drips of paint and half-sawed planks of wood littered the floor. The light sensitive CVs had ceased their endless chatter and the commuters snored on the floor like children having nap time. Glitter shone from their skin and suits, which were beginning to look a little untidy and sweaty. All the furniture had been moved to the back of the room including the VP, who sullenly gazed into space. Alan looked out at insurance who still watched patiently. Little Sally stood beside the Negotiator and both stared unnervingly at Alan, moonlight glinting in their eyes. Alan shuddered and turned back to the VP. "Do you...need a drink or anything?"

He seemed to consider a defiant reply before dropping his head. "Yes, please." Alan quietly fetched him a glass of water. The VP chugged from the glass held out to his lips. "Tomorrow they're going to measure me for new clothes," he said hollowly, "apparently I'm having a makeover."

Alan rubbed his brow with the tips of his fingers. "I-I'm sorry about this." Then he remembered the drones. "But why did you have to kill them? There's always another way surely."

The VP looked up at Alan with sad eyes. "I was just following orders. The Big Boss tells us what to do and we do it, or the same happens to us."

Alan sat cross-legged in front of him. "You don't get killed for not doing your job," he scoffed.

"Oh, don't we?" A wild look seeped into the VP's expression. "God help anyone who doesn't do what they're told." Alan thought of the townsfolk who disappeared and the drones that were destroyed. A worm of doubt wriggled through his thoughts. "You understand, don't you?"

Alan curled up in a chair in the corner, trying not to think of the man tied up in front of him and how much the ropes must be chafing at his wrists or how his bones must ache after sitting in the same position for hours. He ignored all of this and the constant tingle in his left hand which was now a throb encompassing his entire arm. He rubbed it, clawing his fingertips for a satisfying scratch. He checked under his top –hard edges framed his arm and a ridge was forming between it and his stomach. Shakily he lifted the material from his belly. The 16th of May was emblazoned onto his skin with what looked like black ink, but it didn't smudge when he rubbed at it. It was a part of him. Other dates in May were faintly visible in rows, but the 16th was encircled. Not again, he thought, not again. When he pulled his hand away strings of stomach skin connected to his fingertips and he swallowed a whimper. He had to leave it alone; if he left it alone and didn't think about it, The Problem would go away. He placed his hands on his knees and stared at the wall until the sun rose.

The shriek tore into his nightmares. "What are you doing to him?" he scrambled to his feet and dove into the crowd as they oohed and aahed in a circle. Standing miserably in the centre, with a rope tied to his wrist proclaiming efficiency on Adobe software, the VP wore a monstrosity of an outfit made from sugar paper and scraps of denim. His quiff was larger than any possessed by the Commuters and his lips blushed with delicate charcoal. His cheeks were smeared with Gris and the rest of his skin was perfect alabaster white.

"Oh wonderful, daaarling," purred a lady resembling a slug, "now let's see you do a runway walk."

"Brilliant," a toad woman croaked as she reached for a mirror in her purse, "I'll record it for my makeover website."

"Oh, rather!" squealed a man with cherub features, "I'll review it for the fashion section on my own website. I'm bound to get a job in the industry after this."

Their squawking laughter bumped and slapped against Alan, pushing him back into the corner of the room. He sank down with a haunted look;

was this what man was capable of, could they sink to lower depths? The crowd parted to form a rudimentary catwalk. The VP's shoulders were hunched and his eyes glistened with tears as he stumbled in his new heels. However, as the crows of encouragement surrounded him, his chest puffed out and he pursed his lips in a kiss to the air. His strides took on a purpose and when he reached the end of the runway he posed, hand on hip, face full of attitude. "Yeah," screeched the commuters, "you work it." The VP clicked his fingers to one side then the other, and repeated the process. On and on it went. There are too many to stop them, Alan reasoned, I couldn't stop it if I tried. He covered his eyes with his hands. On and on it went, back and forth.

When the commuters had tired of this game they trussed up the VP once more so they could remodel a selection of tables into 'shabby chic.' Alan crawled like a submissive dog to the captive's feet. He tried to say he was sorry, that it wasn't his fault, but nothing passed his lips. The VP looked sadly down at him. "I've got nothing to go back to," he said calmly, acceptance in his face. "It's out there now, everybody saw. It's funny," he gazed mistily at the commuters squawking over their newly sanded furniture, "but once the worst happens it never feels quite as bad as you expect it to."

"I'm sorry," Alan sobbed at last, tears coursing down his cheeks.

"No, it's alright," the VP said with a melancholy smile, "I would never have had the courage to do anything like that under my previous circumstances. It was so…freeing."

"I – really?"

"Yes," a new strength seeped into the VP, "I feel as if I've been hiding myself for a very long time and it's finally been forced out. Now I've nowhere left to hide, this is it, here I am."

Alan didn't know how to reply. The VP closed his eyes and hummed a tune softly. It took a moment for Alan to recognise it: "I am what I am." He felt himself relax, even if the itching on his arm didn't stop. Beyond the wood shaving and squeals of pleasure, beyond the self-realisations of the VP, a little girl watched and beside her stood the interrogator, their eyes unblinking.

"We need to take action," Alan stormed. "We need to send them a message out there, a message telling them we won't give up. And we need some proper demands. Where's that mirror? I just talk into it and they'll receive it on theirs, won't they?"

"Uh, well, yes," quiff boy said. The commuters stood dumbly.

"Right, give me that," Alan perched himself on top of the table. His eyes met May's poison-filled ones. "Hello? Are you getting this?"

"Receiving you loud and clear, you worthless scum!" Boomed the megaphone outside. "Ignore him," said the same voice slightly lighter, "he's old school marines, I'm the one you should listen to. Tell me your thoughts and we can help you."

Alan paused before turning back to the mirror. "Right, er, we need a safe passage out of here, and we will release the hostage." A roar of shock and outrage issued forth.

"Well done," said the megaphone, "you have made the right choice. You will see no pity from us – we'll blow you to kingdom come soon as you set foot out of those doors. You are safe with us, you have nothing to fear."

An anxious silence followed. "Well," said Alan, "which is it?"

"Don't worry, you can trust us. Maggots."

All eyes crawled over Alan. "OK," he said, "we release the hostage after we're at a safe distance, then you let us go." Several of the commuters joined hands. "We'll be alright," said Alan, "you can trust me." He saw some of the tension drain from them. May's hateful expression only deepened and Alan tried not to look.

When the CV rope was removed from the VP he twirled and pirouetted, screeching "faaaaabulous!" Alan gestured for everyone to line up at the door and he reached for the door handle, swallowing hard and stepping out into the square.

"You're doing the right thing," said the interrogator, "you worthless Commies."

"We're going off this way," said Alan, pointing to the woods on the right, "with the drones, and the VP will be given back to you."

"With the drones? Ah geez."

"That's right," Alan motioned to the shell-shocked little folk as they peered from the bushes. They shuffled past their captors and when all were by his side Alan led everyone across the silent square, towards the path entrance guarded by two man-sized flowers.

"Well," Alan saw one of them whisper, "we all know what's coming next, don't we?"

Alan turned in time to see the newfound joy slip from the VP's eyes. "Destroy them."

"Quick," barked Alan and dove into the bushes. He pulled himself through on all fours, checking his cohorts were behind him.

Stabbing sentences attacked Alan's shoulder, "Don't you feel you've let yourself and your team down? What can we do to make this situation better?"

"Oh God," wailed one of the Commuters, "It's the Team Leader." Alan glanced over his shoulder to see the shadow of a clawed hand. The fingers lengthened over the figure of a drone who curled into a ball, putting his hands over his head.

"Come on, move!" Alan yelled. The others obeyed but the frightened drone remained and, before they turned the corner, Alan saw the clawed hand drag him back, leaving only his plaintive yelp.

"We have to keep the statistics up," stabbed the voice of the Team Leader.

Alan pushed himself forwards with energy he didn't know he had. The ache in his arm, the tiredness in his limbs all disappeared – all that remained was moving forwards in the undergrowth and keeping the others doing the same. "Oh, thank heavens," said a wild-eyed man wrapped in vines, "I'm sure I'll have lost my job by now. Could you give me a hand old boy?" Alan debated agonisingly for a second, until he heard a distinct rumble about working together to get better results behind him.

"I'm sorry," said Alan, pushing himself away, "we'll come back for you I promise." On he went into near darkness, hearing the cry of the trapped man behind him. In the twisted branches to the left was a battered suitcase, almost overgrown with moss. It sprang open, revealing wormlike creatures with gargoyle faces, sharp teeth and enlarged gums. The things giggled maniacally and squirmed towards Alan, catching up to him fast and sinking tiny, sharp teeth into his side. "Oh God," yelled Alan, batting them furiously with his hand. More writhed from the suitcase, three wriggling clear before a commuter threw itself over it and clicking it shut, chopping several in half.

"It's I.T.," he said, hitting out at the dark worms. The other commuters followed suit while the drones rushed to Alan's side, pulling at the creature who was now wriggling into Alan's flesh.

"We need to have a chat about your attendance," the Team Leader's words spiked around the corner.

The drones pulled the I.T. monster free. Pain tore through Alan's side as it took a large chunk of his flesh with it. A number of the commuters fainted at the pooling blood as the Team Leader's voice drew nearer. Her words wrapped around the furthest commuter, tearing at her face and squeezing her until all that remained was an empty grin. A drone smashed a rock against the I.T. creatures until they were nothing but spattered goo. Alan shook the shoulder of one of the unconscious commuters and several drones grouped together, kicking them repeatedly until they rose, bright and perky. "Goodness, how unnecessary," they griped, following Alan once more.

On and on through the darkness they crawled until the vegetation around them was soft and spongy. "Try not to touch anything," said Alan, squeezing past an empty teacup with a fungi stem groping its way outwards. A thick wall of mushroom trunks blocked the way on the right.

"Where are we?" May whispered.

"You're here, dickhead," said a passing rabbit, "at the Old Bag's house. Have a nice time, she's a right bitch." It dived down a hole.

"Shit, what do we do?" May was borderline hysterical. Alan peered through the mushroom trunks in front of them, the tea table was empty aside from one figure, the goon whose head growth was now a trunk reaching into the ground, burrowing into nutritious soil.

"I need to check your time sheets," crackled a voice to their left.

"Ok," Alan stood, "we're going in." He surged into the open, the others following blindly. "Just keep running," Alan called, his heart matching his pounding footfalls. Across the clearing he tore until he was within arm's reach of the trees on the other side. Elation coursed through him until he was knocked back by what felt like a battering ram. Confused, head throbbing, he tried to get up but the Wise One's face peered down at him, blocking the sky.

"I'm so glad you decided to have tea after all," she grinned, "Timmy, round 'em up."

They were led into the cottage by a floating tape worm, his stringy body making them cringe every time it got too close. No-one wanted the smell of stomach acid and festering stench from its wrinkled skin touching them. "Good boy," simpered the witch when all huddled inside the cottage, "here's a treat." She threw a chunk of chewed up bread outside and Timmy followed. She slammed the door behind him. "Lovely pet but makes one feel a bit ill, no?" Her reply was a horde of frightened eyes. Alan's mind whirred for a way to escape and he knew May was doing the same. He had to put a plan into effect before her or doubtless she would use their deaths to her advantage.

"Maurice," the witch called to a grim looking butler with grey mutton chops, "come and help me tie them up." Maurice did so and before long silver ropes chafed at their wrists and ankles as they sat in a shaking group. Alan had a bad feeling about the cauldron bubbling in the kitchen. "Now," she clapped her hands like an excited child, "time for us to enjoy ourselves." She spooned a few mouthfuls into a wooden cup and loomed over them, playing a game of eeny meeny miny mo. "You," she pointed to a commuter with a comb over an enormous egg-head, "Yes, you'll do."

"Wait!" yelled May.

'Damn,' muttered Alan.

"We'll tell you anything, just please let us go. We're on a really important mission, the world is ending you know."

"Yes," snapped the Wise One, "I know about that. Who cares? Goodness, do stop going on about it." She sat the commuter in a chair while Maurice stood guard over him.

May's mouth remained open until she caught herself. "Well, that affects you, you know? If the world ends, you won't…be here anymore."

"Good," she fumed, "then you people won't keep bothering me." She resumed cackling over the terrified commuter. An insane thought struck Alan.

"You hate visitors, don't you?"

The Wise One turned to him. "Yes, idiot, I dislike intruders."

"Well," Alan shifted uncomfortably, "what if your land was to become Private Property?"

The Wise One loomed over him, her shadow encasing him. "It *is* private property."

"No," Alan's voice was small but firm, "what if it was made Private Property by law? The council would put invisible walls up and no one could pass through here without a verbal and written appointment?"

The Wise One retreated from her fearful stance, tapping the hairs on her chin in deep thought. She swilled the liquid in the cup in circles. "And...there'd be no way people could get in?"

"Absolutely none," Alan nodded.

"How do you have this power?"

"Well," Alan swallowed but his throat was dry, "here, you can check my credentials on this form." He looked down at his pocket. The Wise One gestured to Maurice, who approached Alan with resignation and hands outstretched. He produced a Necromancy fine after much unnecessary fondling.

"Look Maurice," the Wise One scoured the paper, "the paper is council headed. Just think, no more intruders kicking up the mud and destroying my flowers. Oh, won't that be beautiful?"

"Brilliant," May leapt up, "now you must let us fetch the forms."

"Well," the Wise One looked uncertain, "I suppose that makes sense." Maurice untied them all and they wrung their tortured wrists, Alan taking care to hide his. His heart was a powerdrill against his ribs, this was going to work. They scurried to the door and waited for her to release the tied up commuter, but instead she merrily poured the misty liquid over his helpless head.

"Oh my God!" wailed Alan. The man's forehead bubbled. He shook with fear and confusion as the liquid skin ran down his face and spattered down his front.

"Oh dear," he whimpered as the top of his head plopped onto his knees, leaving his brain exposed. It, too, was liquefying. Cries of disbelief and disgust issued from the onlookers when he looked up beseechingly at them, the muscles and sinew from his skull bleeding through his eyeballs and mouth. Eventually his body's infrastructure collapsed and his body degenerated into a pile of slush.

"Well, wasn't that nice," the Wise One wiped her hands on a kitchen towel. "Maurice, get the dustpan and brush. Now you know," she turned to them, "what will happen if you fail me."

"Y-yes ma'am," they mumbled in unison.

There was no conversation during the walk back into town. The townsfolk greeted them with cheers and applause and Alan couldn't help feeling important. "It's the Great One!" they wailed, touching his hair and face, "he returned to us!" Lilly the ice-cream girl embraced him, giggling.

"Thank you everybody. Well," he addressed his travelling band, "I propose what we do now is have a..a meeting about the next plan of action."

"Good idea," said May, and Alan didn't notice the ice in her eyes. "But, I've been thinking. Head Office are clearly enraged with us, aren't they? Otherwise they wouldn't want to destroy us." There was a general mutter of assent. Alan's joy faded. "I went to the library once, and a book said anyone wanting to appease Head Office had to make a sacrifice."

Fear prickled Alan's skin. The burning returned. "Really, that sounds daft. How old was this book exactly?"

May turned to him triumphantly. "It was written only last year." She flung her arms into the air. "Who should we choose for this great sacrifice?" A roar of suggestions immediately followed, each person desperately pointing at someone else. "No!" May's fury cut through the words, "who better than a Great One?" Think how satisfying that would be." She nodded her head towards Alan.

"What? After all this, you're going to murder me? You total..."

"No!" May was horrified. "It's not murder. We're sending you to a hero's paradise. We'll put you up in the Town Hall while we build the temple," several groans issued regarding the effort required, "and we'll give you a whole room and your own comfy chair." Surrounded by townsfolk, commuters and grief distracted drones, he limped alongside May to a dull stone building in the town centre. Inside a bland office room a dusty armchair waited for him.

"Thank you very much," he said, falling onto it when May's hand pushed him hard in the small of his back.

The townsfolk surrounded him. "May we fetch you cups of tea, my lord?"

"Perhaps a scone?"

"No," Alan shook his head, "thank you, I just want to be left alone for a minute."

"Of course!" Everyone shuffled out whispering excitedly about their new plan. May leaned against the door.

"You'll find we've taken extra precautions for your safety. The windows have been boarded up and sentries will guard this door at all times."

"Thank you," said Alan through gritted teeth. When the door was shut he yanked up the sleeve of his shirt. The skin on his elbow bubbled and the ridges had sharpened. He spent the afternoon checking the room for escape holes but the council had been thorough after the Draught Debacle of 62. He even had an ensuite, ruling out any toilet related plans. Alan slumped into the chair, defeated. For a further 20 minutes he picked at the fluff on his trousers, devoid of all thought, and made miserable noises.

The hammering outside nudged his eyelids, gently at first and then enough to sting. Running his hands over the wooden slats covering the windows he searched for a join to peek through. "Oh shit," he muttered. The Temple the townsfolk were building would be a disappointment to all but the neediest of Gods. Marble or similar material was apparently in short supply and instead the base was a row of rotting logs with three broken fence segments pointed into a pyre. Surrounding it was a collection of mildewed objects which must have come from the tip – a broken toilet, four issues of Reader's Digest and a nail gun.

He spun round guiltily when the door opened. May's smile was an odd mixture of relief and fury. "Look," he cut in before she could speak – the itch on his arm was unbearable, "this has gone far enough. When can I go?"

Fear pooled in May's eyes. "You can't! We need you!"

"You need me in here, you mean, for you to be their leader."

May's cheeks flushed deep grey. "We need you more than ever. You're the Great One, you bring us prophecies."

"May, we both know this isn't something you believe. They might," he pointed to the crowd kneeling before the alter, "but you know better."

May raised an eyebrow. "It'll all be over soon," she soothed. "You know, in another situation, I like to think we could have made it work between us."

"I doubt it…I prefer men. And people who aren't trying to kill me." As May slammed the door behind her, Alan clawed at the handle. "May!" he bellowed until his throat was sore, "I didn't mean it!" After ten minutes of hammering and begging, things seemed a little better in the foetal position under the table.

Darkness oozed in and Alan uncurled himself. Something rustled nearby but he detected no other movement. He pushed away a pile of clutter and crawled back out into the open space; nothing. Peeping through the wooden slats he saw nobody.

The adrenaline was like a pure injection. He tugged and pulled at the shutters one by one but nothing budged. He felt along the walls, still nothing – until he reached the far left corner. Dust came away from the bricks when he nudged and scrabbled at the loose ones, making a small hole. As he searched for a heavy object to slam into it he doubled over in pain. Holding his stomach he tried to find a position where the agony was less intense, curling into a ball and willing his body to go limp. It wouldn't listen, and he continued mutating.

In the silver dawn the door crashed open. "What?" May struggled to compose herself as the goons stumbled after her.

"What's that?" one demanded.

"Uh…" a quick answer was at the forefront of May's mind, but it hid behind a vessel. Before them stood a four foot by six oblong calendar with a date circled – tonight.

"Gaah," the bodyguard shakily pointed at it before running out to the other townsfolk.

"Jesus, what a girl," May tutted and followed him out. She stood on the steps of the Town Hall and held out her palms. Her gesture of authority ended, or at least subdued, the arm wringing and wailing. "The Great One himself has predicted our doom, it's true," she held up a hand when her audience flailed their limbs and sank to their knees. "But if we continue with the sacrifice he will absorb it all and everything will be fine, trust me. Then we can go on living for ages."

"That doesn't make sense," Lilly the ice cream girl rose from her knees. Everyone turned to her.

"A doubter!" shrieked Bill.

They bundled her, shrieking and flailing, into the room with the now silent, faceless Alan. When they locked the door and she was alone she listened to his rhythmic breathing. Nervously she approached him. "Great One?" she whispered. Nothing. She reached out and felt his corners. The rhythm of his breathing soothed her and she lay down next to him, pretending she was by the sea, until she fell asleep.

The pile of rubbish on the Town Hall lawn had grown to a disturbing height, stacked with electrical equipment and phone books and sandwich packets. The townsfolk beside the rubbish dump had sorted various objects into piles and passed them piece by piece from person to person in an assembly line.

In the Town Hall Alan stood, silent and oblong, the date still firmly circled on his chest. "You see," said Lilly, lying on her back with her arms folded beneath her head, "it's been a constant struggle to figure out what I want to do, where I fit in. Since mum went on holiday and didn't come back I've just been thinking about what else is out there, you know?" Alan loomed over her. "No one has ever listened to me the way you do." She sighed and rested a hand on his lower corner. "They're going to kill us, but as long as you're with me I don't care." Alan continued looming. "I've never known anyone like you," she laid her head against him. The door jerked open.

"Tea and a packet of biscuits," sang May carrying a tray. The flowers sprouting from her words dissipated when she saw Lilly's embrace. "Oh," she said sharply, "I see you two have become well acquainted."

"We have," said Lilly, flicking her hair dramatically, "Alan is a very caring man."

"You know he's... he's a calendar, right?"

"When love is real it knows no bounds."

"Right," May slammed the tea tray down on the table, "let's hope those bounds include death because the Great Fire will be lit tonight."

"Oh," Lilly was knocked slightly, but she regained composure. "Well, we don't care as long as we have each other." She pushed her face into his page folds, her tongue writhing against the card. May shook her head and shut the door behind her. Lilly rested her face against Alan's cool surface and sighed deeply, humming as she traced her fingers over the frayed corner. "Perhaps we could run away together," she mumbled, but made no effort to rise. Darkness fell and shrieks permeated the wooden slats. A soft light flickered. "I'll check it out," she whispered.

Through the cracks she saw the crowds circling a pile of rubbish that stretched precariously up to the night sky like a diseased finger. "There's too much wet stuff," said Milkman Mike, "where did you get it from?"

"The lake," replied barmaid Sally, "that's not a problem is it?"

"No," Mike grumbled, turning his attention to piling on the broken furniture. The rest of them formed a circle and held hands. The words to a song drifted gently up to the stars, "Oh Great One we like you, you have dreamy eyes..."

"Well," said Lilly, "this is it, my love." She ran back to Alan and hid in his shadow. Heavy footsteps appeared under the door and she tried to hide her shaking when the keys rattled in the lock. The shadows loomed behind May and all Lilly saw of her followers were the whites of their eyes in sooty blackness.

Lilly's hands were held behind her back out on the Hall steps while the goons carried Alan high over their heads. When the people saw him they gasped. Several women wept and a small boy pointed and laughed. "No!" Lilly wailed, "We're in love." She struggled weakly against those restraining her but her small frame wasn't a match. The goons held Alan up to the fire, his pages illuminated.

"Stop!" The word tore through the ceremony and a small man with white tufts on his head pushed his way to the front. The goons jumped back, eyes darting to May for instructions. Her mouth opened and closed a few times but, faced with genuine authority, she was stuck. "You can't burn him," continued the man, "he's too valuable. Why is today's date circled?

Shouldn't we find out?" he appealed to the crowd. They shrugged and turned to each other. "I'm studying his condition for my thesis. It's known as auto-mutation." He cast a loving gaze over Alan. "It's a very rare, stress-related disorder and I'll be the first to write about it. Uh," he changed tack, aware he may be losing his audience, "so we need to know what brought on his attack, it could be very important."

The townsfolk muttered amongst themselves. "So," May said, "stress turned him into a calendar?"

"Precisely!"

"Right, so the date could be the cause of his stress?"

"Exactly. Either that or the imprisonment and burning, but we won't know without asking him."

May's left eye twitched. Aware of everyone waiting, she ordered him back inside. "What about our burning?" the townsfolk roared.

"What?" said May, "you can't have it both ways.

"Burning!" They roared, their faces a deep grey.

May suddenly longed for a week in bed. "Alright, burn her," she pointed vaguely at Lilly, whose eyes widened in terror. She was carried, screeching and kicking, to the fire where she was unceremoniously dumped. The onlookers cheered and clapped their hands at the wails and the scent of melting flesh and singed hair while Alan was ushered back inside the Town hall. "I don't know if that will be enough for them," she said as they burst into his cell. "OK," she turned to her goons, "get cushions and blankets. Mark, put the kettle on. Dave, find some kittens from the shelter. OK doctor, he's all yours."

The doctor kneeled beside Alan's resting place on top of a nest of dusty cushions. "There, there," he said, patting him gently, "they've promised not to burn you." He realised his hand was possibly resting on a sensitive area and moved it. "Now they've said you can go home, everything's fine." The room was still save for one of the goons gazing at his toes. May sighed.

"Nothing's happen −"

"Shush, look!" Alan's corners were rounding. His bulk melted like hot cheese into the cushions, gloopily forming the shape of a man. Black hair sprouted messily from his scalp and soon Alan sprawled, his spindly legs splayed and his arms stretched over the cushions.

"Oh God," he wailed, "I'm still here?"

"No," soothed the doctor, "it's all over, you're allowed to go home."

Alan's face collapsed in relief and he sat up sharply. "I can go? Right…"

"Well," the doctor leaned in conspiratorially. The effect was unsettling, especially when Alan could see a splay of nose hairs. "As soon as we figure out what's happening tonight."

Alan lay back down, his eyes flicking from the doctor to May. "Well, what does happen tonight?"

There was a pause. "Well," said the doctor, "that's what you need to tell us. Tonight's the 16th, if that's any help."

"Erm," Alan put his fingers to his temples. He thought back over celebrations, plans, everything, but nothing seemed to stand out. His temple rubbing grew increasingly frantic. The doctor turned desperately to May.

"Where are those goddamn kittens?!"

Milkman Mike burst in with a mewling basket and Alan's face resembled an ecstatic child's as they were tipped onto his stomach. Everyone watched with pursed lips as he tickled the silver one's ears and rubbed the black one's belly. May's left eye twitched again. "Look," she grabbed his shoulders, "what the fuck is happening this bloody Thursday?"

"Oh, it's Thursday!" realisation seeped into Alan's face. "My Pig Fancier Monthly magazine arrives on Thursdays. This week it's all about the saddleback!"

The doctor sat back on his haunches. "Your…a magazine…so, the end of the world, you don't actually know anything?"

Alan pursed his lips. "Well," he said cautiously, "not exactly. I mean, I know the situation's in hand. I just – I'm not entirely sure how."

May stood straight. "Right, the burning's back on." Alan was lifted away by rough hands to the crackling fire where Lilly's charred remains glowed. Pieces of paper lined the edges, and as he was pulled closer he noticed they were all letters from relatives on holiday. They had been written with the same handwriting.

The goons carried Alan towards the flames and singing hit the sky once more. Sweat from the heat and fear poured from his face and a scorch mark crept over his jumper. "That's right," a screech issued from the forest edge, "you burn him! Then you'll all be next."

"Oh, ballbags," muttered May; it was the Wise One.

They were inside a high domed building with warm ash walls. An old gramophone span lyrics into the air while a fire crackled in the grate, and there was no sign of the hideous snow storm. Small Elflike creatures with pointed ears and shoes attended to an assembly line of products, all of which fell through a shoot at one end of the room which presumably took it to the next stage of readiness. Elenor narrowed her eyes at the items that travelled from busy hand sticking on a label to busy hand adding the price. One was a bottle of shampoo, behind it was a cereal box and after that – her heart did a forward roll – was a box of non-bio detergent. Before she could gather her thoughts Sam was already heading for the elf assembling the cardboard box. "Excuse me," he said, "we've been asked to come here and fetch some non-bio, I wonder if it would be possible to pick some up? How much would you be asking?"

The elf didn't move his focus from the task before him, "there is no selling."

Sam's brow furrowed in confusion. "Not…for sale?"

"No." The elf continued his task, shut off now to Sam's presence. Holly charged forwards.

"Look," she said to the elf, "we're very tired, we're very busy and we don't have a lot of time. Please," the word left her lips with great difficulty, "can we have a box of non-bio and just be on our way. Look," she indicated the products on the conveyer belt, "you've got stuff to last for centuries, you won't miss it."

"OK," Elenor took a place beside Holly, "we'll pay whatever the supermarket charges for a bunch of them, how about that?"

"Sooper…makket?" The elf's expression was blank. The elves nearby tried their own pronunciations with varying success.

"What do you make these for?" asked Elenor.

"For the Great One," he said, lowering his voice reverently.

Holly leaned in to whisper to the others, "Why is there always a Great One?"

"OK, how about this," Sam was business itself once more, "we have a word with your Great One, explain the situation, get the non-bio and be on our way?"

The elves murmured amongst themselves as the trio waited. After a long moment the elf turned to them, hands blindly operating his task. "We will take you to the Great One. Jerry is about to embark upon a ten minute break, he will lead you." One elf in a small group folding cardboard stepped forwards, beckoning them. They followed him to a dark corridor, the shadows leering down as they passed the stone walls. Elenor grabbed the first hand nearest to her, Holly's, and noticed she and Sam were already holding each other's. At the end of the corridor was another flight of stone steps leading into blackness. Elenor was surprised to feel Holly's grip tighten as they descended, eventually reaching a heavy wooden door bolted with steel locks.

"We have reached the lair of the Great One," Jerry knelt to the ground reverentially before trotting back up the steps. "He will see you now, go right in."

Holly reached out to the steel lock, turning it on its side and pushing open the door with an almighty creak. Darkness waited and the three stepped inside. "Look," Sam whispered, pointing to the floor. At the back of the wall was a vast pile of products including several packages of non-bio and, sat before them looking up from a soft warm basket, was a black kitten. Its bright silver eyes blinked.

"Aw, look at the kitten!" squealed Holly, rushing forwards to tickle its chin. It purred and the other two joined her. "Don't you just want to squeeze it to death?"

"Never have cats," said Sam.

Elenor eyed the pile of stuff. "I suppose we can just take it," she shrugged, removing a box and sticking it under her jumper. They rose reluctantly from the purring creature and headed for the door. A rumbling sound followed them out. "What's that?" asked Elenor, turning to see the kitten not looking so cute anymore. It was swelling like an inflating balloon, its eyes pinging from their original position outwards and its fur splitting.

"Help it," wailed Holly.

"I don't think it needs help," said Sam. By now the kitten had swelled to the size of the room and expanded outwards, its head almost reaching them. "Run," Sam ordered, Holly had already bolted. The kitten's body was now an undulating, pale segmented blob, the only thing resembling a face on its body being a tiny set of sharp teeth at its forefront.

"It's a maggot," gulped Elenor in disgust as Sam pulled her up the stairs. It's bloated, pulsing body followed them. The maggot was still growing as they reached the top of the stairs and the floorboards began to split. Holly beat the creature's face with a chair. It barely noticed, breaking through the ground and rising like unpleasant dough. The elves cowered in a corner.

"One of you has it!" shrieked an elf, "you must replace it or our workshop will be destroyed!" The maggot extended itself to reach an elf standing nearby, taking its feet in its hideous maw. The screams were unbearable as the beast sucked it in.

"I'll put it back," said Elenor, her face tear-streaked.

"No," said Sam. He picked up a piece of broken machinery and dove towards the rampaging grub.

"Stop!" yelled Holly, and they watched as the tiny mouth opened and sucked him inside. Holly went to run after him but Elenor grabbed her. They waited for what felt like a year, an age. The first sign something was wrong was the shaking of the maggot's head. It ceased its pulsing journey forwards, instead bunching its body in apparent discomfort.

"What's happening to the Great One?" muttered the elves. Their answer was given with an eerie, winding howl and a geyser of blood pouring from the top of its head. Its body deflated and shrank. When Sam pulled his head free from the skin he took a long breath, falling to his knees as the remains around him shrank to the size of a kitten once more. Holly and Elenor ran to him but he held a hand up.

"I'm covered in gunk," he explained. They looked down at the kitten, torn apart on the ground.

"We ought to go," said Holly. The other two followed her gaze to the elves. Some looked openly outraged, others simply lost, like their security blanket had been ripped from their arms. The trio sidled to the door as though hoping to slip away unnoticed. Elenor was stopped by a tug on her jumper. She tried to pretend she hadn't felt it but it grew in insistence.

"What do we do now?" asked the elf. There was no self-pity in his demeanour, only fear and confusion.

"Well," Elenor said, "you could carry on what you were doing, only sell them to supermarkets." Curiosity and hope flooded their eyes and Elenor spoke with more confidence. "Sell them to supermarkets and repair the damage, or build an even nicer place. You'll be alright. Take all this stuff around town and find someone willing to buy for a decent price." The elves waved them off and they sped over the white wilderness, passing all that was left of Mr Charles, a dark figure soaked in blood by the Cliffside.

The gates opened for them and the runners trotted inside, the dead springing back to life. "They don't really die out here," the queen explained with a chortle, "they have a penance to complete and complete it they shall." She took the non-bio powder box from Elenor and held it aloft, the crowd roaring in triumph. "You have succeeded," she cried, "stay and become Lord and Ladies of the court. We will dance until sunrise and feast on Snow ogre and, above all, wear clothes as smooth as silk and itch-free!" The court erupted once more.

"OK," said Holly.

"We're terribly sorry," said Sam, "but we have an important mission to complete, otherwise this world might not exist much longer." The Queen nodded her head sadly. "Truly you are the heroes from the prophecy." She led them to an ice encrusted door in a hidden corner, opening it to reveal a swirling vortex. "We will honour your good deed by erecting statues of you holding up the mighty box," she assured, and the trio took a deep breath and stepped through.

"Oh good," said woman at the desk, "you came back. Now, fill in this form with your education and previous employment."

She crowed once their forms were returned. "Oh wonderful, I've just the things for all three of you."

"Oh, thanks," said Sam, "we'll buckle down and not get distracted by each other. It'll be as though we're alone."

"Well," the woman removed her glasses, "you will be alone. You can't all work together – your skill sets are completely different."

"Oh," Elenor's stomach crawled with caterpillars.

"Yes, you see, the young man here," she indicated Sam, "has worked in retail and is good with people. Elenor here will be placed in tallies and Holly will be placed in the crèche."

Holly gasped. "I'm not that bad."

"No," the woman said impatiently, "it says here you worked with children and animals." The other two glared at her.

"Well," she shrugged, "they were there on the commune."

"Wonderful, I'll show you to your posts." She opened a side door and grabbed Holly's arm. "It's just through here. Don't look so worried, all you have to do is watch them and make sure they don't start killing each other or burning effigies again. There we are," She shoved a frightened looking Holly through the doorway. "Just watch out for the clowns, the children sometimes like to tie them up and hide them places. It's ever so much fun but sometimes their husks aren't found for several months."

Elenor waved goodbye to Sam when a tiny, shrivelled prune of a man showed up to lead her away. Keys jangled at his side as he hobbled along and his jump suit was less wrinkled than his face. "This way to tallies," he muttered, "that department has the most beautiful tables in the entire building."

"Oh, really?" Elenor wasn't sure what else to say.

"Oh yes," a vague light appeared in his otherwise dim eyes as they passed rows of office spaces, "they're just lovely. Floor 56 has attractively carved filing cabinets but the tables here more than make up for it. Mind you, I'd give up working on this floor if I could just sample the computer desks on Floor 189 for a day." his eyes softened as though he had fallen into a dream. Elenor struggled to think of a polite response, but the moment stretched into an embarrassing silence so she decided to leave it. They reached a side room. The back wall was covered in shards of mirror, each showing a different section of the building. "This is Magrav The Terrible," he indicated a shadowy, gaseous figure with a hooked nose and staring eyes, "he's your buddy for the day." The man with the keys made a quick exit. Magrav wafted slowly into the corner. Elenor hesitantly sat in the chair, keeping an eye firmly on her supervisor.

"Er, shall I just start on the tally list here and work my way down?" Magrav didn't respond, his watchful gaze seething with rage. "OK…" Elenor decided to list the amount of bald men that had passed through corridor F that morning and how many looked under-confident. She reached for a pen. "No," said Magrav.

"N-no?"

"No."

"What should I-"

"No."

Elenor sighed, feeling the sweat on her palms intensify. She spotted a second pen holder and removed a biro. Magrav gave a tiny nod. Releasing her breath she gathered a pile of paper before her. "No." Frustrated, she slammed the paper back and pulled out some more from the drawer. "This is not how we deal with company property," he rumbled firmly. Elenor ignored him, trying to find the zone where time passed at a satisfying rate. Her mind whirred as she surveyed each scene; a man hugging the wall of hair, whispering "I'll never leave you, mother," a lady in the toilets pirouetting gracefully until someone entered, a young salesman geeing himself up to make a phone call – all fascinating, all useless, until she spied a familiar ruckus on floor 17. Figures paced back and forth along the corridor and the bottoms of the walls had been painted a strange colour. No other personnel seemed to be present, except…Elenor looked again – Severed limbs littered the ground along with organs and strips of security uniforms. It wasn't paint on the walls but the vestiges of a bloody massacre. An idea waved its flag.

Somehow she lasted until the first break time. With relief she found the staff room where attractive young men with chins almost as large as their hair chatted about their new houses with attractive young women who chatted about their mortgages. Distinguished, handsome older men chatted with sleek older women on the state of Commuterville and how things were once better. Elenor passed all of these, focusing instead on the man with skin like a prune.

"Hello again," he said when she sat down. "How are you finding it? Don't you think the cupboards in that room lack the depth and workmanship of the cupboards on the fifth floor, but I suppose the wood grain pattern in the wainscoting is really a hard thing to beat."

"Oh absolutely" Elenor leaned in, accessing a happy memory to stop herself running all the way home. Sam's face swam into view, asking her to go on a bike ride. To her embarrassment her eyes welled up and she blinked furiously. "I'm new here and I was wondering if you could show me around?"

"Oh, uh," a flush of pleasure lit his face, "well, I need to go on my rounds in a moment, but I'm free later."

"Brilliant, I bet you have some fascinating stories."

The prune blushed deeply. "Perhaps," he looked as though he were about to do the bravest thing he had ever done, "we could meet at lunchtime?" Elenor agreed, feeling guilty but telling herself it was for the greater good.

The afternoon passed like a slug. Elenor recounted all possible outcomes of her plan so many times that she counted the same bald man twice and Magrav's "No" was large enough to block the hallway for several minutes. By the time lunch arrived Elenor was shaking with nerves and a determination she had never felt before. Not since she had won the yearly local crab collection had she felt so charged.

She waited outside the break room, sensing after a few moments that all was not well. She sidled to the corner and peeked around at the office space desks. He was chatting to someone from Security, squinting at a handheld mirror which Elenor was quite sure portrayed security footage of all three of them. She prepared to run when she noticed the blank expression of the prune. He shook his head, seeming confused, before blinking short-sightedly. The Security Guard marched his way around the office, showing the mirror to all around him. His hand seemed quite keen to reach for his rifle and the next worker he showed the picture to didn't seem so confused. The prune headed her way.

"This is very kind of you," smiled Elenor, edging away as quickly as she politely could.

"That's quite alright," he said shyly. He pointed to a room beside them. "Here is where the drone facilitators work. I once borrowed a chair from that room," his expression became wistful, "it turned so smoothly, didn't make a single squeak. Still," he lowered his head, "she went onto to better things. The boss upstairs took a shine to her." He led her on, Elenor listening impatiently to story after story of furniture and fixtures.

"That's wonderful," she said, leaning in until she could smell his breath mints, "but what about the really exciting stuff?"

The prune looked confused. "Exciting? Isn't this exciting?"

"Oh, no, of course it is," Elenor patted his arm reassuringly, "it's just, you know, everyone likes to hear about the juicy stuff don't they? Like a chair an important person sat on, or a cabinet that holds, I don't know – a lot of important information."

"Well, yes, I suppose some people prefer salacious gossip. I prefer facts."

Elenor sensed she was losing him but her blood fizzed now. "No, come on, what's the most secret cupboard? What's the cabinet that holds information about the way things are really run?"

"Well," the prune shrugged, "you must mean the Cabinet in the Little Room, but nobody goes in there."

"Do you go in there?" Elenor leaned closer.

"Well," he smiled a little, "I went there once many years ago. It does have one particularly magnificent drawer with a beautiful oak panel."

"Could we…look at it now?"

"Well," his eyes took on a haunted expression, "I'll show you where it is." He led her through several corridors, making many twists and turns Elenor tried to store in her memory. Finally they reached a hallway that rolled and dipped like a boat on a choppy sea. Doorways leading to office spaces were just visible from where she stood; melting hands reached out and people in suits wailed and begged for help. The end destination was a shadowy point in the distance. "It's down there," he said with a small voice. "Well, that's enough. This place troubles me and there is no other furniture worthy of the trip. Come on, let's get you back."

At her desk she searched the mirrors for Holly and Sam, finding Sam serving coffee and information surrounded by worryingly happy co-workers. Holly was apparently involved in a princess' tea party. Several clowns were huddled in the crèche corner weeping, their running make up giving them a melting impression. Now and then Holly and her wards would go as if to hit them before falling about laughing.

Elenor glanced sideways at Magrav and tapped her pen on the paper. "No," he said. Elenor bristled.

"Sir, I heard some things in the break room you ought to know." His eyes bored into her, almost making her lose her nerve. "Yes, uh, I heard that some people were going to the stationary room after lunch and picking some of the seeds to take home."

"What?" he fumed, smoke billowing from his eyes.

"Y-yes, they're probably in there now, filling their baskets with pen pods and stapler saplings. It was a whole bunch of them."

His eye smoke now streamed out and two small flames flickered inside them. "Noooo," he bellowed, bashing his way through desks and walls leaving all in a state of shock. Elenor held her breath until the lift doors closed behind him, releasing it as she tapped on the mirrors containing her friends. "Please let this work," she mumbled. "Holly, you need to go to Floor 17 and lead everyone there to the Top."

"What about these?" she pointed to her charges. One toddler had a clown by the throat.

"Bring them."

"Alright!" She tore the quiff from her head and ran a hand over a clown's face, smearing the make up across her own.

"Hello, happy time coffee house, how may I help?" said one of Sam's co-workers. "He's serving at the moment," he said when Elenor requested him.

"His mum is very ill," said Elenor, crossing her fingers and hoping that people couldn't be jinxed in real life.

"Oh, dear," the worker's grin became a worried frown, "I'll get him." After some shuffling, Sam peered out at Elenor. "It's at the end of corridor 50," Elenor barked, "You need to go to the Top Floor." Sam nodded grimly just as an old lady waved her hand in his face, screeching for service.

Elenor ducked out of her seat and tore down the hallway, repeating the directions in her head like a mantra. "Left at the water slide on the corner," she mumbled, aware that she was drawing stares from everyone passing. "Right at the tadpole sale," she took care not to upset the buckets of wriggling creatures. She pushed gently through the gathered crowds.

"George," said a lady shaped like a wheel barrow, "isn't that the one they're looking for? You know, the one in the photo they're showing everyone?"

"Yes," said a glittered mirror ball, "you're right. You know, I heard she tries to sleep with everybody's husband too."

"Oh gosh, well I just heard from Susan and you know Susan never says anything about anyone well Susan says she eats puppies and…"

Elenor didn't stay to hear more, breaking into a run. "Left, then right, then left…"

Still the voices behind continued, threatening to break her concentration, "Well I heard she turns up to all parties drunk and no one can stand to look at her and…"

"Oh, dammit, no, left then left then right…" she turned another corner and another, risking a look over her shoulder. A mass of twisting, rolling and bouncing Office Workers were trailing just behind.

"George, Margaret, who's got a mirror? We need to call security!"

Elenor felt a hand brush her back. She bolted, sure now that she had lost her way, but just as groping fingers pulled at her sleeves she launched herself into the whirling, undulating corridor. Elenor steeled herself to run further but the followers stood anxiously still. "Go on, Rita," urged the mirror ball, but Rita didn't budge and nor did anybody else.

The air was stagnant. In the offices beside her lost and frightened workers called for help; a young man's tie was caught between the teeth of an angry desk and a young woman wept uncontrollably while a malfunctioning computer listed all her faults. Elenor kept her gaze firmly ahead, much as she wanted to stop and help them she had to keep going.

A young woman was draped over a dozen men whose tongues dangled to the ground. Beside them another woman took apart a computer, muttering curses under her breath. The men groped the writhing vixen busily while she tormented their clothed nether regions in a tableau of frustration. The computer woman looked up to roll her eyes and tut loudly before falling back onto her pointless task. "Would any of you boys like a cup of tea?" purred the vixen.

"Oh yeah," said one of the men, his hands rubbing her chest.

"Can I drink it from your tits?" said another.

"Oh," she chuckled, "I'm not wearing a bra so yes you could."

"I'd like one," said the other woman, but she was ignored.

"Yeah, that's it," said the vixen to a man squeezing her thighs, "now who wants me to piss on them?"

Elenor kept moving, kept her eyes firmly ahead, ignoring the acrid stench of urine behind her. A hand grasped hers and she yelped. A man had pressed a button on a fax machine and was being sucked inside. "Help me, can't you?" Elenor searched for an off button but it was too late, he was emitted from the other side as a sticky goo. Elenor backed away slowly, ordering herself to continue, don't think about it don't…

More fingers grabbed her skirt and wrapped around her ankles. They were unattached to anyone, just hands. She kicked them away and the nails of one pinged off, its bloody stumps flailing like tentacles. Elenor heard cries, wails for help and they seemed to be getting nearer. She put her hands to the side of her face to blinker her eyes but when she turned, they were dragging themselves towards her. People without legs pulled themselves along the ground, torsos without arms used chins and broken teeth and parts used anyway possible. "Would you like to hug me and stay here forever?" wept a man whose body had melded with the wall. "Please, just hold my hand, I used to have friends I know I did." Elenor shrieked, breaking into a run until she was at the Cabinet, and the figures kept on coming.

"Shit," she whispered. She opened drawer after drawer but found nothing of interest. "Please," the wailing continued, "please…" she found it – pages and pages of correspondence and plans filed alphabetically for The Big End. Elenor kept going, trying more and more until she found the files accounting for disappearances. She felt a tongue on her ankle and kicked instinctively, sending a severed head crashing into the stumbling figures. She flicked through the disappearance files, reaching a name that was all too familiar.

"Mum?"

"Mrs Allbury, incinerated April 674. Reason: filing complaint 90003, inconsistent refuse collection."

Elenor's hands shook violently. She stared and stared but the words didn't change. Her jaw set and she grabbed a pile of the Big End files along with several Burning Room orders. She leaned her head down like a battering ram and crashed into the oozing figures. Their mouths sucked at nothing like starving babies and their digits groped for something solid, falling wetly onto the floor. Elenor bit and scratched and fought against hands and feet that tried to pull her into an eternity of the Corridor, punching through rib cages and head butting faces until finally, soaked in blood and drenched in organs she fell at the feet of the Office Workers. Elenor rolled onto her back and looked into the eyes staring down at her, finally throwing a handful of the papers in a shower over their heads. "What are they?" shrieked the workers as they scrabbled to read them, "What do they say?" The last thing she saw before slipping into unconsciousness was a mirror screen showing Sam knocking three times on the wall until a door appeared.

Blood was smeared over the walls on The Top Floor. People begged for mercy as they were savaged by wild-eyed call takers and children. Underneath the screams and the begging was the regular, rhythmic chant of "Leads, leads, leads…" and the squealing laughter from Holly's wards. Sam fought his way through the corridor until he saw it, the Great Door.

The room was in almost total darkness were it not for the eerie glow of the lights behind his father. "Welcome, son," He smiled. Sam had never noticed how falsely bright, how even his teeth were before. He raised a hand in welcome and the shadows of his fingers crept up the wall to the ceiling behind him. "You've decided to come see where daddy works, have you?"

Sam snorted in a bitter laugh. "Daddy murders people for a living."

The Big Boss looked offended, his dark charcoal face creased in horror. "No, that's not true. I run a tight ship so one day my boy can take over. Just think, you at the head, me popping in for visits – perhaps bringing the odd bottle of brandy?" Confusion muddied Sam's anger; his father wasn't behaving like the Evil One, he was the man who had once bought him a singing taxidermy diorama for Christmas. He steeled himself.

"Yes, you do. What about all the drones? The call takers?"

The Boss shrugged his shoulders, perplexed. "The drones are created to work, they have no feelings, and the call-takers are free to find work elsewhere." He paused, sitting back in his seat. "Ok, you want to have a chat. I'll lock the door," a button was pressed on the desk. "There, now, what exactly is troubling you? I'm always here for you."

Sam noticed how the skin now sagged at the corners of his father's face and almost couldn't speak. When had this man grown so old? "What about the townspeople?"

The Big Boss placed meaty fingers at his temples. "I work day and night to keep order. It's really quite a lot harder than it looks. I admit," he held his hands up, "I would like some things to be worked out better and perhaps we can do that together in the New Year. Now, Sammy," he tilted his head, curiosity in his eyes, "don't you want to make things better in the Town? Create a better life for your friends?"

Sam shook his head. "I don't know."

"Come on Sam," his father reached out his arms appealing to his boy, "you know I'm just trying to do my best." He rose and stood in front of his son. Sam wanted to push him away and embrace him simultaneously. Instead he just stood, helplessly, as The Big Boss crushed him in a terrifying grip. "I just want you to be happy." Sam noticed for the first time how watery the old man's eyes were. He reached his arms around him. "There we are," said The Big Boss, "that's better. Wait…" he said sharply, urgently, "What are you doing?"

"I'm sorry," whispered Sam, "but I want to do things my way."

The Boss shot out a hand and pressed the button for his guards, but no one came. He whimpered as Sam's arms twisted around his waist. His whimper became a full scream as his son lifted his top half clean off. Inside The Boss there was no blood, no organs. Instead, glaring at Sam through unseeing eyes was a smaller version of his father. Sam reached out to twist the top from this one as well, on and on, until all that remained was a tiny china version at the bottom of a giant trouser seat. Sam picked it up and inspected it. He felt too many things to feel any at all and sat at the desk staring at the tiny, lifeless figure. From the corner of the room a cloud appeared, spreading like a powdery trail, snaking outwards and creeping under the door and through the windows. "You've learned to rule for yourself," whispered his father's voice from somewhere in the ether, "I'm proud of you, you'll be just like me." The world was ending, it was here.

In its wake the carpet wasn't grey, it was something else, something bright – but not white. Sam watched it wash over the room and sprinkle over the walls. He didn't resist as it crawled up his skin, tingling like a million cockroaches. The screaming had stopped outside, everywhere was still. Sam opened the door and stood face to face with a blood stained crowd. "Baaa," said Sam. He had meant to speak a sentence but instead something had rumbled up his throat and vomited into the air.

"Aaaaa," said Holly, looking equally as troubled.

The cloud undulated through the streets, the woods, the houses and the air. At first people screamed and clung to each other, but afterwards they stared at their fellows calmly. "Kkkkk," said one woman.

"Ffff," said a man.

On it went, winding through towns and cities and villages, striking everyone and everything. At first they ran but, once it hit, nobody could remember what had been so troubling. "Yyooouuu," said a woman wrapped in a live fox, the first person to speak a complete word. She would go on to appear on Mirror News, after a live performance by The Queen VP.

The cloud spread to the town where The Wise One was reaching into a bag of curses. The cloud hit and she couldn't remember what she had wanted so badly to do. The townsfolk dropped Alan and scattered. He yelled for help, trying to pull his hands free of the ropes, but when the cloud covered him he lay quietly, watching new shades fill the world.

May charged ahead, leaving her followers calling out to her. The cloud struck and running didn't seem so important anymore. Instead they flopped to the ground burbling like babies. It was Milkman Mike who cracked it. His first attempts sounded like mumbling but he concentrated hard. "Hell...o," he said and all eyes turned to him. They knew now how it worked and Mike would show them.

Sam and Holly found Elenor lying at the entrance of the corridor. Their arms were wrapped around each other and when Elenor saw them, she knew they were happy. Holly grimaced as she helped her up, unwilling to smear lung and kidney on her dress. "Sam," said Elenor after a few tries, "you...you in charge now." Sam beamed. "But, you good...leader?" Holly laughed, as though it was a daft question, but Sam didn't answer straight away. Instead he raised an eyebrow, and Elenor had a bad feeling.

THE MARZIPAN KING IS A DICK

I can hear Simon breathing behind me. His black body is as comforting as it always is and his shadow joins the others in the dark early morning room, a contrast to my pale flesh and long blonde hair. His warmth reaches me from his side of the bed. I decide to stay awake otherwise I'll be groggy when I get up. I blink.

When I open my eyes again I see I've not managed this simple task. In the distance is a marzipan kingdom with a marzipan castle, and the sugary ground stretches out as far as the eye can see in white, baby pink and soft blue. A flesh and blood terrier yaps at my feet and I know he's mine, even though I don't own a dog in real life. I lean down to pet him and he licks my face. When I straighten up he's standing in front of me, the Marzipan King.

"Yum, sweetmeats, thanks!" he says as he picks up the dog, swallowing it in one mouthful. I feel annoyed as I'd started to get attached to him.

"That's fine," I say, hoping he notices the sarcasm in my voice.

"Want to come to my magic kingdom?" he says with a leer and a wink. I realise he's kind of a dick.

"Not really," I say.

"Oh." He looks disappointed and folds his arms. "Well, I thought you were ugly anyway."

I want to hit him but I'm too shocked to move. "I think I'd like to wake up now," I say eventually.

"Fine, whatevs," he says dismissively. As I feel myself fading his Marzipan hand shoots out. "Poob," he says in a high pitched voice as he grabs my breast and squeezes. I simply stand there and let him as this isn't the kind of thing that's supposed to happen. When I open my eyes I'm back in bed. I'm relieved and turn to Simon, snuggling into him. I'm a bit troubled when I smell sugar in his hair.

The morning is bright as I rise and begin my usual daily tasks; look for a new TV research job and do the washing up before lying on the sofa moping. I daydream about my old job and the frantic phone calls and the too-busy-to-think days when I'm looking at the media listings. That, and Jack – Jack and his too confident attitude, Jack and his disrespectful way of speaking to the team, Jack and his exciting habit of pulling me into secret places when no-one else was looking. Today though I can't stop thinking about Marzipan and its sickly sweet smell. I imagine the Marzipan King saying the same thing about his magic kingdom to every girl that appears by his castle and the thought makes me angry, but not for the reasons I expect. "God, he was really a jerk," I tell myself but it sounds hollow. When Simon comes home I'm telling him about the dream before he has the chance to speak.

"Really?" he chuckles, "how weird. So anyway, I've been given another project at work, which is a pain."

"Oh, but that's good," I tilt my head and I almost believe my own response, "it must mean you're doing really well."

"Well, yes, I suppose so." He hunches his shoulders awkwardly, unwilling to show his pleasure. Then he hugs me and my nostrils twitch for the scent of sweets but all I smell is coffee and our pomegranate shower gel. I feel slightly disappointed.

Simon suggests watching TV and I agree, like it's not what we do every night. I secretly enjoy it when the evening's underway but I feel if I don't complain I'm truly not the media tiger between jobs, I'm just a contented housecat. And I can't ever be that, it would be humiliating. I already have to inflate the projects I'm working on as it is whenever I run into old colleagues.

That night I hope for the Marzipan King and for once I get what I want. The flat, sugary kingdom stretches out for miles and the trees are intricately twisted statues of sweets. In the distance stands the castle, the tallest object the eye can see. I turn my head and there he is, standing so close I can smell his sickly flesh. "You came back then," he says in an "I'm not that interested," kind of way.

"Yep. It wasn't really my choice though," I explain.

"Yes it was," he says, suddenly defensive and confrontational, "or you wouldn't be here."

I shrug. "I was curious, I suppose."

"They always are," he leers and again I think, what a jerk. He leads me by the hand towards his castle and I'm overwhelmed by how beautiful it is inside. The ballroom is a vast expanse of glittering surfaces and the Main Hall is as vast as Henry the 8ths court, everything in different coloured Marzipan. He kicks the stool from under one of the violinists and we guffaw as he scrabbles to pick up his broken rock candy violin. "Let's get pissed," says the king, and together we chug down barrel after barrel of fermented sugar. When I wake the next morning I actually have a headache. Simon's already left for work which is a relief; it saves the awkwardness of being the one left behind.

I barely glance at the media listings, instead thinking about marzipan lips and marzipan fingers. When Simon walks through the door his skin seems grey, his clothes so dull and the words he speaks are the same I've heard every evening for the last two years. Yes," I reply curtly to everything. "I don't know," I snap. He pulls away from me, trying not to look hurt. I almost feel sorry for him but my anger is too strong. It's his fault, he shouldn't be so boring.

That night, in the Marzipan Kingdom, I dance with the king alone in the ballroom while a string quartet plays. "You're a great shag," he says loudly enough for the musicians to hear, "can I do you up the arse later?" I laugh because he's so funny – we are a pair of rebels. We don't live by anyone else's rules. I carry on dancing and chuckle at the slightly disgusted sneer of the cello player.

I barely notice the days at home now, I've given up looking at the listings. Instead I stay in bed all day trying to get back to the Kingdom. It only happens at night but I keep trying. Simon is starting to look at me strangely but I don't care, he's probably seeing someone else. I would be.

Friday night he brings home a DVD from the shop. "They're too expensive," I say, "you might as well download."

"I wanted us to watch something together," he said, "without any whiskey or wine or anything."

"Oh God," I sound like a teenager, "it's Friday night, that's what you're supposed to do." He looks at me as though I've said something terrible about his mother so I relent and promise I'll only have one beer. I know I've got at least three in the fridge and he won't notice if I open them in there. We start watching, him lying at one end of the sofa and me at the other, our legs entwined.

An overly dramatic programme about a young murdered girl begins. "They all sound the same," I grumble, beer sloshing in my belly, "How can they all light up a room with their smile? It's like a production line of victims that come with their own internal light bulbs." Simon's face speaks of horror and disappointment. I roll my eyes. "Look, I'm tired, can we argue about my terrible behaviour in the morning?" Taking my cue he stomps, tight-lipped, into the bedroom. "Whatevs," I mutter, and sink down into the couch.

I arrive in the Great Hall where the Marzipan people are feasting at the long table. A sugary fire crackles in the hearth and the ground drips with blood from meaty delicacies. Some of the Marzipan knights nudge each other and make breast honking motions when I walk past and I make sure I swing my hips extra hard. I feel my blood fizz as I make my way through the crowd to the head of the table but I stop dead. Sitting next to the king is a girl, a human girl like myself. The King looks up and I swear I see him roll his eyes.

He waves me over and shoves the priest sitting on his left onto the floor. This at least raises a smile from me but I'm shaking. "Alright tits," he says as I take the empty seat. He piles my plate with the raw, quivering flesh of a pig whose empty eyes glare at me. "Shove that down you. Oh, this is Kelly."

"Hi there," she offers her hand, leaning over the King who tilts his plate to drain the pooling blood. I accept it, smiling politely. I'm shaking her hand when all I want to do is tear it off.

"I'm not really hungry," I push my plate away, eager to get the King alone.

"Oh really?" Kelly looks surprised, "it's really nice." She lifts the leg of a puppy and rips off a chunk, licking at the blood smeared over her face.

"This is fucking boring," says the King, "why don't we all go to the ballroom?"

We're followed by the entire court and I keep my gaze firmly on Kelly as everyone twirls to the music. I can't keep the smirk off my face when the King gestures to me, pulling me to him and launching us through the dancing couples. I breathe in deeply his sickly scent which had so disgusted me at first. I lean my head against his chest, sensing something is wrong but not wanting to look up at first. When I do I see his face connected with Kelly's, their tongues writhing like poisonous slugs. I've never been punched in the stomach but I imagine it creates this same winded, airless feeling. I smack his shoulder, leaving a dent. "What's your problem?" He is furious. People nearby are looking and Kelly just seems confused.

"Why are you kissing her?" I shriek, all pretences torn away.

"I wasn't, duh," he says, "she was going to faint, I was giving her mouth to mouth. Christ, how selfish can you be?" He raises a hand for one of the courtiers to high five him and my anger erupts.

"I'm not stupid," I shriek, "I saw you!"

"Well," he shrugs, "it's not her fault, look how drunk she is." Indeed Kelly is swaying, her eyes unfocused.

"That's not the point," I'm spitting unattractively "you're not, what were you thinking?" He groans and turns away and I can't bear the lack of his attention. "No, stop," I grab at his shoulder, "maybe we can talk about this."

"Yeah," he says with disinterest, "we probably can."

"Look," I push one of the courtiers to the ground. It works; the King raises a half smile. "Look," I'm begging now as I tear off my top, "watch them jiggling around!" I'm ecstatic with his renewing interest. He reaches out and fondles them. "That's not all," I try to sound erotic but I know I sound frighteningly desperate. I pull my trousers down and shimmy in the nude, trousers round my ankles. Everyone claps to the music and I throw my entire being into the performance. I feel all eyes on me and my skin is bathed with attention.

Behind me I hear a muffled chortle. The courtiers beside the King are smirking and my movements become less fluid. I want to cover up but if I do they'll know how humiliated I am. The King breaks into raucous laughter and the rest of the room erupts. I stop still, my arms covering my breasts. I chuckle weakly and furtively glance about for my clothes. "These what you're looking for?" The King holds them up and throws them over my head where they're caught by one of his subjects. The game continues and all the while I force the laughter until tears run down my face. Someone kicks me in the back and I fall to the floor still laughing, laughing or weeping I no longer know which, and they stand over me and I can't see through the tears and their faces blur…

I wake in mine and Simon's bed and stare at the wall. It's the calm darkness just before dawn and I sense Simon lying behind me. I turn, excited that I've been given this chance to make everything better and right again, but something's wrong. Simon is still and the sickening smell of marzipan hasn't gone from my nostrils. When I reach out to him I feel his sugary shell and notice his lack of breath. Feeling as though it's my own heart being eaten, I do the only thing I can and slowly chew my way through.

THE PROBLEM ROCK

The Problem Rock lay in a lonely mountainous range between Kingdom A and Kingdom B. Each morning the people from Kingdom A left their lush green paradise, carrying their egg shaped bodies on their pink legs, their only eye a balloon held aloft by a single pink hand, to tell the rock their problems with the mouth that nestled in their chests. Equally the people of Kingdom B – their only eye a lollipop clasped to their blue egg shaped bosoms – left their rich industrial city to queue on the other side of the rock. "It's always been this way," an elder would say if an impertinent youth asked why. "Don't you feel better for getting your problems out in the open? Now stop pestering me, I've got arthritis."

The rock patiently listened to trouble after trouble year after year, generation after generation and millennia after millennia. One day, on a bright spring morning, it got bored. "They expect me to sit here saying nothing, they have no idea I'm even alive," it thought as a boy from Kingdom A whined on about not getting enough time to play after dinner. The rock said nothing, hoping it was going through a phase.

By the third decade, however, it definitely didn't feel any better. A man, clutching the string of his balloon which gazed intently at the rock with a large blue eye, was relating his current concern. "So yesterday my fiancé asked me to feed her pet Gribble, but I didn't know what to answer because I didn't have my tally chart to hand. Last week I remember she brought me a spoon from the kitchen so that's a point on her side, but I'm quite sure I did three nice things for her so if I'd fed her Gribble she would have been in debt by four nice deeds. I just had to say no and now she says I'm being unreasonable."

"What shall I do?" thought the rock. "They've never heard me speak before. They might get cross. And who else will they tell their troubles to? I serve a purpose; I can't just give it up like that." It waited another decade before thoroughly being certain that enough was enough.

The sky was a brilliant blue and the two queues were still miles long. A woman from Kingdom B, her lollipop eye an arresting green with a bright red edge, was telling him quietly that she had been visiting Person F in Kingdom A once too often, and her husband Person N was getting suspicious. "He knows, you know," said the rock quietly so no-one else could hear, "he's just waiting for you to tell him."

The woman stepped back. "Did anyone hear that?"

"Hear what?"

"Oh," she bit her lip, "nothing, it was nothing."

The other lollipops and balloons pretended to concentrate on other things, on the horizon of grey and white mountains or tiny rocks on the ground, or the green paradise and vast city in the distance – anything to avoid appearing as though they were staring at a lady in the process of a breakdown. She stepped closer to the rock, "Are you sure?"

"Definitely," said the rock, "I never forget a face, especially if it's weeping."

"Oh dear," the woman pulled at her lip with her fingers. "Th-thank you." She sloped off, her eye held close to her chest. The next person, whom it recognised as Person Q, stepped forward.

"Well," he began, "my neighbour won't admit that the leak came from her cave, but it dripped down into my cave, and it got flooded and now I have to fix it all by myself."

The rock listened, impassively, as the people expected it to. Then, in a low voice, it said, "Your neighbours always complain about you. In fact, I think they might be plotting."

Person Q stood straight, almost releasing his eye into the clouds. "You can"-

"Yes, yes I can talk. Now, while we stand here talking your neighbours are discussing what they can do with the extra room. Person J has already decided where she'll put her new vase of flowers."

It watched Person Q scuttle back to the sunshine and trees with a growing sense of satisfaction. It felt better than rain after a summer of dryness. If it had had eyes like those surrounding it they would be glowering with naughtiness. Instead its expressionless grey surface reflected nothing; the beetles continued to tickle it's crevices with their tiny feet and the roots of moss continued to search for new and exciting spots of minerals. And all the while it offered caution after caution, complete fabrications that made the rock wish it could hug itself with glee. When the last person finally left for the day, it was thrilled at the idea of doing it all again tomorrow.

Next morning the queues were back, this time with caution in their single eyes. Nonetheless they stepped before the rock, one by one, to be taunted, tortured and japed, each little story getting more outrageous. "No, actually I heard your mother never loved you," it told Person D, not quite a teenager, his egg-shaped blue body standing in the awkward manner youths often do. "So the fact that she didn't let you have any-more liquid jolly juice is neither here nor there." The rock had to admit it did feel an odd sort of twinge, a mild apoplexy of the crust as it watched him trudge hesitantly back to Kingdom B, but it didn't last very long.

The queues changed considerably over the next few weeks. The people no longer waited quietly or patiently, each member bickering with another nearby or accusing others of butting in. Balloons floated into the air and lollipops fell to the floor amidst cries of, "she pushed me!" "He made me go blind!" The rock chuckled quietly and doled out the same warnings and ill-conceived advice.

"Rock," wailed a woman groping blindly in front of her, "I'm certain my parents adopted me but they say I'm wrong. What should I do?"

The rock looked out on the two lines of barely concealed chaos, people either openly bellowing or hissing between clenched teeth. "You should confront them with the evidence you found. What was it again?"

"They don't have any baby pictures of me," she said, "none at all! They say they're in the attic but I've never seen them."

"Well," the rock said, "it's irrefutable."

In the second month everyone in the queue had bruises and wore sour expressions. The ones still with eyes glanced at each other suspiciously and the others elbowed those in front when they could, but the rock still wasn't satisfied. "Kingdom B said your balloons look silly," it said to Kingdom A, and "they say lollies are for kids," to Kingdom B.

"Oh really?" they each said, "oh really?"

The next morning the two Kingdoms marched once more to the desolate mountains but instead of queuing at the rock they formed two opposing walls, staring each other down with makeshift eyes. "Oho," thought the rock, "my luck is in!"

"Ready," yelled a man standing apart from Kingdom B.

"Ready," cried a woman standing apart from Kingdom A.

"Go!" They launched into each other, arms flailing and knees jutting outwards, doing all they could to inflict harm on the enemy. A man from Kingdom B was being pummelled by two ladies from A and a lady from A had her knees kicked by Kingdom B children; it was pandemonium.

"Run, my baby," shrieked a Kingdom A woman to her daughter whose hair was being yanked by a Kingdom B boy.

The rock sat back and watched, satisfied for the first time in its existence.

"That's it!" fumed the Ruler of Kingdom B. The fighting continued.

"That's it!" The Queen of Kingdom A was not to be outdone. At last the subjects began to take notice, and waited breathless and exhausted for orders. "From now on we divide ourselves up, and we use this rock as a divider."

"Quite right," said the Kingdom B Ruler, "That's exactly what I was going to say. We'll just have to tell each other our problems from now on." The King and the Queen shook hands, glowering at each other suspiciously. "Right!"

"Right!"

The Kingdoms marched back to their lush paradise and their big city and the rock waited excitedly for the next event. In the next decade more moss crept over its surface. A Century went by and a colony of beetles made a home of one of its hollows. By the third century, reality hit. The rock stared at the mountains in the silent plains, and listened to the sounds of the chirruping insects, bored and alone.

TIME TASTIC TOURS

I'm sitting at the bar, acting real calm, waiting with the others for the guide to arrive and usher us onto the Time-Tastic Tours train platform. My bag burns a hole on the barstool next to me and I feel as though everyone can see what's in it, but of course I'm being paranoid. If they were to see inside I'd be in a whole heap of trouble and it wouldn't do to raise suspicion. No doubt my fear is heightened by Valium withdrawal; it's been three weeks since my last one and everyone feels like the enemy. I remember the way the doctor's eyes licked my curves and short blonde hair. "There's nothing wrong with you, Lin," he said, "at least try to wean yourself off." Nothing wrong, he said. I just shrugged. In my game you learn to quit making trouble.

Well I did try and now I'm here. I look around at the other patrons. The bartender hums a tune as he dries and replaces glasses like something from a musical made many moons ago. Leaning against one of the comfy fuscia sofas, elaborate cocktails on the table in front of them, sits a couple from the 20th century 20s, gesturing wildly in conversation, no doubt loaded up on 'smelling salt.' On a table nearby a small group of pygmy warriors show each other tourist photos on cameras while right at the back, drinking rowdily, is a large group of Vikings. I notice one sitting a ways apart from the others, studying the wall and tugging at his beard with a resigned expression. Elsewhere an Egyptian princess is checking her diamond studded nails and two long-skirted women with the furtive look of suffragettes share a table.

There's the usual parade of modern folks like myself in temperature controlled onesies, puppy patterns and kitten pictures on those worn by a small group middle aged women. One of them, I notice, has had her silver Persian cat's head grafted to her stomach, its silver ears twitching nervously from the specially cut hole in the cloth. Each time the old broad nibbles her Battenberg she feeds the poor bastard. After a while they all fade from my thoughts. I'm here, with my bag, to do what I've gotta do.

"Hey, toots," he says, my throat closing when he picks up my bag. "What's a pretty gal like you doin' alone?" He's dressed in the be-wigged, flouncy Georgian style but clearly likes hanging out in the forties. As if to prove this, he sparks up a match with his thumbnail and lights my cigarette. I try to appear nonchalant, real friendly like, as if I'm there for a holiday too. I focus on the TV set fixed high on the wall. "Don't you just love that show?" he grins, showing cavities and gaps plugged with papier mache. He nods towards the live feed of Days of the Stone Age, a live feed of a band of poor bastards in the current Ice Age above the miles of reinforced ceiling, living life the ancient way for our entertainment.

They're trying to look happy in a cave surrounded by animal pelt. One is carving fur from a lion corpse, mangling the thing but trying to appear as though it's easier than cheating at cards. To me it was so blatant a piece of television propaganda that I always wondered how no other shmuck could see it. "We don't send terrorists into history to disappear," I could almost hear the government say, "Look how easy it is to survive even as far back as the stone-age. Those criminals choose to hide there to avoid prison."

I keep my eyes on the screen and half smile, screaming inside at him to put down the bag. Finally he places it on the floor without mishap, sliding in next to me. "The easy money's on Hadley to win, he's a man's man. Keeps his trap shut and gets on with the job, no messing. Plus he knows how to treat a dame." He glances at me, hoping I've been bowled over by his experience with women. I don't react and he blusters on. "I mean, he knows what he's doing, he just takes charge of a situation." He takes a long puff of his cigarette.

I shrug. I'm unwilling to enter a full conversation or next I'll be hearing about his family and drinking problem.

He gestures to the barman and orders a chocolate truffle liqueur. You can take the Georgian out of his time zone…"They say Time Tastic Tours is the best," here he leans in close enough for me to smell tooth decay, "they've got special bunks at the back for lonely types."

"You don't say."

He senses I'm tired of his company and looks awkward a time. "I don't know how you cope in the future, cooped up underground like this, just knowing everything outside is dead and frozen. It's like being in a coffin."

I look him in the eye for the first time, "Well, at least everyone I know at the moment is still alive." He winces.

"OK, well, how would you like to sit next to me on the tour, shoot the breeze, cheer me up over all those dead relatives of mine?"

"Maybe," I say, unwilling to be a total bitch in case people notice. I was about to say more when our guide strolls in from a back door, a petite Asian lady in faded get-up of the upper class; an elegant dress with noticeable repairs, glass costume jewellery and a bug-bitten fur coat past its best days. She smiled with lips caked in red liner and bats peeling false lashes.

"Afternoon ladies and gentlemen, this way and the tour shall commence." Speed drinking and excited chatter ensues and I snatch my bag, checking the zip over and over with sweaty palms. We follow her like prize cattle down a corridor lit with fairy lights and painted with corny suns and stars. "Welcome to the past, present and future," proclaims a sign hanging over the tunnel opening onto the underground platform. I high tail it to the front of the group to avoid the Georgian; the last thing I need now is for people to notice my actions.

The train pulls up beside us, its see-through body glowing pus yellow in the false light. "Don't be afraid of breaking this," says the guide, "this stuff is as strong as crystal." She demonstrates by tapping it hard and I imagine her crashing through onto the seats inside, but nothing of the kind happens and everyone scrambles aboard like the train might screech away and leave us all behind. Before I make my way on I catch a glimpse of her sipping from a whiskey bottle hidden in her coat.

I find a four person seat with a table in the middle all to myself. The purple cushion beneath me is created for luxury and I sigh in relief, clutching my bag in my lap. Just then the bored Viking sits opposite me. "Hope you don't mind," he says in a low voice, struggling a little to speak English, "I can't take them anymore."

"Not a problem," I smile tightly, wishing I could reach across and slap him.

Those needing language translations insert earphones and the guide takes her place at the front of the carriage. Her eyes look real vacant now and her grin is just a little too spacey. In the back somewhere a mother reassures her kid that yes, we'll be moving soon but no, the seat covers are not for chewing. "Toilets are located through that back door," the guide points vaguely over our heads, "and the emergency buttons are above you. If during the tour you wish to exit in a different time zone please present your boarding pass and we will fit you with one of these," she holds up a contraption no bigger than a button, "for the company to monitor conversation for your safety. Any mention of time travel will result in imprisonment. Any problems and please do press the button on the back. Please do not be alarmed by the suddenness with which we pull away from the station."

We launch from the platform with a violent jerk and the view surrounding us blurs. A couple of dames squeal in phony fear and a child starts crying for real. "Normality will resume imminently," said the guide, taking another secret swig. When our ride slows down we're surrounded by an open market crammed with chickens and oxen, mosaic pottery and spices as colourful as the tunics of the people passing through. Our guide presses a button and we hear the chatter of a hundred languages and smell earthy sweat underlined by perfume. The city of Rome's heat, however, can't touch us in this air-conditioned vacuum.

"You can't wave at the people, George," one lady laughs at the back, expecting everyone to be just as tickled by her son, "they see us as a wall. The train is invisible to them."

"They're stupid, aren't they?" said George, and I bite my lip when his mother explains they're not stupid, just uneducated. As if in answer to the boy's comment the doors beep and a tall Nubian woman wrapped in electric blue steps on board. The Romans nearest us don't even notice she's disappeared, each focused on his or her transaction. The guide checks the woman's boarding pass and allows her through. I beg her silently not to sit near me, not to mess around with my plan any further, but what do you know? She sits right next to the Viking. I sweat as the train lurches into warp speed once again.

On we go following detours, all the while I'm trying to remember the route told me without whispering it aloud. Finally we encounter a terrain that's been explained to me so many times I know it before it's announced: endless green plains and hills on the horizon. Ashen remains of a log fire sat in the middle of a cluster of round hovels with thatched, pointed roofs. "Iron Age," the guide calls brightly, her blood apparently at the right alcohol level.

"Get up slowly," I tell myself, "you're here on holiday, none of these people have seen you before, you don't look suspicious." I stand real calm, brandishing my boarding pass. I smile with vacuous excitement as I pull on the long, shapeless cloth dress supplied by the Tour Company and am fitted with a monitoring brooch. The doors slide open and the coolness of the air flushes my body with goose-pimples and fills my nostrils with the comforting shit smell of livestock and earth. I step onto the green grass but I know I'm being followed. I turn quickly and there they are; the Viking and the Nubian right behind me. I try to shake them by striding off purposely but they keep close. My heart on my ribcage feels like a bull charging a fence.

"Good day," says the Nubian in a velvet voice, "it seems we each have business here, why not accompany each other?"

"I am very pleased by this," says the Viking, eyeing her muscular frame.

"Yeah, sure, why not, let's have a ball," I say, proving to myself once again that any situation can be handled, Valium or no. But by God I wish I had some. We make our way past log fences enclosing sheep, goats and a small group of cattle. We sit on logs next to the fire and I think over the instructions from the guide on surviving the Iron Age without needing rescue: Don't wake them, explain you are travellers passing through who will work for supplies and don't ask too many awkward questions. If all else fails press the button on the monitor. Everything feels too real, too goddamn present.

"I lost my brother in this place, you see," says the Viking so loud it startles the goats, "and I made a promise to my father that I will search him out and bring him back to us. At first I wandered the land but, in my despair, I fell against the stone wall that protects my village. Only, it was no longer a stone wall. At first I thought I was mad but I could see it for the first time. I tried to show my brothers but they saw nothing. I waited for hours but they left me there alone, and the next train pulled up and the doors opened. The guide said I must be special." He looks as though he's actually inflating with pride and I think, goddamn it, finding the train means nothing. You were just the right idiot in the right place at the right time. The Nubian raises a finger to her lips hoping to silence him but he carries on, "The Gods have frowned much upon my mother this year, I cannot bear her suffering. I will find or avenge my brother." I stealthily reach for the knife in my stocking and can already feel its leather sheath when the Nubian throws her hand over his throat.

"Your mother shall suffer more when I send her your entrails if you do not keep silent." His eyes are so large I picture them falling from his skull, but he seems placid when she lets him go.

"Very well," he grumbles, "your point is made, a little more violently than necessary."

Our commotion has not gone unnoticed and my worst fears are realised; the faces that greet us at the roundhouse entrances are not happy ones. My eyes flick from angry bearded men to exhausted looking women, their weather beaten frowns staring us down, trying to figure out what assholes would appear from nowhere and disturb them this way. Were we attacking? Were we stealing from them? They chatter in a grimy, grating tongue and one large man emerges and looms over the Viking, sickle in hand. "Please, be calm," The Viking holds his up.

I look over the rest of the community; one person stands out, his face smoother than the others, less sure of himself. There he is, Terry Mascapani, sent here for knowing too much. About what exactly I couldn't tell you, but it's enough for a vigilante group to be searching him out, howling for the taste of his blood, and for the Underground to want to move him to a safer place. Though he wears the same get up as the others his blue eyes are hunted and I can tell he's looking for the right time to run. With his dark hair and faerie cheekbones I'd probably be making a drunken pass in another life, but this is now and it's how it is. I don't look at him long – I don't want the others to notice I've singled him out.

"We are but travellers," I say hoarsely in the phrase I'd pretended to learn from the guide, but had actually been practicing for several days. "We are passing through and wish to seek shelter and food so that we may be on our way." One of the children starts crying and her mother picks her up, shushing and rocking from side to side. Two men with suspicion in their eyes and anger in their fists stand beside their friend with the sickle.

"We were unprepared for travellers this forenoon," he says in a calmer tone, "Once you have what you need you will willingly go?"

"Yes," I feel like my insides might leak from my body with relief.

He regarded us for a moment before nodding. "Very well."

The group begins chattering again, too many words to pick up. The leader sends us in different directions with different camp members, the Nubian with a group of women to spin cloth, the Viking with men to tend the animals and I'm shown how to grind flour for bread. The toothless hag leans over the device, a wooden stick pointing up through a hole in the centre of two large stones, one on top of the other. She gibbers gummily, drool leaking from the corners of her mouth, and I want to hit her, to stop this disgusting display – that, or take a Valium so I don't care. She turns the stick and the top stone grinds against the bottom so flour trickles from the sides and collects in the wooden bowl underneath. I nod and take over, glad to be rid of the old broad. Now all I have to do is keep my eyes peeled.

It doesn't take long; Terry's drawn to me like a whore to a violent pimp. He crouches nearby, hammering farming tools on a flat anvil beside the fire. I admire his tenacity; if you've got to hide out effectively make yourself indispensable. His eyes were fixed on me and his face so pale I wondered if he wouldn't just die on me anyway.

Eventually it just becomes too much and he approaches me, eyes darting this way and that. "What…brings you to our land?" he asks, not quite hiding his accent.

I point to the monitor on my dress collar and put my finger to my lips. "My friends and I have a great many miles to travel and had need of some friendly assistance," I say, all the while writing a message in the flour. When he reads it his eyes bulge: "Here to help. Trust me." He looks into my eyes, a mad hope igniting. After a few seconds he remembers to speak; I hope the silence hasn't been long enough for the listeners to notice.

"Very well," he says in an impressively even tone, "If you need anything further I shall be at my station."

The hours crawl by and I have to get this damned monitor off. Whenever I think I'm alone someone walks past or offers me a cup of water. Eventually I make a show of announcing a call of nature and stride into some nearby bushes. I wander until the camp is hidden by leaves and remove my bag from under my woollen sack. My fingers find the cool metal nozzle of The Detacher. Gently as a detective threatening a nun I clip the vice like claw around the button on my tunic and unhook it. I catch it before it falls to the ground, stashing it in my stocking, just like I've been taught.

I take my place back at the grinding stones, waiting for the moment when I can make my way to Terry. I stroll over real casual, cooing with admiration over his handiwork, trying to sound like someone making an embarrassingly obvious play. "Show me how you use those tongs, won't you?" I say, sliding my hand across his back. I smell his sweat from weeks of not washing and endless fear, and it speaks to me of excitement and primal things. I nod down to my bag, make him look down. When he catches a glimpse of the detacher I feel his entire body spasm. The device has been the stuff of legend for decades and few have actually seen it, and here it is. I delicately reveal my stocking, to show him not to get rid of it completely just yet. He nods to say he understands but not before he gets a full eyeful of what's on show. I don't mind. He hides the bag beneath his own smock, loudly extolling the details of blacksmithing for all those around us for several more minutes.

"I found you at last," says a voice rich in accusation. Terry and I look up guiltily at the Nubian. Dammit, how long has she been there?

"Yes, I was just getting to grips with the, uh, this stuff, and this man here was being so very helpful." I'm sounding as flirtatious as I can but there's an amateur edge in my voice I haven't heard for years.

"I will set up my spinning beside you while you make bread, so we are not separated. We may become easily lost and bad things could happen, no?" She arranges her spinning implements, a long spindle sticking up from the centre of a flat stone and a pile of stinking sheep wool, and sits cross legged while I resume my task. I smile blankly and make small talk, grinding rocks together until they scream.

From the corner of my eye I watch Terry make odd, twitching movements as he hammers the objects in front of him until I know he's managed to break free. I have to get to him somehow, to lead him away from the others, but just as an idea comes to me I'm pushed to the ground by the Nubian. So this is it, I've let things slip and now it's time to bite the big one. Instead of finishing me off, however, I look up to see the Viking slump forward, axe in hand and dagger in his chest, dark blood draining into the ground. The Nubian looks me square in the eyes, "you were distracted."

"We gotta get out of here but quick," I grab the target and the three of us make a run for it across the field to the train station. Behind us women are screaming and I know the men won't be far behind us. We ditch our monitors in the bushes, diving towards a cluster of rocks beside an abandoned fort.

We push our way through the crowds at the station, me holding Terry's hand, knocking aside groups in onesies, families in Renaissance splendour and a gaggle of freaked out hippies. We keep our heads down when we step onto the train and catch no eyes while we try to stroll casual but real fast to the bathroom compartment. "We need to get him to the stone-age," I say to the Nubian, "they're waiting for him there."

"My orders were to bring him to the Chinese Dynasty."

"I spoke to them not long ago," I whisper, trying not to sound frustrated, "they've had to change plans and we don't have time to monkey around." She defers to my years of experience and reputation with the Underground but I can see she's not happy. We've only got a stop to go, but a lot can happen in a stop. We make our way past the showers and smile politely at a middle aged woman sitting on a comfy seat, her onesie pulled down to expose a deflated breast and a miniature dachshund in her arms, its little lips suckling at genetically added milk.

The far handle to the compartment begins to turn. I stare at the lady and hold a finger to my lips, hoping my glare is meaningful enough. We dive into a toilet cubicle and I gesture for Terry to crouch on the toilet seat. After I lock the door he grabs my hand again, his grip almost blinding me. Light heeled footsteps and the sound of a cane tap their way towards the breast feeding lady. "So cute at that age, aren't they?" rasps an ancient female voice, wispy as cobwebs.

"Oh, they are," says the woman in the chair.

The Nubian heaves herself to the top of the cubicle in a single, graceful movement and flings a knife downwards. A small scuffle and a quivering shriek follows but I know it doesn't belong to the intended victim, who attempts to scale the toilet door to reach us. I heave it open as hard as I can onto the old crone who drops like a sack of genetically modified kittens. In her arms is a very shocked dachshund with milk around his chops. His owner is looking from him to the old lady on the floor to us in such rhythmic succession she looks like an automaton – an automaton with a flappy breast hanging out.

I push open the door as far as the fallen body allows and we hurry past, but from the corner of my eye I see her sit sharply up and pull a gun from her pocket. The shot dents the door as I shut it behind us and I turn to the frightened eyes of the tour group and their guide. "Relax," I say, "everything is under control." They almost look ready to believe us until the old lady bursts in.

"You are in direct violation of government proceedings," she says, all traces of quiver gone from her voice, "so don't be stupid, give up the prisoner and come with me."

"Can you promise him a proper trial?" says The Nubian.

"Of course, this is what we are working towards."

She didn't notice the woman behind her, breast still dangling and industrial breast pump held high in the air. She didn't, that is, until it clattered down onto her head. When she fell there was a furious gleam in the dog owner's eyes. "She used my Moompsy as a human shield."

The train screeches to a halt and the three of us step out into ice and snow. The cold attacks our faces with tiny, sharp hands. Ahead is a small rock mountain with a cave entrance and we trudge on till we see a number of glum looking people watching another try to light a fire with damp wood. We dart behind a rock, holding our breath, and watch. After a few moments one of the watchers gets up impatiently and takes over, rubbing a stick which catches alight almost immediately. I point to a secluded spot behind some tough looking ferns and we creep towards them. Now all we can do is wait. Terry has a funny look on his face. "Didn't you say we had to wait in the stone-age?"

"Yes," I snap, "that's what we're doing."

"What is it?" The Nubian too sounded frustrated.

"It's just," Terry hunches his shoulders, obviously saying something he doesn't want to. "I recognise those people. This isn't the real stone-age it's the ice-age now in our time. It's where they film that TV show. They won't be waiting for us here – we're in the wrong place."

The Nubian looks at me, her eyes dark molten. "Is this true?"

"Not true at all, mon petite Cherie," booms a voice from the forest. We're joined by a slender man in a black outfit, flanked by a horde of the most evil looking bastards I've ever seen. It's Herve Herst, once a French philosopher from the sixties – till he discovered the Time Trains and how much money he could make as a TV executive in our time. Plus he isn't really French. "Au contrair, we're right here waiting." The goons grab Terry by his arms. He looks like one of those possums that die as soon as it gets into a sticky situation.

"Where are you taking him?" The Nubian stands beside me, brandishing a dagger and glancing at me for further instruction.

"Just somewhere he ought to be," the faux-Frenchman man says, "his body will become an atom of time and space which exists forever in memory, although the physical form has ceased to be."

The Nubian loses patience, "now!" she launches herself into the goons, stabbing and hitting and kicking, but when she sees me standing perfectly still the anguish is distracting and she's overpowered in minutes. I try to show her I'm sorry but she doesn't seem to buy it.

"I'm afraid there's a group who's paid good money to meet you," said the exec, and Terry was carried off. He didn't even struggle, I found myself no longer attracted to him. "As for you, ma petite poire, I think you will enjoy the Triassic period." The Nubian is dragged away, kicking and fighting. The TV exec turns to me. "Your country thanks you."

"Yeah, yeah, a criminal bunch of psychos thank me you mean. My cut had better be there."

"But of course," he sidles just a little too close, smelling of breath mints and cheap wine, "I trust you'll think of me?"

"Who knows, I often get Night Terrors." I gesture to the group surrounding the fire in the distance. "What about Hadley, will you get him back to the stone-age when the show's over?"

"Nah," the exec wrinkles his nose at the thought of such an unpleasant task, "his parents'll probably club us to death."

I leave the next question unanswered, I don't want to know. I head off to catch another train, to find my money and make my way to where people don't have to hide underground like bodies in coffins, and maybe I'll buy a stately home during the Regency. I feel good; I guess the doctor was right about not needing Valium after all.

WE INTERRUPT WITH THIS MESSAGE

The praying cut through my sleep and nothing infuriates me more than being woken. Dreams are like gold from a mystical realm; they fade in our world from pure beauty to dusty crap. From the beginning the religious fanatics and those I met afterwards were not going to be friends of mine.

The muttered chants stopped when my eyes opened and I caught their shadows scurrying into the next room. "Don't you steal my TV," I yelled, leaping from under the covers. My front room had expensive items which weren't welcome to the sticky fingers of strangers, religious or not. "Why are you here?" No answer came.

My eyes fought the dark while I located the light switch but, once on, there was no sign of them. I checked behind the sofa, the chair and the adjoining kitchen but they'd gone. There were no breakages in the windows and no clues on the carpets, and when I went back to bed I jolted at every sound.

At work the next day I knew my eyes were red. My head set squeezed my temples more than usual and the customers used words like 'overcharged' and 'lawsuit.' One lady promised to meet me at the office with a baseball bat. "You're not listening to me," she raged as I spotted Alicia and Kevin passing me on a time wasting trip to the hot drinks machine. I waved them over and they checked for supervisors before joining me. I held the microphone away from my mouth, "hi."

"What's up Gemma?" A fleeting look passed between them. Was that impatience at talking to me? Well, fuck you both then.

"Oh, nothing much," I replied, pulling the shrieking woman away from my ears, "have either of you ever had a problem with…religious types? In the home?"

Alicia flounced away, arms swinging and hips swaying. Kevin stared longingly after her like a St. Bernard and I realised I was interrupting his hormones. "Oh, don't mind her," he said, "I think they overran her flat too a while back."

"Oh. Well, why are they there? What did she do to get rid of them?"

"Look," Kevin lowered his voice and leaned in, "people don't talk about that sort of thing. Maybe let them know you don't want them there. Just don't go on about it, OK?"

I heard their droning prayers through the front door. "God dammit," I muttered as I struggled with the key, eventually bursting in to find my front room packed with people praying and weeping and rocking back and forth in exaltation, wrinkled bits exposed and all over my floors. "Why are you here?" I yelled, but no one even looked my way. They wailed on and on until my ears felt as though they were melting. I ran through to my bedroom but it was the same in there, nude people squeezed in from corner to corner, praying and chanting in dreary repetition.

"You had to come from somewhere," I checked the walls once again for holes. If they hadn't come from outside they had to come from within. I tried to step through the bathroom mirror, expecting a mystical light and my digits to disappear through the surface, but nothing. My nails clicked against the glass and all that stared back was my untidy reflection. I persevered; nothing. I tried to think of something and got a headache at the base of my neck before hearing the sound of a battery running; the laptop. The shop had told me not to leave it in standby all the time and now I knew why.

I tiptoed my way through the fanatics until I stood in front of the dark screen on the desk. I reached a hand forth but pulled it back quickly – what if my particles rearranged in an unsightly manner? Or my arm was pulled off? "Stop being such a pussy," I told myself, and plunged headfirst inside.

It didn't hurt. All I felt was an enveloping of warmth as though a blanket had been thrown over me. I felt enveloped and safe, like I was in a womb of cotton wool. It ended all too soon and I wondered briefly if I would ever feel such contentment again, and then I landed on my head with a thud. My limbs were no longer mine to control and an unfamiliar smile stretched over my face as I strutted through a sunlit space with tasteful white walls and pine floors. Individuals of all weights, colours and ages both cheerful and sad stared at me from photographs adorning the walls. "What's going on?" I tried to say, but my mouth barely moved and all that emerged was a strangulated cry. An attractive woman in a well cut suit waited for me at the far end of the room, accepting my hand when I thrust it unwillingly into hers.

"Welcome to the Museum of Very Important People," she said in an oddly stilted manner. "This person was important," she pointed to a photograph of an angry looking fat man, "and so was this one."

I said in a clear voice not my own, "This is very interesting, but not quite what I'm looking for." It felt as though I had vomited without warning.

"Oh dear," said the woman as if she were reading lines, "Perhaps you ought to try next door."

Everything faded to black and my body was again adrift, only this time in the uncomfortable manner of a fairground ride. I was once more at the furthest end of the same museum, only this time moustaches had been drawn on the subjects with pen; handlebars, Edwardians, toothbrushes, pencils and more, even on the women and children. "Welcome to the Museum of Important Moustaches," said the same lady, greeting me as before only this time our smiles were wider and her make up fresher.

"Yes, this is fascinating," I said, "please do tell me all about them."

An excited male voice boomed throughout the room whilst the lady pointed to photographs and mimed telling a story, "For a day out you'll never forget come and visit The Museum of Important Moustaches."

It was very quiet – the museum had disintegrated and I lay in the foetal position on a white ground. The sky as far as I could see – which wasn't far – was black and the only sound was the distant hum of the laptop like a static ocean. A sobbing noise forced me upright. The land was empty save for the odd cluster of bare, twisted trees and a puffy nude man sitting on a bench holding something, his arm drawing back and forth slowly as he wept. When I approached he looked up, face sharp as an angry fox and eyes black and hollow. "Um, hello?" I said. He continued staring for a moment before going back to his task.

What was he doing? Some kind of oil was spilling over the floor, seeping from his leg, which then plopped onto the ground. No, clearly it was a fake leg. Legs don't fall off. Or maybe they do here. I took a step back. "I don't know what else to do," he said in a small voice. He began the same process on his other leg. It wasn't oil.

"Stop it, for Christ's sake!" I screeched. He looked up with hopeful eyes.

"You want me to stop?"

"Yes," I couldn't stop looking at the plump white leg on the floor, "what the Hell are you doing it for anyway?"

His shoulders slumped and his face looked suddenly tired and old. "I don't know what else to do," he repeated.

"Well, don't do that. What was all that about moustaches?"

"Oh," he rolled his eyes, "You took part in an Interruption. You just have to wait until they're over. It happens to us all now and then." He looked up suddenly, a new light shining from his face. "We must get you to the Mayor."

A sense of misgiving crawled into my stomach. "Oh, I really can't, I've got…work to finish, and then there's the cat, and…"

"Please," he begged, almost wept. His forehead was wrinkled like a Shar Pei, and I could never refuse a Shar Pei. I reasoned that if I spoke to the Mayor I could probably get him to recall the fanatics, so I followed the strange puffy man as he hopped across the white terrain, watching him disappear for moments into the dark before reappearing, shadows making craters of the folds in his flesh, and all the while the battery hum of the laptop whispered reassuringly in the background.

"There it is, the Mayor's office," my companion pointed ahead at a stocky white building. I went to knock on the door but a chubby hand barred my way. "That's not how you do it," said the Shar Pei incredulously. He threw his head back and yowled a bizarre, laboriously long howl. For several seconds I considered running home but he was then answered with an equally unearthly wail. The handle to the door turned and out popped a man wearing a top hat and nothing else…aside from the small tree growing from his belly button.

"Ah, visitors," he beamed, "it's been a while. Would you like an apple? Fresh batch just grown." He gestured to the fruit sprouting from the branches just above his head, which looked suspiciously dark. "Oh, go on," he reached up and plucked one, handing it to me. I yelped and dropped it – it was soft and fluffy. When I saw how offended they both looked, I picked it back up and pretended to take a bite – it was definitely black fluff.

"Well don't eat it off the floor," scoffed the Mayor. The Shar Pei snuffled with laughter.

"He told you off," he said with approval between chuckles. I decided this was the most annoying alternate universe I had ever been to. "She told me to stop chopping my leg off," he pointed right at me, the tip of his finger brushing against my face. It was slightly sweaty and smelled of vinegar.

"She did?" The Mayor appraised me with new interest. I held my hands up.

"Look, if I've transgressed some law I can go, I just want somebody to help me get rid of the…"

"But don't you see what this means?" The Mayor's arms stretched out dramatically, like an old-fashioned actor giving a speech. I shrugged.

"Not really."

They looked at me and back at each other before settling back on me, all the while making small 'I can't believe it' whimpering sounds. "Come with us."

I followed them as they hopped their way towards the town square, giggling and squealing like a pair of large flabby children. Now and then I spotted a figure watching from the shadows but before I could catch up with them, if only to attempt a sensible conversation, the Mayor would throw an apple in their direction and scream "meeting, meeting at the pillar – maybe if you're passing by but don't if not!" The battery still hummed above me.

We arrived at a giant stone statue of a seven headed frog in a town square where a nude crowd had gathered. Some had odd, melted faces. A dog grew from the side of another. Still more were as flat as paper and floated through the air while others walked on four legs, their fingers stretching down to their toes. A hot dog vendor with zips for eyes pushed a cart and called "get your hot dogs here, if you like, if not then don't and perhaps purchase a nice ice cream instead from someone else. It is quite warm so maybe you should do that." Their hopeful staring eyes were like a weight I couldn't carry. What was it they wanted? Some sort of speech? To know what life in the other world was like?

I blinked and found myself sitting in a booth in a 50s style diner. My body once again felt like it had been lifted awkwardly through the air and I just wanted a second to hold my head still. I was hanging on to the arm of a boy I had never met and staring at a burger. "Aw, gee, what will we do?" I simpered, "we have no relish."

"New, easy to use and portable," announced a smooth voice, "simply strap it to your head and cover your meal in the delicious topping of your choice. Now comes with milk for that emergency hot beverage." Strapped onto one side of my head was a salt shaker and on the other was a tiny jug of mustard, while sticking out from my forehead was a spoon.

"It's so easy to use," assured my boyfriend as we leaned down and tipped the mustard onto our meals. The table was sprayed with salt.

"No fuss, no muss," I agreed perkily, stirring my tea and ignoring the big gob of mustard falling into it.

"Condiments-to-go, available at all stores now."

"I suppose you could always start by doing what you did earlier," whispered the Shar Pei from the front row.

I took a very deep breath – I was back in front of the stone frog being stared at by a throng of naked people. I didn't feel much better off. I had the horrible sensations preluding a panic attack; a dry mouth, shaking hands, veins aflame and an urgent need to run or hide in a toilet. I opened my mouth and a hush went over the crowd. Nerves had always made me hungry but that last 'Interruption' hadn't helped. "Um, could someone just get me a hot dog or something?"

The entire crowd dived for the cart and by the time I was covered in a pile of hot dogs the vendor appeared to be dead, blood seeping outwards and limbs pointing in hideous directions. I probably should have been put off but honestly, once I smelled the hot meat and mustard, I was starving. I grabbed one from the pile and took a big bite. It tasted of power and victory. "So, you just want someone to tell you what to do?"

"Yes," squealed the Mayor, "we've been waiting for years! Aeons!"

"Well, can't you tell people what to do?"

"Oh, no," the Mayor held up his hands, "I haven't been able to do that for years."

"But you told me to have an apple."

"But that's it," he shrugged, "I can't advise any further than that. In the early days when the Great Confusion began that's all I did, offer apples – when I'd run out of apples it all got a bit embarrassing. Oh please, I beg of you to stay."

I leaned against the statue behind me. Something felt odd and I whipped my hand away. The silver from the frog's surface was smeared over my hand – was it wet paint? The crowd was still waiting as I pressed against the statue's leg. It was spongy and I knew this was important but I couldn't figure out why. I shrugged. "Everyone…hug the person next to you." Their eyes widened and they turned to their companions, who were already engaging in an embrace of those nearest them, and piled together to form an even larger hug. It was like adding layers to a piece of string until you had a ball of wool – wool that yelped and chortled with unadulterated joy.

I felt a fleeting moment of embarrassment – the reconstruction of my requests felt almost as though people could see into my mind. Some of my followers fell to the ground in a faint. "Er, that's probably enough." They waited once again. A fizz ran through my blood and my brain crackled with possibility. "Make a pyramid," I yelled, and they clambered over each other, heels pressing in faces and hands crushing toes, as they piled higher and higher to appease me. My stomach wriggled when I noticed eyes bulging and faces contorting, but nobody else seemed worried.

"That's great," I said after their third circus formation, "now do a tap-dance – the best ones will come up here and perform to everyone." While they shrieked and yipped and practised madly I heard footsteps behind me. I turned to see the fanatics, beaming with joy and eager to join the melee. That was it, my house was free. They had found a reason to come home. I felt unusually disappointed. "Er," I shuffled, "everyone who arrived late, get on with dancing. Are there animals? Make the animals dance too." I leaned back on the statue with satisfaction. It seemed less spongy than before and the surface was now only tacky. What did it mean?

One of the women, a crooked old hag with teeth like a piano stretching up into the air, pulled a tiny gold key from between one of them and opened a door in her chest. She deflated as a flood of creatures spilled out; several headed furry beasts with great talons, small leathery land fish and anemones floating through the air. The others kicked her flattened body aside and set about herding the animals to train, many of course being led about by the creatures themselves, blinking in confusion.

A new kind of person appeared at the side-lines. They held cameras and clustered in small groups, filming the madness whilst a beautifully coiffured individual with a microphone performed interviews and asides. Now and then they would briefly remove someone who obliged them with stories of tears and torment. The interviewers and crew would champion some only to snicker once their backs were turned. All of this I watched with growing, bursting, exploding joy. Who would have thought Gemma from customer services had caused all of this? I laughed and I laughed and fell to my knees, hugging my sides and slapping the ground. I was almost sick with happiness by the time I realised they had stopped altogether and were staring again. There was silence, a horrible silence.

"Where's the humming?" I demanded. Blank faces looked back at me.

"The humming, oh Great One?"

"Yes, the bloody laptop, the noise of the portal or whatever, the way out." I turned this way and that, checking the floors and few trees dotted about. Finally I turned to the statue, running my hands desperately over the concrete. It was dry. "How did you get back in?" I asked the fanatics with a tongue like a dried leaf.

"Through the Frog of Greatness," they said, "it opens but once a generation."

"Of course," I said, "of course." I slumped to the ground.

"What will you have us do now? We can hum for you if that is what you require." The air was filled with the most desperately irritating sound like a swarm of giant idiot bees.

"Stop it!" I yelled and silence immediately followed. They were waiting, hoping, happy for the first time in years. I felt my body fading again.

"We've all at one time wished for psychedelic talking wellingtons…"

"Oh, go fuck yourselves," I snarled as I was sucked into another Interruption, managing just before I disappeared to see my eternal subjects leaping gleefully onto each other's privates.

ABOUT THE AUTHOR

Madeleine Swann has had articles in magazines including *Bizarre* and *The Dark Side*, ranging in subject from church restorations to toe wrestling championships.

Her anthology, **The Filing Cabinet of Doom**, is published by Burning Bulb Publishing.

She writes from her home in deepest, darkest Essex and has surreal comedy and horror in *American Nightmare*, *Polluto* magazine (issue 10), *LegumeMan Books*, *Black Petal* magazine, *The Strange Edge* and *Bizarro Central*. She also has erotica published on the *Forbidden Fiction* website, *The Darker Edge of Desire* anthology, *Weird Year* and *Strange Saturdays* (by Strangehouse Books) and her short story *The Gathering* was published in the **The Big Book of Bizarro** by Burning Bulb Publishing.

Madeleine's website is www.madeleineswann.com. Also, Madeleine blogs at: http://madeleineswann.wordpress.com and follow her on Twitter @madeleineswann.

OTHER GREAT TITLES FROM

WWW.BURNINGBULBPUBLISHING.COM

ANTHOLOGIES
BIZARRO AND TRANSGRESSIVE FICTION

THE BIG BOOK OF BIZARRO

The Big Book of Bizarro brings together the peculiar prose of an international cast of the most grotesquely-gonzo, genre-grinding modern writers who ever put pen to paper (or mouse to pad), including:

NIGHT OF THE LIVING DEAD horror writers John Russo & George Kosana; HUSTLER MAGAZINE erotica contributors Eva Hore, Andrée Lachapelle, & J. Troy Seate and established Bizarro genre authors D. Harlan Wilson, William Pauley III, Wol-vriey, Laird Long, Richard Godwin and so many more!

From Alien abductions to Zombie sex, The Big Book of Bizarro contains OVER FIFTY STORIES of the most outrélandish transgressive fiction that you'll ever lay your capricious and curious hands upon!

WARNING: This book may be one of the most controversial and dangerous books you'll ever read.

WESTWARD HOES

Nine outlaw writers rode into town from obscurity to pen nine tantalizing tales of horror and fantasy, and leaving once they branded their own personal marks on the weird western genre and became living legends of the American Frontier experience.

Like drunken Indian scouts, the writers fervidly tracked down and captured the Western genre, tore off its fashionable veneer and ravished its exposed essence.

So belly up to the bar with your favorite soiled dove and enjoy perusing these thrilling tales of Old West debauchery, danger and desire; compiled by the publisher of The Big Book of Bizarro and featuring the bizarro novella *Big Trouble in Little Ass* by Wol-vriey.

Burning Bulb
PUBLISHING

ANTHOLOGIES
BIZARRO AND TRANSGRESSIVE FICTION

THE BIG BOOK OF BIZARRO SPECIAL KINDLE EDITIONS

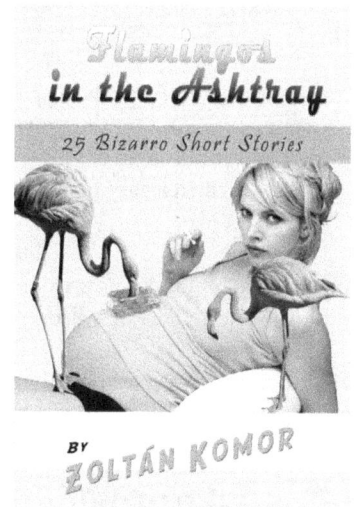

Burning Bulb
PUBLISHING

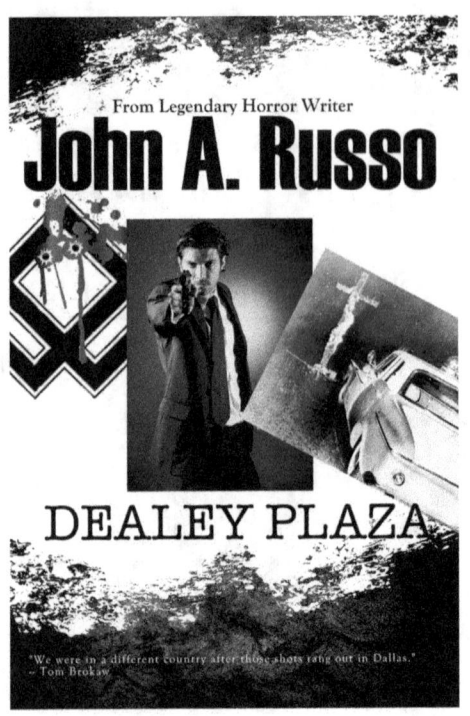

DEALEY PLAZA

From legendary horror and suspense writer JOHN RUSSO comes a harrowing tale where no one is safe!

Dealey Plaza is one of the most notorious places in America, and when youthful conspiracy buffs go there in 1964 to stage their own reenactment of the Kennedy Assassination, four of them are brutally murdered ~ the first victims of a hate-filled legacy that continues for four more decades.

The survivors of that long-ago Dallas trip, each of them now icons of the American way of life, are about to be honored ~ or killed.

Who will live and who will die? Will it be country-western star Lori McCoy? Her loving husband? Her scheming ex-husband? Or the case-hardened FBI agent and longtime friend who risks his life trying to protect them?

www.DealeyPlazaBook.com

Burning Bulb
PUBLISHING

Bright little children, at school and at play,
until their minds are stolen away...

A Novel of Terror by

JOHN A. RUSSO

THE ACADEMY

THE ACADEMY

The Academy. It's every parent's dream, turning their little
darlings into geniuses, superachievers, perfect little
children.

And if there's a problem, the Academy fixes that too. It's a
simple operation. Just a little device. Then a teeny pink scar
on a tender little skull . . .

One boy knows the secret. Now he wants his mind back.
But it's much, much too late. Too late for anything but the
ugly feelings. The bad feelings. The messy sexy feelings. The
knife-cold hatred, the murderous rage, for total, screaming,
blood-drenching revenge . . .

www.TheJohnRusso.com

Burning Bulb
PUBLISHING

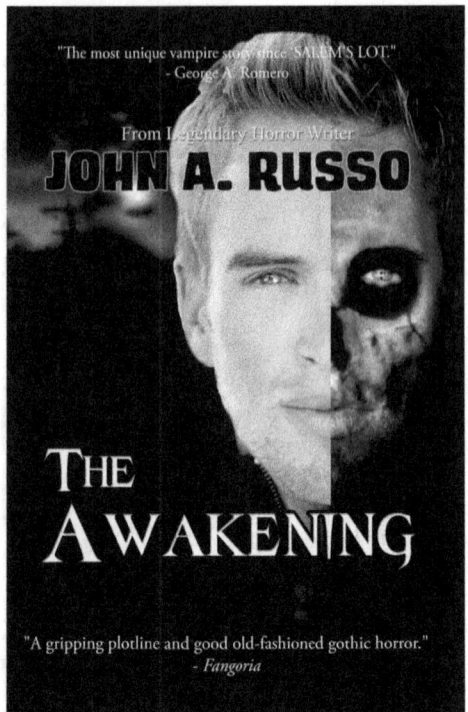

THE AWAKENING

For two hundred years, he has rested. Now he rises. Now he will be satisfied. Nothing can stop him. No one can resist him.

Benjamin Latham is young and handsome, his eighteenth-century mind wakened to a bizarre twentieth-century world. And there is the need deep within . . . an animal need, frightening, murderous, unholy . . . a vital need that must be fed.

And with his need comes a power over men and women to do his bidding, to quiet his dark craving . . .

Until the murders begin. And the inquiries. All suggesting the same hideous truth.

Now Benjamin must find a sanctuary: a lover, a partner, a friend. Someone who can share his darkness. Someone he can lead to . . . The Awakening.

www.TheJohnRusso.com

Burning Bulb
PUBLISHING

GARY LEE VINCENT'S
DARKENED
THE WEST VIRGINIA VAMPIRE SERIES

DARKENED HILLS

When evil descends on a small West Virginia town, who will survive?

Jonathan did not start out his life to become a rambler, it just worked out that way. William was a troubled youth with something to hide. Both were from Melas, a small town tucked away in the West Virginia hills... a town where disappearances are happening more and more frequently.

After the suicide of a wanted serial killer, the townsfolk thought the nightmare was over. But when a centuries-old vampire is discovered they find out the hard way it's just getting started. Dark secrets can only stay hidden for so long and when the devil comes to collect, there will be hell to pay. Can Jonathan and William find a way to stop the vampire before it's too late? Find out in *Darkened Hills!*

DARKENED HOLLOWS

In the heart-stopping sequel to the award-winning *Darkened Hills*, Jonathan and William must return to West Virginia to face possible criminal charges stemming from their last visit to the damned town of Melas, where both had narrowly escaped the clutches of a vampire seethe.

And as livestock start mysteriously getting murdered with all of their blood drained, worried farmers are searching for answers - leaving the local Sheriff and his deputy racing against time to learn the cause before a more violent crime is committed.

Burning Bulb
PUBLISHING

WWW.*DARKENEDHILLS*.COM

GARY LEE VINCENT'S
DARKENED
THE WEST VIRGINIA VAMPIRE SERIES

DARKENED WATERS

When the world goes to hell, the chosen must arise!

As Talman Cane orchestrates a flood of epic proportions in this third installment of the *Darkened* series the towns of Melas and Tarklin are caught completely off guard by the deluge. Hell-bent on finishing what they started, the evil brothers return to the lunatic asylum to take care of the witnesses and add to the ever-growing army of the undead.

Aided by Lucifer himself and the insane vampire demon Legion, the stage is set to channel all of the forces of hell to come forth. In an all-out race to survive, Jonathan, William, and Amanda soon discover they are up against impossible odds as Lucifer opens the Gateway to Hell, ushering in the zombie apocalypse and the End Times.

DARKENED SOULS

Melas and the Madison House are about to be rebuilt.
True evil is about to be reborne!

Young ex-priest and vampire-killer William is drawn back to the West Virginian town that almost killed him, where his vampire arch-enemy Victor Rothenstein still stalks the earth.

The town of Melas lies destroyed after the battle of the End of Days. But why is wealthy Jackie Nixon so eager to rebuild it using the bone dust of murdered souls?

Terrible evil has visited before, but the Gateway to Hell is about to be reopened in a horrific climax. And this time – it's personal.

WWW.DARKENEDHILLS.COM

Burning Bulb
PUBLISHING

WEST VIRGINIA-THEMED HUMORROROTICA

BY RICH BOTTLES JR.

HELLHOLE WEST VIRGINIA

From the heights of Mothman's perch high atop the Silver Bridge in Point Pleasant to the depths of Hellhole Cavern in Pendleton County, evil lurks within the shadows as the sun sets upon the haunted hills and hollows of West Virginia.

Bizarro author Rich Bottles Jr. blows the coffin lid off horror genre clichés with this tour de force cast of Eco-friendly vampires, beach-yearning zombies and sex-starved she-devils.

LUMBERJACKED

If you are easily offended or do not possess a truly depraved sense of humor, this story may not be the light summer reading fare you desire. As for the four feisty female freshmen stranded on top of West Virginia's third highest mountain, they have no choice but to experience the sick, twisted debauchery and perverted mayhem described deep inside the tight unbroken bindings of this horrific missive.

Lumberjacked takes the reader to a nightmarish world where character development and aesthetic integrity are prematurely cut short by the swinging axes of maniacal lumberjacks, who are hell bent on death and destruction in the remote forests of Appalachia. And at the climax, when paranoia crosses over to the paranormal, Lumberjacked makes Deliverance look like a family raft trip down the Lower Gauley.

THE MANACLED

What happens when twin brothers lease out the former West Virginia State Penitentiary with the false purpose of filming a documentary on supernatural phenomena, but their true intention is to make a pornographic movie?

Chaos ensues as the disturbed spirits of murdered convicts, along with the reanimated dead from the neighboring Indian Burial Mound, take their vengeance on the unwary and undressed trespassers.

Zombies, ghosts, mobsters and porn collide in this bizarro tale from horror author Rich Bottles Jr.

Burning Bulb
PUBLISHING

WOL-VRIEY
BIZARRO AND TRANSGRESSIVE FICTION

BOSTON POSH

In 2028 AD, the USA is a nation ravaged by hungry dragons and dinosaurs. In Boston, Massachusetts, private eye Bud Malone is hired to rescue a kidnapped heiress. But nothing is as it seems. Malone works to unravel a tangled web involving Boston China-town, a 200-year-old woman with a 9-year-old body, white robots, a human-liver-eating psychopath, a golem, a porcelain dragon, and a snake goddess with a crush on him. There's also a woman obsessed with chicken sex. Then Malone meets Posh Lane, a gorgeous call girl who's desperate to quit her pimp. Romantic sparks ignite be-tween Posh and Malone, but Posh's past suddenly catches up with her in a BIG way. To save Posh, Malone agrees to run a quest for Earth's new rulers, the Forks. But, Malone has no idea that agree-ing to the Fork's odd request will send him on the weirdest trip he's ever been on in his life.

VEGAN VAMPIRE VAGINAS

The biggest bank heist in US history. And Tom Palmer can't remember pulling it off. And no, this isn't your standard case of amnesia. After a one-night-stand gone horribly wrong, Boston salesman Tom Palmer wakes up with a vagina implanted in his left hand. Then his day gets worse:

Tom is transported across space-time to a nightmare version of Boston, one where the Bizarro virus has transformed half the population into cannibals. Worst of all, Tom discovers that in this new Boston, he's the infamous gangster Pussypalm, wanted for robbing the Federal Reserve Bank of Boston a year ago. He also learns that the vagina in his hand is prophetic, i.e. it talks . . . after sex. With 130 people left dead during his bank heist and six billion dollars missing, Tom knows he's living on borrowed time. It is in his best interests not to remember anything. Because once he does . . .

VEGAN ZOMBIE APOCALYPSE

In the post-apocalypse worlderness, zombies rule the earth. They're allergic to meat, and brains literally make them explode. Zombies now eat blood potatoes, parasitic tubers grown in the flesh of humancows corralled in maximum security farms. Two fugitives meet in the ancient ruins of Texas. The first is Soil 15-f, a womancow who's escaped her farm a week before she's due to be killed and her blood potato crop harvested. The second fugitive is Able Kane, former head necros food technician, now sentenced to death for heresy. But Soil is no ordinary humancow. Unknown to herself, she's the vegan zombie agricultural revolution, and the zombies desperately want her back. And the necros equally desper-ately want Able Kane dead. He's fled with a forbidden discovery which will reshape the world for the worse if used. And Able is just hardheaded/misguided enough to use it.

MINOR CONFESSIONS OF AN ANGEL FALLING UPWARD

by Planner Forthright, as edited by Joey Madia

Confession. Revelation. Rant. *Minor Confessions of an Angel Falling Upward* is all of these... and more. Set in modern times and spiraling back to the swirl of Pre-Creation, this postmodern blend of genre-bending pop-prose and socio-political commentary is a classic tale of the (anti-)hero's quest for Reason and Redemption in a Universe gone mad.

Who is Planner Forthright? A fallen angel made Man. A once-winged evil with un-Divine purpose on this Plane. A cannibal prince chosen to inherit a castled landscape of destruction and despair. An Alchemist of sorts—a mental magician; a mortar-and-pestle wizard converting carbon lies to golden Truth, whose language is his own. A Vampire by nature and condition whose been walking the waters and thorny highways of our planet for over 40 years. And he's seeking a way out...

PASSAGEWAY

by Gary Lee Vincent with illustrations by Andy Hopp

When an archeological dig goes horribly wrong, the team is trapped in an alternate world where evil awaits them at every turn. Find out who will survive the *Passageway*!

From Gary Lee Vincent, the author of supernatural vampire thriller *Darkened Hills*, comes an unforgettable tale that spans four continents and takes the reader to the very realm of Hell itself.

Skeleton warriors, zombies, other undead beings and were-wolves are allvery real inside the *Passageway*! In this Bizarro-genre tribute to H.P. Lovecraft and Indiana Jones, this deadly tale will keep you guessing and leave you breathless to the end!

THE TWELVE STEPS

by Zachary Crabtree

"A Man who Cannot Keep Awake Cannot Keep it Together." There is always something that pulls an alcoholic deeper into his unquench-able thirst – something degenerative to the human spirit. Indeed, there have been incidents in my life that carry tragic significance to me, yet I know they pale in comparison to the tragedies experienced by others.

When the jagged pieces of a disfigured past become a troubled, broken-up, glass-bottled mosaic in one's present life, all the innocent souls affected along the way become entangled in one's conscience; while the depression, pills, manic behavior and soul-searching co-alesce in a series of twelve steps.

Alcohol affects the lives of hooligans, stubborn old fools, lovers, and families torn apart by drunk drivers – drunk drivers like me.

Burning Bulb
PUBLISHING

THE FALL OF TOMORROW

Hopelessness... How do you protect your loved ones when Hell itself opens its insidious mouth?

Horror... Nightmarish Creatures invade your world and there is nowhere to hide.

Blood... How long can you hold out before they come for you?

Pain... Where do you run to avoid being eaten alive by monsters with a voracious appetite for your flesh?

Screams... While you selfishly run for your own life.

Questions... Who is to blame? Where did they come from? How many people survived...and how does the human race find the means to fight back?

THE FALL OF TOMORROW is man's last tale of desperation told by those that are striving to salvage some hope against a ravenous bastion of evil beasts bent on ruling our world.

"David Fairhead writes compelling stories that offer very human characters and very inhuman monsters. There is no subtlety in Fairhead's imagination - he is simply dying to scare the hell out of you."
- Nelson W Pyles - author of DEMONS, DOLLS AND MILKSHAKES

Burning Bulb
PUBLISHING

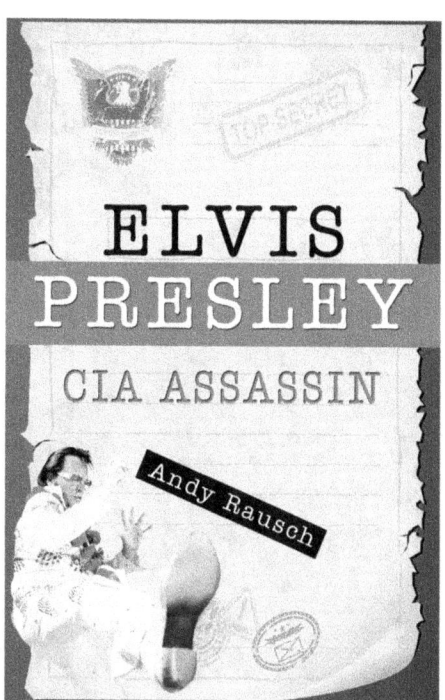

ELVIS PRESLEY, CIA ASSASSIN

"I can guarantee you. Read this book and you'll never look at Elvis the same way again!"
~ Douglas Brode, author of ELVIS CINEMA AND POPULAR CULTURE

SOON TO BE A MAJOR MOTION PICTURE

In 1970, singer Elvis Presley secretly met with President Richard Nixon. This new comedic novel imagines that Presley became a Central Intelligence Agency operative, eventually moving up through the ranks to become a skilled assassin.

Presented in an oral history fashion, the book tells us about Presley's secret transformation by the people who knew him best.

Did he fake his death in 1977? Was Presley involved with the Watergate scandal? The Iran hostage crisis? Communicating with aliens?

Read this book to find out the answers to these and many more questions.

Burning Bulb
PUBLISHING

THE TAILSMAN

From the creators of *The Big Book of Bizarro* and *Westward Hoes* comes a new comic unlike anything you have ever seen!

He's hot on the trail, looking for some *tail...*

Sly Franko was a man of the West, a forger of the wild frontier. Like the Country Western song that would be written years after he died, the words, "Faster horses, younger women, and more money," seemed to be the anthem of this horn dog cowboy.

Franko would ride into town on a blazing saddle, find the closest saloon to wet the whistle, belly up to a good card game, and find him a hot-loving hussy to get his cowpoke on with.

However, Sly might have met his match when a visit to bathroom leads to terror and death. Can Sly and his poker buddies solve the mystery before more of the townsfolk are murdered? Find out in this exciting premier issue of *The Tailsman!*

WWW.BURNINGBULBCOMICS.COM